You wouldn't expect murder to be much of a problem in a small city on the Niagara Peninsula. You wouldn't expect it, but it is . . .

Large french windows let what was left of the spring day into the room, but I didn't get to admire the view because of the mess the apartment was in. There were papers flung in every direction. Beside the desk the file drawers were open and red filing folders stood half down from their moorings. In the midst of this mess, the first, not the last thing we noticed as we came into the room was Dr. Zekerman lying stretched out on one of the leather chairs that dominated the room. There was blood around the top part of what used to be his head. His mouth gaped open adding to the look of surprise frozen on his frightened eyes . . .

This one they couldn't call suicide.

"The Suicide Murders introduces Benny Cooperman, a character who manages to combine unforgettably the elements of sleuth, klutz, and standup comedian . . . Cooperman is as uniquely Canadian as Van Der Valk is Dutch, Martin Beck is Swedish, Travis Mc-Gee is American. That makes him decidedly special, nothing less than the hope and direction of the best of Canadian crime fiction."

—*Books in Canada*

THE SUICIDE MURDERS

A Benny Cooperman Mystery

Howard Engel

SEAL BOOKS
McClelland and Stewart-Bantam Limited
Toronto

*This low-priced Seal Book
has been completely reset in a type face
designed for easy reading, and was printed
from new plates. It contains the complete
text of the original hard-cover edition.*
NOT ONE WORD HAS BEEN OMITTED.

THE SUICIDE MURDERS
*A Seal Book / published by arrangement with
Clarke, Irwin & Co., Ltd.*

PRINTING HISTORY
*Clarke, Irwin edition published September 1980
A Selection of Canadian Reader
Seal edition / September 1981*

*Seal Books are published by McClelland and Stewart-Bantam
Limited. Its trademark, consisting of the words "Seal Books"
and the portrayal of a seal, is the property of McClelland and
Stewart-Bantam Limited, 25 Hollinger Road, Toronto, Ontario
M4B 3G2. This trademark has been duly registered in the Trademarks Office of Canada. The trademark, consisting of the word
"Bantam" and the portrayal of a rooster, is the property of and
is used with the consent of Bantam Books, Inc. 666 Fifth Avenue, New York, New York 10103. This trademark has been duly
registered in the Trademarks Office of Canada and elsewhere.*

to
Janet

ONE

I was looking for a four-letter word for "narrow path," when I heard high heels on the stairs. High heels usually means business for me rather than for Dr. Bushmill, the chiropodist. With men on the stairs, it was only guessing. I put away the newspaper in time to see a fuzzy silhouette through the frosted glass of the door hesitate for a moment before knocking. I called "Come in already!" and she did.

She was the sort of woman that made you wish you'd stayed in the shower for an extra minute or taken another three minutes shaving. I felt a little underdressed in my own office. She had what you could call a tailored look. Everything was so understated it screamed. I could hear the echo bouncing off the bank across the street.

She took a chair on the other side of my bleached oak desk and played around with her handbag. It matched her shoes, and I thought that the car outside probably matched the rest of the outfit. Sitting in the sunlight, with the shadow of the letters of my sign caressing her trim figure, she looked about thirty, but I put part of that down to decent treatment, regular meals, baths and trips to Miami, things like that. When she raised her eyes to look at me, they were gray.

"You're Mr. Cooperman?" she asked.

"Would I lie to you?" I said, trying to help her over the awkward stage. The sign on the door told the truth too: BENJAMIN COOPERMAN, LICENCED PRIVATE INVESTIGATOR. "What can I do for you, Miss . . . ?" Her lips smiled suddenly, like a puppeteer pulled the right string and then released it. Her eyes didn't change.

"I'm Myrna Yates," she said, looking to see if that meant anything. It didn't, but what I don't know about the upper crust in this town could fill a library. I hated to lose her respect for me so early in our association by not raising an eyebrow, but the hour was early and the day was hot. She tried it another way, with more luck. "Chester Yates is my husband."

"The contractor?"

"Among other things, yes." She looked down at the handbag again, just as things had started rolling.

"Sure, I guess I've heard of your husband. He's not missed too many chances to be interviewed in the paper lately, has he? Still, if I were in his shoes, I'd see that it was probably good for business. How can I help you, Mrs. Yates?" She sighed like I'd asked her to write *War and Peace* on a credit card, and then looked like she was about to plunge.

"It says in your advertisement in the Yellow Pages that you do private investigations." I nodded encouragement. "You do civil, criminal, industrial and domestic investigations?" She was rapidly moving to the top of the class.

"That's right, Mrs. Yates. I do all that, although between the two of us, I leave the industrial stuff to Niagara and Pinkertons. They can afford to keep all those guys in uniform and pay for the fancy electronic equipment. Me? I'm just a peeper. Divorce is my meat and potatoes. I could be wrong, though. I heard that Niagara set up six TV cameras to catch a fast operator a month ago and I hear he got away with all six of the cameras. And frankly, since they've been fooling around with the law on divorce, I've been having to cut down on meat and potatoes. Don't listen to me. I talk too much. Is it something about those articles in the paper? Something about that subdivision he's involved in, maybe?"

She shook her head like we were playing charades and I'd wasted thirty seconds not catching the conventional gesture for *the*. "It's not about that at all. May I smoke?" She dug into her bag and brought out a pack of menthol cigarettes. I could have guessed. I tried my top drawer for a book of matches, but by the time I came up with one she was already exhaling her first lungful. The smoke added cotton-candy wisps to the sunlight streaming in from over the second-storey rooftops of St. Andrew Street. She looked around at my licence hanging in a black frame behind me and then studied the clutter on top of my filing cabinet. When she had satisfied her curiosity, she examined the end of her cigarette for a minute. Then she looked at me quickly, her gray eyes widening. "I think he's seeing another woman," she said, "and I want to know for sure. I want to know who it is and I want pictures and dates and times and . . ."

"The whole schmeer. I get the picture." I lit a Player's Medium and took it all the way down. Then I gave her my standard speech intended to scare off clients who were just playing around "Tell me, Mrs. Yates, have you and your husband quarreled? Did something happen this morning or last night? What I'm trying to find out is, are you really looking for a divorce? If you are, there are easier ways of going about it, God knows, than putting a tail on him. Are things that bad? Look, even though I can use all the clients that can climb these stairs, I think you ought to be honest with both of us. I don't want you to come to me in a year's time pointing at me and saying that if it wasn't for me you'd still be pouring tea at the Junior League." I could see that she wanted me to finish, so I did.

"Mr. Cooperman, I know that I could go to a lawyer. That's not what I want. Not yet. As you guess, I'm reasonably comfortable and going to a lawyer at this stage, in this town, well it just . . ." She let the unfinished sentence hang there between us as though we both regularly had to face throwing up one hundred thousand dollars a year in exchange for the Russian roulette of the courtroom and golden dreams of alimony. She threw in one of her mechanical smiles, which still didn't light up her eyes. I brushed fallen ash off my still unmarked pad of yellow foolscap on to my shirt and tie, a klutzy gesture but maybe it lets clients relax and open up a little.

"Okay, I've got it so far. You are not flying out the window after a fight. You are oyster calm and collected in limited editions. What makes you think your husband is playing around, Mrs. Yates? You can be frank with me."

"I came here to be frank. It's the only way."

"Good. Why don't you start at the beginning and tell me the whole story from the top, as they say." She took a long drag on her cigarette and let the smoke find its own way out while she collected her thoughts. I picked up a ballpoint pen and looked as serious as a graduation photograph.

"We've been married for nearly twenty years. When we met, I had just given up on a business school after having made a mess of high school. I was popular and I ran with a pretty wild bunch. When I say *wild*, I don't mean like the kids today with their pot and drugs. We drank a little and fooled around, but mostly in groups, so nobody got in too deeply." I pictured Myrna Yates at eighteen, trying it on, not getting in too deeply, and held that image in my mind while watching this immaculately tailored Myrna Yates talking at me from across the desk.

"I don't remember when I first met Chester. I can remember a gang of college boys moving in on us. They had newer cars than the ones we were used to, and had a better line. Chester was one of them, and I remember slowly becoming aware of him being around. You know what I mean? He was just there: chunky, dependable and smiling. He was always hanging around, and soon he was running out to buy me cigarettes and freshen my drink. That sort of thing. I don't think I ever saw him as my dreamboat. I had lots of other interests. In the summers we all went necking in the dunes down by the lake. Chester was always breathing down my neck. I could tell he wanted me, and for a long time I strung him along, not giving in to him, and not taking him very seriously. I guess you think I'm just getting a little of my own back, Mr. Cooperman?"

"Tell the story."

"Well, soon I noticed that all my friends had paired off and I was the only one still playing the field. The field was Chester. So, to make a long story short, we started getting serious. We were married, we had a child, a girl, Ellen, who is in a home. She's severely retarded. We didn't have any other children. Chester came from a good family, and let his father set him up in his factory. But Chester had always liked machines and trucks, and soon he bought one and rented it out to a contractor. In a year or two he had a number of trucks doing excavation work mostly. It grew to be a fleet of them and Chester and I moved from the west end to a place on South Ridge. He left his father's job and got into the real estate boom at the end of the sixties. I guess he had a piece of every deal around. He had the big earth-moving machines by then. Is this any help?" she asked, her eyes rounded.

"Take your time."

"I guess we were never a deeply loving couple, Mr. Cooperman. I was fond of Chester. He was always good to me. And we went through a lot with Ellen together. He was a dependable, open sort of person. He had no secrets, he never called me out for trespassing, if you know what I mean. Then, recently, beginning a couple of months ago, that changed. He started getting moody, secretive, and that's when the lies started."

"The lies?"

"I discovered it by accident to start with. Then I confess to checking up on him. I phoned the office on a Thursday afternoon about something. Two months ago. His secretary told me that Chester was over at City Hall meeting with Vern Harrington. Well, I know Vern and Doris quite well, and I thought that what I had on my mind—I forget now what it was—was important. So I phoned Vern's office and there wasn't a meeting at all. Chester hadn't been there and wasn't expected. Vern thought I was checking up on my husband. We both laughed. That night I mentioned Vern —not that I'd phoned or anything, but just that I'd been thinking about him and Doris—and he didn't turn a hair. That's not like Chester. He usually gets beet red if somebody says 'brassière.' His face doesn't hide much. One week later I called again about something and I was told that he was keeping a dentist's appointment. Again that night I mentioned that I should see my dentist, and he let that sail right past without comment. He wasn't at the dentist's I'm sure. I got more and more suspicious and I began phoning or stopping by the office when I was out shopping and discovered that most of the times he wasn't there the reason given was a lie. Do you think I'm being silly, Mr. Cooperman? Have I been watching too much television? I don't want to be the last to know if he's been playing around. What do you think I should do?"

I wish about then that I had a pipe to use as a prop. I needed something to enhance my dignity: a streak of gray at the temples, fifteen thousand dollars in the bank, that sort of thing—just so she'd know everything was going to be all right. I shifted myself around in my swivel chair and leaned back. I knew just how far I could go before I had to pick myself up off the floor. She was still asking me questions with her big gray eyes.

"Well, it may not turn out to be as mysterious as it looks, Mrs. Yates. There are hundreds of things he might be doing without endangering the sanctity of your marriage. My father, for instance, for years was a secret gin rummy player. He used to take two-hour lunches and when he got back to the store had to duck out to the United Cigar Store for a sandwich. My mother caught up with him in the end, but they celebrated their thirty-fifth wedding anniversary recently." I waited for the anecdote to take hold and then made a suggestion. "Tell you what I'll do, let me nose around a little and report back to you in a couple of days. If I turn up anything interesting, we can have another talk. If it's just business or something like gin rummy, then you'll have to take my word for it when I say 'Don't lose any more sleep.' How does that sound? If you like it, it's going to cost you a hundred a day, say for three days, if it takes me that long, and expenses."

She pulled her handbag open and put fifteen twenty-dollar bills on my blotter. I put the money in my billfold without actually jumping across the desk and hugging her. Since the first of March when I had to put up my annual licence fee, a nick out of my almost non-existent income adding up to five hundred dollars, things hadn't been lively around the office. I'd traced a runaway couple to Buffalo, I'd found evidence that the poor abandoned Mrs. Furstenberg was getting a big one on the side every month from a former basketball all-star. And I'd taken on a lot of crazy things that I shouldn't have of course. I could do worse than spend a few days tailing Chester Yates. A guy like that goes into a lot of fancy places in a day.

"Tell me, Mrs. Yates," I said, wagging my star sapphire ring in her direction, "have these absences of your husband formed any sort of pattern? Have you been able to anticipate when he is going to be away without leave?"

"Yes. It's always a Thursday and always after lunch, from around two-thirty to four-thirty. Sometimes he doesn't come back to the office."

"Fine."

"Mr. Cooperman, today is Thursday. I wonder, could you see where he goes this afternoon?"

"As a matter of fact, Mrs. Yates, I'm going to move some other files off my desk for a few days and concentrate on this one. Where is your husband's office?"

"It's on the seventh floor of the Caddell Building."

"That's on Queen Street?"

"No, James."

"Oh, near the market."

"Further down."

"Well, don't worry. I'll find it all right. When I have anything to tell you, how do you want me to get in touch?"

"You may call me at home. I'm there all day most days."

"Right. That's in the book is it?"

"It's unlisted. I'd better give it to you." She gave me the number which I added to the doodles on my yellow pad, then I got up with what in a taller man would signal that the interview was concluded. Since she remained seated, I walked around my desk and took her hand. It was a strong and determined grip, which she released with one of her puppeteer smiles. "I'll hear from you, then," she said turning. I beat her to the door.

"Yes. And in the meantime, let me do the worrying."

I listened to her receding footsteps down the stairs to the street, and looked at my watch. It was nearly noon. I had a couple of hours to kill until I had to pick up my man at the Caddell Building.

TWO

It was two-thirty, and the day had turned from hot to hotter. I was flipping through a pile of paperbacks in a bookstore with a clear view across the street to the big glass doors of the Caddell Building. In my pocket was an eight-and-a-half-by-ten glossy of Chester Yates in a hard-hat shaking hands with the mayor, also wearing a hard-hat and with a vote-getting grimace. Both of them managed to look as though wearing hard-hats wasn't regularly part of their day. Chester wore a three-piece out-of-town suit. His big frame needed all the help a tailor could give it. At about two-forty, just when I was getting re-acquainted with Miss Wonderly on page five of *The Maltese Falcon*, Chester came out the double doors and blinked in the sunlight. He wasn't wearing a hat, but I thought I might be able to follow his blond head through a crowd anyway.

I let him get about a half a block ahead of me. I thought I could keep tabs on him without endangering the backs of his imported brown shoes. He didn't look around once. From behind, as he wove in and out of the pedestrians and waiting at the end of the block for the light to change, he looked like an ex-football player going to flab gently. He wasn't carrying a lot of beer fat on him, but his muscles were turning to marmalade. We were back on St. Andrew Street again, heading west, with the one-way traffic of the main street running against us.

At the newspaper office they'd been very helpful when I asked for the photograph. I'd seen it in the paper a couple of days earlier. The woman with the pink hair behind the desk thought it was just wonderful that I wanted a picture of

Mayor Rampham. Thought I set a good example and didn't care who knew it. I listened patiently until she finished and still had to pay up two dollars for the print.

Chester had stopped in front of a sporting-goods store. The window was filled with baseballs, baseball mitts, a selection of bats, bikes, golfing things and in front of everything, an assortment of imported English toys, model cars, trucks and buses. Chester pulled at his chin for a second, then entered the store. Through the glass I could see him talking to the owner. He was too old to be a salesclerk. They went to the back of the store among the bicycles and bicycle parts where they jawed for about ten minutes. The owner walked him to the door and I preceded my suspect west along the north side of the street, until I stopped to eject a stone from my shoe and he passed me again.

With the single stop at the sporting-goods store, Chester had gone in a straightforward manner to Ontario Street, where he walked north past the green expanse of Montecello Park with its bandstand gleaming in the sun, and little kids running around while their mothers gossiped on the park benches. Chester kept to the sidewalk, maintained a steady pace—not too fast, although I'm out of shape and wheeze after sharpening a pencil—and went into the Physicians' and Surgeons' Building across from Hotel Dieu Hospital. It was one of the newer buildings on the street. It had replaced a hundred-year-old mansion with sixteen-foot ceilings and peacocks painted on the inside shutters. About twenty-five years ago, my mother sent me to take drawing lessons from a painter who lived in the dying mansion. The things you remember.

Chester sat down in the open vinyl splendour of the lobby. I was sure he hadn't spotted me so I marched in too. The cushion breathed out as I sat down behind a plastic yucca plant. Chester looked at his watch, frowned and picked up a magazine. There was traffic in and out of the gift shop near the entrance, but the air conditioning kept the heat and noise outside. At three o'clock on the nose, Chester got up and pushed one of the eight-hundred buzzers on the solid marble wall by the elevators. It buzzed back, he said something and a voice croaked through a speaker. Chester went up the elevator to the tenth floor. I went over to the wall and tried to locate the right button. It had been fourth or fifth from the top in the third row. The fourth was a Dr. Chisholm on the eighth floor. The fifth was Dr. Andrew Zekerman on the tenth. There was a pay phone in the lobby. I looked up the worthy Dr. Zekerman and discovered that he was a psychiatrist. I could also see that I was going to have to return at least ten of those twenty-dollar bills.

I killed exactly fifty-five minutes in the gift shop looking at quilted mauve dressing gowns and bed jackets, avoiding the hostile stare of the lady with her glasses on a string behind the glass counter. Zekerman wasn't giving away any free time by my watch. At fourteen minutes to the hour, Chester came down from the tenth floor. Playing a hunch, I let him walk out the glass doors, leaving his tail behind him. If he had another secret, it could wait until next Thursday. In another five minutes, a stringy, fortyish woman with sunglasses and a wide-brimmed straw hat came in. At exactly four o'clock, she pushed Dr. Zekerman's buzzer and rode up to the tenth floor.

I mentally noted "solved" on the file of the Chester Yates caper, and walked back to the office. I ducked into Diana Sweets for a chopped egg sandwich and a marshmallow sundae. Across from me, in an identical brown gumwood booth, Willy Horner was half-way through a hot hamburger sandwich. I've been living away from my mother's kitchen for over seventeen years, and I still think that the gravy is the wickedest part. Willy nodded at me, I nodded back at him. We'd been in grade eight together. That's the way it is in a small city like this, you never really lose sight of anybody. That was the year the manual training teacher announced to me, "Cooperman, you've got two speeds: Slow and Stop. Who are you trying to fool? You people don't make carpenters." On the way back to my bench I thought of one, but decided the hell with it. He was right, the breadboard I'd been working on for the last eight weeks was lopsided.

Once back at my office, I decided not to call Mrs. Yates. In the morning, it would look as though I'd earned at least half of what she had advanced me. Dr. Bushmill's door was open. I walked into his empty waiting room. The good Irish doctor was where I saw him last, with a glass in his hand and a noggin of rye mostly in the doctor.

"Hello, Benny, how's the boy?" he grinned at me, missing eye contact by several focal lengths. "Sit down and have a jar." I sat down, and filled a reasonably clean glass—which on balance was also reasonably dirty—with about three fingers of rye. He did up a bottle a day, starting right after his last patient left, and not closing the door until it was gone, around nine or ten. The office smelled like most doctors' surgeries, but this one had a stale smell of old wood, old medicine, old magazines and Frank Bushmill added to it. The word on the street was that Frank was gay, but to me he just looked miserable. My mother was always trying to get me to bring him home for a good meal. He could use one, but let her invite him on her own time.

"What are you reading, Benny?" His fingers around the glass were yellow with nicotine and the fingernails ridged and thick. "Did you look up that Simenon book I was telling you about? He's the deep one. And everybody thinks he's just a detective story writer. Did you know that Gide was writing about him at the time of his death? That's a fact. Have you read any Gide at all?"

"I'm still working my way through the Russians." Slowly.

"Gogol," he said, rolling his eyes with meaning that didn't need further elucidation, except to me. "It's all in his *Overcoat*. You know that?"

"Whose overcoat?" I'd lost him.

"Gogol's."

"Ahhh," I said, nodding sagely. I sat a minute more, looking at the shining instruments in their glass cases, and then drank up quickly. "Well," I said, "I'd better be off. Thanks for the drink."

"Anytime, Benny. Anytime. Good night." He didn't get up, just went on staring at the spot I'd been sitting in.

"Good night," I said.

I closed the office door behind me and looked up Lou Gelner's number. Dr. Lou was a pal, and he knew everybody.

"Hello."

"Lou, it's Benny Cooperman."

"Hi, Benny, how's it hanging? What can I do you for?"

"Lou, what do you know about a Dr. Andrew Zekerman?"

"He's a shrink. What's to know? Has an office across from Hotel Dieu and sees a flood of patients every day."

"What else?"

"That's it. He's not cheap. He's sort of popular right now. You know, if there's a vogue in shrinks, this is his year. How'm I doing? You hear the one about the New Zealander and the plaster-caster, Benny?"

"Save it. Whenever you start to ramble on the phone,

...te wearing a little rubber finger glove on your

...gular Sherlock Holmes, Benny. I never let my right hand ...w what my left hand's doing. If you pick up a dose, call me." I put down the phone for a minute, lit up a smoke with the last match in the office, and broke down and called my mother.

"Hello, Ma?"

"It's you. I'm watching the news."

"I thought I'd come over tonight. What are you doing?"

"I told you, I'm watching the news."

"Well, if you're not doing anything special. I thought . . ."

"Benny, it's only Thursday night. You can't wait for Friday? It's only one more day. Your brother should drop in as often as you do. I got to go. Goodbye."

I stared at my yellow pad for a minute and then decided to take a run over to my mother's place just the same. She sounded a little down to me. I closed up the shop and walked to the stairs.

"Good night, Frank."

"Good night, Benny."

My car was parked behind the building. I went down the lane to where I'd left the Olds. For once I wasn't blocked in. By the time I parked outside my parents' condominium, it was getting a little purplish in the sky, but the heat hung on for dear life. It was a record spring for heat, the paper had said, and it caught everybody with his long underwear still on. The house wasn't really a house, it was something called a unit. This unit looked like all the other units on what looked like a street, but it wasn't a street, since all the units shared the same street address. It saved on numbers. I let myself in with my key. There were no lights upstairs and none on the main floor. She had been down in the recreation room watching television since the early afternoon. I walked over the high pile of the broadloom and went downstairs. She was where I expected to find her, where she had been since 1952 as close as I can remember.

"That you, Benny?" she asked without turning her head.

"Yes, Ma."

"I thought it was you. Your father's playing cards at the club tonight. This is his night to play cards."

"Uh huh."

"Did you eat?"

"I had a sandwich downtown about an hour ago."

"Good, because there's nothing to eat around here."

"Uh huh."

"That was too bad on the news, wasn't it?"

"What?"

"Too bad."

"Too bad about what, Ma?"

"About Chester Yates."

"What are you talking about?"

"I just told you." I went over to the set and looked for the button to turn it off. She protested, but I found it. I looked at her half expecting to see a decreasing circle of light end in a pinpoint of brightness and then go out, but she just sat there looking at the blank set.

"You shouldn't do that, Benny."

"You started to say something. I'm trying to help you finish it. Tell me and I'll turn the set on again. Cross my heart."

"Don't get funny with your mother."

"Ma, for God's sake tell me what you saw on the news about Chester Yates."

"He's dead, that's all. Now turn it back on again."

"What do you mean he's dead? I just saw him this afternoon."

"Well, about an hour ago he put a bullet through his brain."

THREE

For a full minute I just looked at my mother. Her face looked old and drained of colour under her blonde curls. I sat down hard on one of the vinyl stools in front of my father's other hobby, his bar, trying to get the fact through to the right terminal in my brain. I couldn't believe that the guy who'd carried all that overweight and a three piece suit for ten blocks, leaving me huffing and puffing like the Big Bad Wolf behind him on the hottest day this spring, had suddenly become work for the undertaker. It didn't make sense. Do people get up from their hour on the shrink's couch and quietly plug themselves? It didn't jell somehow. I looked around the room, hoping that something somewhere would have an answer. There was a bookcase full of all the books I'd ever bought, except for the dozen I had in my room at the hotel. There were some of my brother's medical text book discards: Histology, Dermatology and all the other ologies which a chief of surgery can safely discard. But no answers. Right about then I would have settled for a couple of good questions. I wasn't getting anywhere, and I had that itch at the back of my knees that said "move." I have good ideas only at the back of my knees. So I moved. I flicked the switch and turned my mother on again. The colour came back to her face and she smiled at a familiar commercial.

Upstairs, in the living room, with a portrait in oils of my mother at forty, when she was a brunette, hanging above the fireplace, I sank into a tangerine chair on the tangerine rug looking at the tangerine chesterfield and the tangerine curtains and tried to think. I could call Mrs. Yates. Bad idea. She would be playing jacks with the cops until midnight. I had money to return to her, but that could wait. I had news for her, but I wasn't sure whether news that her husband hadn't been playing around with another woman would exactly light up the sky for her. I could drop by the widow's house. I even wondered whether she was a widow yet. Maybe there was a three days' grace period when she was just the bereaved and bereft. Then I remembered that I only had her phone number and that was unlisted. I'd have to go back to my office downtown to look her up in the city directory. There didn't seem to be any more I could do just then, except make sure that I saw the 11:15 local news.

I let myself out. The moon shining through the windshield had a big bite out of it, and I rolled the window down as I drove through the razzle-dazzle of the fast food traps on both sides of the north end of Ontario Street. *"Chazerai,"* my father would say. But everybody to his poison. I turned left at the light when I got to the end of Ontario, and then joined the one way traffic along St. Andrew. There was lots of parking space where I needed it. I left the Olds in front of my office, a two-storey brick building, with a crowning cornice that jutted out two feet from the front, like all the other places that dated from the same bad year in domestic architecture. The streets were as bare as my bank account at the end of the month. I'd passed a couple looking at the pictures outside the Capitol Theatre. Except for them, everybody was safe and secure behind closed doors, or off in some shopping mall turning pay envelopes into down payments on appliances.

Frank Bushmill had either taken himself home or pulled himself the rest of the way into the bottle. His lights were out. Once, when I'd picked him up off the floor and poured him into a taxi, he half-opened his befuddled eyes from the backseat and said, "Benny, you're a decent old skin and God bless you." Maybe he was off with the gay crowd having a hell of a time. I hoped so, but doubted it. Around here, poor Frank was the gay crowd. No wonder he drank.

My place always looked spooky at night, with moving shadows and lights crawling over the walls and filing cabinets until I found the light switch. The fluorescent light stamped on the shadows. The office was a mess, with everything where it should be. I dragged out the city directory from under the telephone to look up Chester's address. It was in the right neighbourhood all right. He lived up to every dollar he'd earned right to the end. To think of him lying dead, when I'd seen him healthier than me only a couple of hours ago, stubbed all reason. Well, now he can be the healthiest body in Victoria Lawn. And what about his wife? She was sitting pretty. There would be no divorce. No further business for me in her direction. She was going to come out of this smelling of cut flowers, and only I knew how close she came to blowing the whole deal. I tried her number. After three rings, it was answered by a voice deep enough to belong to a police sergeant. She was under a doctor's care and not taking any calls, thank you. "Yeah. So what are you still hanging around for?" I wondered after I'd hung back the phone.

I'd come to a dead end. It was getting late and I'd earned my pay, so what was I worried about? If I had a private life, it was time to be getting on with it. Only I didn't feel like going back to my hotel room yet. If I were a drinking man, this is where I would open my filing cabinet and pull out a bottle of rye from behind the dead files. There was a dried-up orange back there and some dried apricots. The one was inedible and the other gave me gas. To hell with it.

I locked up the door with the frosted glass and squired myself to the car. There were two drunks talking in front of the beverage room of the Russell House. I looked in my glove compartment for matches. I sat behind the wheel, startled by the brightness of my tie as I lit a cigarette in the dark interior, and decided to take a run out past the Yates place. It couldn't hurt. And I'd like to think Myrna Yates would do as much for me.

I drove along the curving length of the main drag, then turned down into the valley where one hundred and fifty years ago the ship canal that the town had grown around had been dug. Now it ran in a filthy black arc behind and below the stores on St. Andrew. The road followed the canal for a while, being choosy about picking a crossing point, then doubled back to climb up the opposite bank to the two-hundred-thousand-dollar homes of South Ridge. Beyond that, on top of the escarpment, I could see a line of lights from streets like Minton and Dover in the South End, just this side of Papertown. The illuminated green water tower stood out as usual above everything.

The streets were wide with pools of light showing the way, while the houses themselves lay well back from the street under maples and birches. Hillcrest Avenue curved along the ridge of the same valley the canal took, but at a point beyond where it was a canal. On my right, the backyards of the rich ran for hundreds of feet down to the clay banks of the Eleven Mile Creek. Driving slowly I could see the house numbers easily, not that it was necessary: two police cruisers were still parked outside the Yates place, where all the lights were still burning.

I slid in behind one of the police cruisers, killed the motor and doused the lights. I was on my third cigarette, when a man came out of the house. He was a big guy, so I was surprised when he didn't get into one of the cruisers. I took a good look at his meaty face as he went under the street-lamp. He walked past my car without interest and headed along the sidewalk to a dark Buick parked about a hundred yards behind me. After he drove off, I had another cigarette, and then I thought, "Enough of this driving around."

The national news doled out its usual helping of international calamities and national absurdities, which I was able to watch in black and white from my bed. I'd closed the dusty curtains to keep the neon out, and lit a cigarette. I'd smoked nearly two packs today without once thinking of giving it up. It had been a busy day. From downstairs came the beat of the rock group playing in the "Ladies and Escorts" section of the downstairs beer parlour. I could feel it through the mattress.

The local anchor man wore a crest on his blazer with the station's logo on it. He looked pretty silly before he started speaking, and then it was the content that looked silly. They seemed to use the same film-clip of the back end of an ambulance three times for three separate stories. The last one was about Chester Yates. According to this account, the body had been discovered in his office on the seventh floor of the Caddell Building about five-thirty on an early security check by Thomas Glassock, who worked for Niagara. Nobody heard the shot. Chester had returned to his office just before the office staff left for the day. His secretary, Martha Tracy, who was the last one to see him alive, said that her boss had not been his usual ebullient self lately. I'll bet Martha Tracy said ebullient. Those TV newswriters are all reaching for a Pulitzer Prize. The gun that he used was his own target pistol, and the police were hoping to wind up their routine investigation swiftly. Chester was then praised for his many public-spirited acts by Mayor Rampham wearing his other expression, and by Alderman Vern Harrington, a close personal friend, and the owner of the face I'd just seen under the streetlamp leaving the home of the dear departed. That's all there was to it. Thank you and good-night.

The sun was illuminating the dust particles in my stale air at eight o'clock next morning, when I rolled out of a dream in which I'd been chased through Montecello park by Chester and his wife followed by a dozen or so Keystone cops. Blinking, I thought that reality couldn't be worse than this. I got up, shaved, put on my rumpled pinstripe suit again and again promised myself to retire it as soon as I could afford to. Once more I knotted my tie so that it made doing up my fly unnecessary. I tried it a second time, but it didn't help. I grabbed a cup of coffee at the United Cigar Store, and looked through the paper to see if there was any more information about Yates' suicide. There wasn't. The solid citizen stuff was pushed to the top, and then the sad loss, and then the scant details about taking his life under the pressure of business and overwork. Case closed.

I climbed the twenty-eight steps to my office, and let myself in. The mail on the floor was unimpressive: "Give our Total Service a try and Save Five Dollars." I wrapped a blank piece of paper around ten of Mrs. Yates' twenty-dollar bills and put them in an envelope which I addressed to her. On the back of one of my remaining cards, I wrote:

> Dear Mrs. Yates,
> I was sorry to hear today of your husband's sudden death, and I extend to you my deepest sympathy at this difficult time. I am returning to you part of the retainer you left with me yesterday because I have concluded my investigation, discovering that your fears were groundless and that in fact your late husband had been seeing a doctor.

I looked at it. I didn't like my cramped words, I didn't like my childish scrawl. I didn't like the possibility that someone other than Mrs. Yates would open the envelope. There are always helpful people around when there's a funeral in the air. I tore up the note and put the money in my inside breast pocket. I'd have to see her in person. But I couldn't decently accomplish that until after the cops and the mourners had thinned out a little. I shrugged to myself and decided to buy myself a haircut. It would set me up for the whole day, and with *my* hair, which had been running for cover above my collar and behind my ears since I was twenty, it wouldn't cut too deeply into my business day.

It was business I was brooding about as I walked up St. Andrew towards the barbershop in the basement of the Murray Hotel. I thought of dropping in on my cousin Melvyn to see if he needed any title-searching done down at the registry office. He could usually be relied upon to throw me some crumbs if I chirped brightly. He was even known to have paid me a couple of times. I can't complain. It leaves me busy and like polio it keeps me off the streets. I remember the little creep sticking his tongue out at me when he was still in his playpen. Now he's graduated and practising, he has learned subtlety. For a while I was his chief good-works project and my mother loved him for it. Lately, although Ma hadn't noticed, his big interest in life was cuff-links made from real Roman coins.

There was a chair waiting in the barbershop. Bill Hall was sweeping up from his last customer and placed the brown curls in a white garbage can, leaving the mottled tile floor with a dull sheen.

"How've you been, Ben?" he asked seriously.

"Can't complain, Bill. Nothing much doing in my line."

"Nor in mine," he said, cocking his bald head and looking at me meaningfully in the mirror.

"Too bad about Chester Yates," I said, playing my king's pawn opening.

"Well, we all got to go," he sighed shaking his head, and trying to line up my ears on a horizontal line.

"Paper said it was business worries. What kind of worries do you get with his kind of business?"

"Real estate, developing and contracting? It's a hustle like everything else, I guess. Most of them are walking a thin line holding their breath most of the time. They make their backroom deals and the accountants and lawyers straighten it out and make it look up and up."

"But, if that's the name of the game, why should he suddenly blow his brains out?"

"I guess even hustlers can have enough," he shrugged in the glass over the bottles of hair tonic which, in the ten years I'd been coming to Bill, he'd never used on me.

"Uh huh."

"I used to know his wife, Myrna. Years ago. She came from the west end same as me. Her father had a wrecking yard out Pelham Road. There were two of them on the way

out to Power Gorge, and her father ran the one closest to
town. She was a saucy little tramp in public school. She, you
know, developed early for a girl, and she knew what it was all
about when the rest of us thought balls were for basketball
hoops. Of course, she's changed a lot now. Settled. Money
does that. Funny thing about money, Ben: it makes people
different, inside. Outside, you can't tell much. I had Lord
Robinson, the newspaper tycoon, sitting right where you are
one time, and he wasn't any different from anybody else. I
couldn't find any trace of his organizing genius in his hair.
Ginger-coloured it was, getting kind of sparse so he liked it
combed across. But where was all that power for making
money? He had dandruff, same as you."

The morning was well advanced by the time I left the
hotel and started back to the office. The sidewalks showed a
few storekeepers leaning against their plate-glass windows.
Without thinking about it, I was staring into the window of
the sporting-goods store at the baseball mitts and English
Dinky toys. I could see the old man at the counter in an otherwise empty shop. An old-fashioned bell rang as I opened the
door.

"Yes?" he said, looking over his glasses. "Say, aren't you
Manny Cooperman's boy?" I nodded. "I thought so. I've
known your father for forty years. He used to bring you in
here when you were a boy. Which one are you? One of you
is a doctor, isn't that right?"

"I'm Ben, the one that stayed at home."

"That's right, I see you go by once in a while. You don't
come in any more. Say, I remember one time your father
brought you in here, you couldn't have been more than three
or four, but walking you know, and I asked you—it must
have been in the 1940s, just after the war started—and I
asked you, just kidding, mind, who did you think was going
to win the war over in Europe. And you thought a minute,
I'll never forget it, and said that you thought that both sides
were going to lose. Now can you beat that? Do you remember
saying that? Did your father ever tell you that story? I know
it was you. You or your brother. Couldn't have been more
than five or six. Yes, sir, I'll never forget that."

He seemed to sink into his private past for a minute,
looking very tall and thin in the tall, thin store with the light
coming in through the bicycle wheels in the window.

"It was my brother."

"Hmmm?" he asked, pretty far away.

"Nothing," I said.

"Is there something special you are looking for, Ben? We don't see you much these last few years. We seem to lose them after high school and then pick them up again when they start tennis and racketball. But there's a ten-year gap sometimes. I didn't catch. Did you say you were looking for something special?"

"Oh, I was vaguely looking at your bikes through the window—it's Mr. MacLeish, isn't it?"

"That's right. You know my brother's gone."

"Oh, I'm sorry to hear that."

"Well, that was a good many years ago now. It gets longer every time I add it up. You were asking about bicycles. Yes, a lot of people your age are riding safety bikes. You know I sell more to young adults than I do to teenagers. Isn't that a pretty paradox for you? I guess it's the gears they have today that they didn't have in your day or in mine. And it's all this play they give to fitness on the television. Don't you think that's so?"

I walked with Mr. MacLeish to his display of bicycles. He had about twenty on the floor and another bunch hanging from hooks on the wall. Behind a partition, a teenager in a mouse-coloured shopcoat was assembling more from wooden crates.

"Funny thing," Mr. MacLeish said, his watery eyes winking over his lenses, "speaking about bikes. You know who came in through that door yesterday afternoon? It just goes to show you that you can't be too careful on the subject of fitness. Well, sir, yesterday afternoon I had a customer looking at bikes, and he was a dead man by the time I closed up for the night."

"You mean Chester Yates?"

"Why how'd you know that? That's right. Isn't that a remarkable thing?"

"Well, I guess anybody can look at bikes even if he means to shoot himself in an hour."

"Ben, I agree with you. It might calm a desperate man about to commit a desperate act. But Ben, looking at bikes is one thing, and buying them's another."

"What?"

"That's what I say. Buying a ten-speed bike and then killing yourself, that's a totally different can of paint."

FOUR

I walked back to the office without seeing anything much. All I knew was that the file I had marked "closed" was open again, and written at the top of the first page inside was "Concerning the death of Chester Yates." It didn't add up and things that don't add up give me heartburn. So, I went to work. I phoned Dr. Zekerman, but got an answering service. It was the same service I use, so I was able to quiz the girl and discover that the doctor sometimes picked up his calls between patients but often didn't bother until late in the afternoon. No, there wasn't a nurse or receptionist who picked up the calls, it was always the doctor. I left my number with her.

Next I called Peter Staziak in Homicide. We'd been in the same class in Chemistry at high school, and I'd been in a school play with his sister. I asked him who was handling the Yates suicide and he put me on to a Sergeant Harrow, who was supposed to have all the answers. I told Harrow what I had and I could hear him breathing steadily at the other end, without any sudden intakes of air. Then he wanted to know who I was and why it had become my business. He seemed to be more interested in that than in the news about a suicide buying a ten-speed bike an hour before killing himself. Finally he said, "Look, Mr. Cooperman. I want to thank you for coming forward with this information, but the case is closed."

"There'll be an inquest, won't there?" I asked.

"Sure, but that's just routine too. You see, sir, we have the report from the medical examiner who says that death came from a self-inflicted wound in the head. The powder burns say that it was a self-inflicted wound, the fingerprints say so and so does the paraffin test."

"That's doesn't mean too much to me. I mostly do divorce work."

"Well, Mr. Cooperman, I think you'd better go back to your transom gazing and let us get on with our work. Thanks just the same."

"Wait a minute! What have you got for the motive? Why'd he do it?"

"Like it says in the paper: he was depressed and overworked. Look, Mr. Cooperman, this is a dead one. If you want to play sleuth, we've got dozens of cases you can go to work on." His irony had the same effect as someone digging you in the ribs with his elbow repeating "Did you get it?" I got it and then got off the line.

I was getting nowhere fast. I looked up the name of Chester's company in the book and dialled it. I asked for Yates' office, and when the noise of clicking and switching stopped I asked for Martha Tracy, Chester's secretary.

"She's off sick today, sir. Can I help you?"

"Can you give me Miss Tracy's home number?"

"I'm very sorry, we don't give out that information."

"I'm sure you don't, under normal circumstances, but this is an emergency." I heard some talking through the palm of her hand which I didn't catch and then there was a new voice on the line.

"Who is this?" it asked, "and who do you want?" I thought that in this instance the better part of valour was retreat. I hung up. I waited ten minutes and dialled again, heard the same noises and clicks and heard the first voice again.

"Can I help you?"

"This is Father Murphy over at St. Jude's and we're after arranging a high mass for dear Martha Tracy's poor unfortunate employer, may he rest in peace. But Sister Kenny can't seem to find the girl's telephone number at all at all. Would you help us out, Miss, and may the blessing of St. Patrick himself be on you for helping us in this sad business?"

"Will you please stop doing that," she said, with a steel edge to her voice. "We don't give out private numbers. If you keep calling I'll call the supervisor." The line went dead. I took that hard, and went out for a cup of coffee. I'd had lines in *Finian's Rainbow* at school. I'd been one of the silent singers. I just moved my lips during the songs. But I had real lines.

I decided that I'd better go down there to snoop around in my own way. It was Friday, so everybody would be anxious to get away promptly at five. That made the muscle in my cheek relax a little, and when I looked at my hands, they were almost dry. I ordered a chopped egg sandwich. In the seat next to me at the marble-topped counter an old geezer was rapidly making notes. I wondered for a second whether they were on to me, but he didn't look up at me or at anyone else; the waitress scooped the soupbowl out from under his nose and slid the ham and eggs under without getting in the way of his pencil. I took a sideways look at his notebook; the writing went in all directions. The waitress saw me staring at him when she brought my sandwich. Without any direct reference to my neighbour she said, "I knew a fellow who wore Reynoldswrap in his shorts, once: to keep the radiation away from his precious jewels."

Back in the office, I put in a call to Niagara. Said I was Sergeant Harrow from Homicide. I found out that Thomas Glassock would be on duty as usual in the Caddell Building beginning at five o'clock. Good. I was back on the track. I didn't quite know what I was on the track of, but I was back on it and it felt better.

To kill the time before talking to Glassock, I wandered over to City Hall. There were tulips in bud in large cement planters in front of the war memorial as I walked up the wide expanse of front steps. I always got a good feeling walking up these steps which rise to a series of eight doors. Eight doors has a kind of New England town meeting feel. But when I got to the top, all but one of them was locked. There was a message there for me someplace; I decided to pick it up later.

I disappointed the girl behind the counter by not having my assessment with me. When I told her that I didn't have an assessment, it nearly broke her heart. I asked her where I could find the elected members of council. She directed me and I obeyed.

The wall to wall rug down the corridor between the offices of the aldermen was thick and green. The doors were blue, I couldn't figure that one. I found Harrington's door, and was about to knock, when a stenographer picked the wrong moment to be efficient.

"Was there something?" she asked as though we were both speaking English.

"Yes, there was. In fact, there is. Is that Mr. Harrington's office?"

"Yes, but ..." I was wondering whether she was just playing a game with me or whether she really cared whether I got in to see him or not.

"Well, is he in it?"

"Yes, but . . ." It was happening a little too fast for her.

"Is he with someone?" She shook her head. "Is he asleep?"

"Sir, do you have an appointment to see Mr. Harrington?"

"No. Is it necessary to have one to see an elected official?" I pretended to bristle.

"Not really, but may I ask what is the nature of your business with Mr. Harrington?"

"Well, I wouldn't tell everybody, but since it's you, I'll tell you. I want to ask Mr. Harrington just exactly what he intends to do about my wife. Call it family business or private business, whatever you like, but if he won't see me, I'm afraid he'll have to see my lawyer."

"Oh! Oh dear. Why, of course, yes. You can go right in. I know he's there. Goodness." She visibly faded behind her pink plastic glasses, leaving only a smear of rouge and lipstick under her permanent wave. I knocked at Harrington's door.

He was a big man by anybody's scale. His face looked like a roast beef dinner with all the trimmings, with a huge portion of nose in the middle. The rest of him lived up to that start. I could see why I'd taken him for a cop the other night in front of the Yates house. He wore a two-piece blue suit with a wide dark blue tie. A brown paper-bag lunch lay spread out in front of him, and he began collecting the evidence in a napkin quickly as I crossed to his desk.

"What can I do for you, Mr . . .?"

"Cooperman. Ben Cooperman." He smiled an election smile and shook my hand until it was raw meat. I took a chair that looked like a cream-coloured plastic tulip and found that I could sit in it without being whisked off to the land of the little people.

"Well, Mr. Cooperman?"

"I'm a private investigator, Mr. Harrington, and I'm looking into some of the circumstances surrounding Chester Yates' death. I know you were a friend of his. I need your help." He smiled, but there was no charm in it. He began to size me up for the first time.

"What kind of circumstances?" He chose his words carefully. "Chester shot himself. What could be clearer than that?"

"Two hours before he killed himself, Chester bought himself a present."

"How official is this?" He looked worried.

"I was there; I saw him buy it. If you were going to kill

yourself, would you buy an expensive gift for yourself that
you knew you'd never live to use?"

"Present, what kind of present?"

"A ten-speed bike. He got it at MacLeish's on St. Andrew Street."

"This is absurd. A bicycle! What are you trying to make
of this, Mr. Cooperman? A man is dead. Isn't that enough? I
spent a couple of hours with Chester's wife last night and now
you insult a fine man's memory with talk of bicycles." His face
was getting to look rare on the outside. He was a big man,
and I didn't want to picture him angry. He looked like he
could do angry far too well.

"Look, Mr. Harrington, the normal assumption is that a
purchase is made to be used. People who kill themselves don't
buy cars, rent apartments or reserve plane tickets. They may
be killing themselves for the first time, but if you check the
books in any insurance office you'll see that every move is
predictable, from the small nicks on the throat of a razor
suicide to the clothes left at the top of Lovers' Leap. It's
all been done before, thousands of times. It's as unlikely for a
man to have bought a bike before knocking himself off as
for a woman to hang herself wearing long underwear or jump
from a slow-moving passenger train. This thing will have to be
looked into."

"What's the difference? Think of his family, Cooperman.
Walk away from it. That's my advice."

"I hear you talking, but I don't think a little nosing
around will hurt."

"Cooperman, I'm telling the truth when I say that it
would be best to drop this. You don't know what you're getting into. It's disgusting, really. Like playing in your own dirt.
I don't want to talk about it any more. I can see that you
aren't prepared to be reasonable."

"What you call reasonable, I call looking the other way."
I heard a buzzer sound. His right hand was moving away from
a button on his intercom. His face was moving from mauve to
purple. I intended to stay out of his reach, as he got up and
started around the end of his desk in my direction. The door
opened and the girl with the plastic glasses stood between us.

"Miss Keiller, Mr. Cooperman is leaving now. I want
you to take a good look at him, because if he ever comes to
the office again, I don't want him to get by your desk. Do you
understand?" She nodded, swallowing her explanation. Harrington grabbed a couple of file folders, and strode past me

and Miss Keiller through the door and out into the real world of civic politics. Miss Keiller and I stood fixed like we'd been bolted to the broadloom until a door slammed at the far end of the corridor. I tried to flip her a grin as I went by her, but I think I missed.

Just before five o'clock I walked through the double glass doors of the limestone-fronted Caddell Building and punched the elevator for the eighth floor. That put me on the floor above Yates' operation. I decided to try walking to my right as soon as the doors opened in case I looked lost when some receptionist looked up. But there wasn't a receptionist. The floor was divided into a number of small offices with doors leading off the corridor. I found the Men's Room and went inside a cubicle for a smoke. At five after five I found the red exit sign and walked down one flight of stairs. Inside the door of "Scarp Enterprises" all was quiet. I found the door with Chester's name on it in stand-out white plastic letters. It was locked. I fished around in the top drawer of the desk just outside Yates' office, Martha Tracy's, I guessed, and found a key in the paperclip box. I couldn't be sure when Glassock would make his first check, so I had to get in and out quickly. I tried to ignore the geography once I closed the door again. I could take it all in again later. What I needed now was some link with the dead man that might carry me along for another couple of days. The desk top was clear. So were all the other surfaces. I pulled out the first drawer that opened: envelopes, paperclips, and company letterhead. If he had a private address book that had been taken with other obvious stuff by the police. I was looking for sloppy seconds, and found them in a middle drawer. It was a clipboard with the agenda of a board meeting on it. A few words were underlined and there was a feeble attempt at a drawing of Mickey Mouse in one corner. He was no artist. That was something. Elsewhere on the sheet he appeared to be trying to design a logo. The Arabic numeral two and the letter "C" were drawn in three different possible arrangements. There was one attempt with the Roman numeral for two, "II." I scanned the agenda and couldn't find anything beginning with "C" or having a "2" or "II" connected in any way. No, the meeting had to do with Scarp Estates, with a sewage contract, with tenders for foundation construction, and others for roofing. I was getting nervous, so I slammed the clipboard back in the drawer and left the room in a middle-sized sweat.

The outer office was still bright and silent. No sign of

elevator noise. I could sit on my hands and wait, I thought, or I could see what useful information might lie out in the open. First I noted down Martha Tracy's home telephone number from a typed list of names and numbers inside the lid of a metal desk-top file. I also found a glossy brochure describing Scarp Estates, a new subdivision planned for the top of the escarpment that runs through the peninsula like a spine, with Niagara Falls which tumbles over it supplying hydroelectric power for the expanding industries of the area. From the brochure it was plain that Scarp Enterprises was dabbling in some of that industrial expansion along with the real estate development. Nice going, I thought. But the brochure didn't say anything about somebody dying in order to keep it running so smoothly.

I could hear the security man let himself into the outer office, and so I leaned back and lit a cigarette.

"Who the hell are you?" he asked, putting his time clock down on the edge of a white metal desk.

"I'm Behan of the *Beacon*. You're Glassock?"

"Yeah."

"You found the body?" He just stood there like someone had given him the prize in the box of Cracker-jacks.

"Yeah."

"My editor thinks that there's a lot of this story that didn't get in today's paper. He wants me to try a new angle, human interest stuff: TOM GREENOCK FINDS CORPSE. How's that for a headline?"

"Glassock."

"Even better. HARDWORKING TOM GLASSOCK STUMBLES ON BODY OF CORPORATE GIANT. How'm I doing?" I hated to take advantage of the poor geezer, but everybody's got to make a living. So, I strung him a little. I wasn't stealing his watch. "What I want you to give me is the whole story in your own words." I picked up a green pad with a spiral binding from Martha Tracy's "Pending" basket and licked the end of my pencil.

"You going to write down what I say? Put it in the paper?"

"That's right," I said giving him my Pulitzer Prize smile.

"Well, now, I don't know about that. I got a family to think of. It's as good as my job if I blab to everybody."

"Well, Tom, the *Beacon* isn't everybody."

"True, but . . ."

"Tell you what. Anything you say is off the record, I'll forget I ever heard it. You've got my word on that."

"Well, I guess it's all right, or they wouldn't have sent you. What do you want to know?"

"Why don't you just walk through it and show me the way it was?"

"Right. Well, I came in that door over there," he indicated the main door leading from the two elevators.

"That was about this time yesterday? A little after five?" He bent his head and studied his leather-bound clock for a minute. I could see the pink of his scalp through his gray hair.

"Later than that. I was on my first round, but this is a big building. I have to answer for the whole twelve floors, keeps me hopping. It must have been same time as usual, that's five forty-five."

"Is that the time on yesterday's card?"

"Well, yesterday, it was a little later. It was five fifty-seven, they told me. That's a little off my regular time but not by much."

"Did you hear anything?"

"No. These places are built with thick concrete floors. I couldn't have heard anything unless I was on this floor somewheres. Well, sir, I came through this aisle as usual and saw that Mr. Yates' door was open."

"Were the other office doors open?"

"Most of 'em. And I saw that Mr. Yates' door was open."

"But you just said . . ."

"I know. Well, it was open, that's all. And I looked in and there he was."

"Could you show me?"

"Sure." He brought out a bunch of keys and studied them closely. "This should be it," he said and it was.

Chester Yates' office, which I now took in for the first time in detail, told the world what Chester wanted it to know about him. He had a corner office with light coming in through windows on two walls. Through the sheer floor-length curtains I could see north to the lake and follow the coast around in a gentle arc until it disappeared in the haze. His desk was a wide expanse of immaculate white, without a paper on it to suggest that these surroundings had a hold on whoever sat behind it. The walls were industrial wallboard, whose covering suggested wood panelling. The wall that Chester faced as he signed his name on the dotted line all day was a busy place. He had one of those credenza things which covered his files, over which a three-tiered bookshelf caught my eye. The chair behind the desk was the same sort of orange that the green broadloom was. The kind of colour that doesn't exist outside an interior decorator's mind. I took a closer look at this handsome object. It was a swivel chair, and from now on when it swivelled would swivel over a dark brown stain on the rug.

"They'll never get that out," Glassock muttered, shaking his head. "They'll just have to junk it. That's where I found him, right there in that chair. Sitting up he was, with his head bent over the top, like he expected the dentist to look at his teeth. The gun on the floor where he'd dropped it."

"Was everything in the room the way it is now, except for the body?"

"Yes, I think so." I saw Glassock's eye go to the book cases. "Yes, it was just like this."

"Why did you look over there? Is something different?"

"Well, yes, there is," he smirked. "It's the bar."

"Bar? All I see is a bookcase." Glassock's smirk opened up to reveal a mouthful of teeth that were aggressively false. He went over to the bookshelves and transformed them.

"He had it specially made. It's got a sink and fridge, and like you see, it's well-stocked."

"And you say it was open last night."

"Yeah. I could smell it too. There was the odour of drink in the air. That's one of those off-the-record things we agreed about."

"You mean you didn't mention this yesterday?"

"Bad enough him killing himself like that. No sense adding insult to injury I always say."

"I couldn't agree with you more. Tell me, was there a glass on the desk, or on the credenza? A glass with a half-finished drink in it?"

"Let me see . . ." He walked over to the bar, stroked his chin and pulled at his earlobe. "He always kept his empty glasses on this tray. Kept them lined up in two rows the way they are now." I counted six highball glasses. They were dry and clean. I backed up and pulled at my earlobe too. Glassock watched me as I looked from the desk to the bar, from the bar to the door, and from the door back to Glassock.

"Did you ever talk to Mr. Yates?"

"Sure." He stretched the syllable out making Chester sound like a regular democrat.

"And you'd seen the bookshelf open before last night?"

"Mr. Yates used to tell me things. He'd invite me in here and we'd chew the fat, you might say." He looked over to me like I should hand out little gold stars. "Many's the night we'd have a noggin and he'd stand looking out the window at the lake, sort of far away in his thoughts, and jangling his keys in his pocket with his free hand." Glassock showed me exactly what a far-away look was and tried to imitate Chester rattling his keys. On a cliff-top, it would have made quite a picture. Under the fluorescent lights, it lost something.

"Where does that door lead?" I asked him, shattering his reverie.

"Just a cupboard."

"May I . . . ?"

"Help yourself." Inside the door was sports wear for all occasions: a track suit, three different kinds of brand-name running shoes, a squash racket, and something that looked like headphones for a stereo set. I picked them up. There were no wires attached. "Them's ear-plugs for the firing-range. He was a crack shot, they say. Used to practise with the police shooting team sometimes." Near the ear-plugs hung a black leather holster. It was empty.

"He was quite a sportsman," I said.

"He could afford to be." Glassock was beginning to shift from haunch to haunch.

"Tell me one more thing: did Mr. Yates like a good time?"

"Same as most, I guess. Never told me anything personal. He mostly went on about the opportunities in this country for people like me from the old country. He'd get a few drinks under his belt. He liked a drink, he did. But he wasn't the sort to . . . play around, you know. But then, you never know." He let his words hang in the air for a second or two, then I broke his beautiful moment again by crossing the room with my hand outstretched. I thanked him for his help. He asked me not to print anything that might get him in trouble and to be sure to let him know when the article was coming out. I backed my way into the elevator while he discussed the best time to get pictures of himself with Violet, his wife, and Alfred and Edward, the twins. When I told him that he had been very helpful, I wasn't telling a word of a lie, as Dr. Bushmill would have said.

FIVE

It was nearly six o'clock when I got back to my room at the hotel. I stripped off my clothes like a snake sloughing last year's skin, and slipped into the shower. I let the water run at full pressure first as hot as I could take it and then slowly I turned the tap around to cold. I stepped onto the white bathmat feeling somehow like I'd deserved the good feeling building up in me. Then I remembered that I was going to my mother's for dinner.

I drove up Ontario Street past the drive-ins on both sides of the road, and finally parked a quarter of a mile beyond in one of the guest parking spots at the condominium.

"It's you!" my mother said, as though she was Stanley looking for Livingstone. I didn't try to figure it out. I was so surprised to see her up, dressed and in the kitchen. "I wasn't really expecting you," she said.

"I told you yesterday I was coming."

"What?" She made the vowel so you could slide it under the door.

"Ma, you knew I was coming. I told you last week, and I told you last night." She frowned and looked hopelessly in the direction of the refrigerator.

"You're going to kill your mother one day with these surprises. You hear? Well, I guess I could put a couple of frozen steaks on. Your father's downstairs. You'll eat a steak, Benny?"

"Sure, Ma, but try not to broil the hell out of it, please."

"So look who's telling me how to cook. Go talk to your father and leave me to be the Mystery Chef if you please." I found the unopened *Beacon* on the tangerine loveseat and took it with me downstairs into the rec room. Pa was sitting

32

in front of the television. My parents spell one another off like that. Between the two of them they don't miss much.

"She said you weren't coming." He was looking older tonight; his gray-black hair, his brow, like onion skin, and the purple ant-tracks on his cheekbones made me go over and give him a hug and kiss on the cheek. He smelled of talcum. He'd been in the sauna at his club. "Are you working hard?"

"A little."

"Melvyn. I saw Melvyn your cousin today. He said that you haven't been to see him like you promised. He could throw some work your way, Benny. He's got contacts. You shouldn't end up like your father a poor man at the end of your life."

"Pa, what are you talking about? You're comfortable, aren't you. So what if you're not a millionaire."

"Leave my brother Harry out of this. Believe me, Benny, if I had wanted to make money, I would have made it. There's nothing easier. Like the poet says, 'Does a rich man sleep as soundly as a poor man? Is he happier?' Still, don't put me off what I was saying. You'll promise me to go in and talk to Melvyn on Monday. Okay? Tomorrow, he and Doreen are going to the Seligman bar mitzvah in Toronto at Temple Sholom."

"Good for them. I've got the paper. You want to see it?" He dismissed it with a wave of his hand.

"I get all the bad news I want on TV. I don't need it in the paper too." I took that as permission to open it myself. In the first section, there was a short editorial about Chester running twenty lines after a long piece on the abuse of higher education by taxi drivers who are actually Ph.D.s in sociology. Writing about Chester the editorial writer mused on the pressures of modern life, the loneliness of the men at the top, and the loss of our ablest citizens because they are always willing to walk the extra mile. For a minute it looked as though he was going to throw in a blast at food additives, but at the last moment he swerved off in another direction. Food additives came in for a column on their own further down the page. On the inside of the back page under *Deaths, Marriages, Funerals and In Memoriam* I discovered that the Yates funeral was slated for Monday. The coroner hadn't seen fit to hold Chester's body while the investigation continued. I was still way out in front in a field of one.

In about twenty minutes, my mother called us to the table. The Friday night candles had been lit, and there were two bowls of soup on the plastic cloth, one for me and the other for my father. It was canned vegetable.

"Where's your soup?" my father asked.

"I never eat soup," she answered. I was still in short pants when I first heard that exchange. "If anyone wants a salad, I can make one," she dared us. I said that a salad would be just the thing. She didn't budge. Pa went into the kitchen to retrieve the steaks from the broiler. "Manny, let Benny have the rare one." He placed the platter of steaming meat in the middle of the table, after I cleared a place. "You know how he likes his rare." He handed me my plate and I cut into the meat. It was liver gray all the way through. The vegetables were canned peas and carrots; lukewarm. Ma repeated her invitation to salad. Maybe there remained in the back of her mind the ghost of a servant lurking in the kitchen who could whip up these trifles at a moment's notice. The meal concluded with the traditional passing of the teabag from cup to cup, followed by the time-honoured squirt from the plastic lemon. After his last sip of tea, Pa pushed himself away from the table observing, "Benny, it does you good to get a home-cooked meal for a change, after the *chazerai* you eat in restaurants."

Later, back at my office, I did a few useful chores. I attached the key I'd taken from Martha Tracy's desk to a piece of paper with Scotch tape, slipped it into a stamped envelope, addressed the envelope to Martha Tracy care of her office in the Caddell Building on James Street and put it with my out mail. Then I tried to reach Dr. Zekerman again. No luck. I left my name for a second time with his answering service. Then I lit a cigarette and dialled the number Myrna Yates had given me.

"Hello?"

"Mrs. Yates, this is Benny Cooperman." There was the sound of some sort of mental process down at her end of the wire.

"Oh yes, Mr. Cooperman." Her voice became metallic and formal.

"I just wanted to tell you how sorry I was to hear about what happened to your husband." I was trying to find a way to tell her what I'd found out without saying too much over the phone. "I wonder if we might meet to discuss some business—after Monday, of course." That was the best I could manage.

"Mr. Cooperman, I don't think we have any business to

discuss. I thank you for what you've done, and I'm sure you understand that there is nothing further ..." At this point another voice, on an extension somewhere, joined in with an authority familiar with the forms and arts of chilling a poor private investigator to the marrow.

"Look here, Mr. Cooperman, I don't know what business you are talking about, but Mrs. Yates is in no condition to discuss business at a time like this. I'm sure you appreciate the severity of the shock she's had and I don't think that I want to see her suffer any more if I can help it. Do I make myself clear?"

"Bill, I ..."

"Let me handle this, Myrna. I think that Mr. Cooperman understands the situation."

"My business," I began to say, "is with Mrs. Yates, Mr. . . . ?"

"This is William Allen Ward, Mr. Cooperman, and I think I've made it plain that Mrs. Yates doesn't wish to be harassed by people just now. I don't wish to sound unpleasant, but if you don't get off the line, I will be forced to report this unfeeling and distress-causing behaviour. Do we understand each other?"

"Sure, Mr. Ward. Have it your way. But since when is a single phone call 'harassment'? I'll bet Mrs. Yates could tell me to hang up all by herself if she wanted to."

"It seems to me I did just that, Mr. Cooperman," she added, filling an inside straight that I'd left wide open for her.

"Okay, okay. I'm hanging up. Sorry to have caused all the commotion."

So Myrna Yates had William Allen Ward running interference for her. I guess the mayor could spare him for a few hours in such a good cause. Ward was a comer in local politics, the mayor's shadow, and the man responsible for adding the Harvard Business School phrases to the most recent crop of official documents. A local boy, he had brushed the hay and alfalfa off his jeans and made good in a way that looked like it was going to pull the whole city into the big time behind him. Even the mayor looked like a cracker-barrel hick when sitting next to Bill Ward on a public platform. I was impressed by Myrna Yates' taste in protectors. She couldn't have picked better.

Next, I thought I'd try Martha Tracy. I dialled her home number. Bill Ward couldn't be in two places at once. I was getting smart in my old age.

"M'yeah?"

"Martha Tracy?"

"That's the name. Who wants her?" It was the husky voice of an original. I could picture her at her desk shooing away unlikely visitors from Chester Yates' door.

"This is Benny Cooperman. I'm a private investigator."

"Come off it, who is this?"

"No, really. I want to talk to you about something concerning Mr. Yates' death. Can I come over to see you?"

"I got a house full of people here."

"Tomorrow, then?"

"M'yeah. But not before noon. And it better be good. I've had my craw full of policemen the last few days. What was the name again?"

"Cooperman. Benny Cooperman. See you at noon, tomorrow."

"Goodbye." And she hung up. Martha Tracy was going to be someone I wouldn't like to miss. She sounded as shaken by the death of her boss as the security man, less. Chester must have been a wonder to work for.

I locked up the office and started for the stairs. Frank Bushmill's light was burning, so I wandered in. The Doc was sprawled in his waiting room, dead to the world. An empty bottle had rolled from where he'd dropped it across the worn carpet to the opposite side of the room. His mouth was open and he was blowing soft bubbles at the glass globe supported by three brass chains above his head. I found a coat on the chipped walnut rack and threw it across the body. He mumbled something unintelligible, which I agreed with, naturally, and then I left him there. He didn't have patients on Saturday morning, so he wouldn't be awakened by an emergency case of athlete's foot at the crack of dawn.

Back at the hotel, it was the usual Friday night din. The beat from the band hammered at the floor like an electric vibrator. Somehow the melodic line was lost in transmission through the joists and plaster, just the amplified bass notes tickled my toes out of my socks like magic fingers in cheap motels. I climbed out of my clothes and into bed. I tried to sleep but got tangled in the loose ends of the bed sheets. I hate loose ends.

SIX

Saturday dawned a hot one. But these old brick walls kept the heat away from me until I hit the street around ten. After some coffee and toast at the United, I went back to the office. The Saturday crowd on St. Andrew Street must have been laid off. Three or four merchants stood at their doorways, wondering what had hit them. Somebody should tell them their former customers are out at the shopping plazas. Out there, the storeowners have customers knee-deep and wall to wall.

The sun cut a diamond-shaped patch through the transom, throwing the reversed letters of Frank Bushmill's name across the stairs as I climbed to my floor. No mail on a Saturday. That meant less garbage. I tried reading an itch at the back of my knees. It seemed to say get in touch with Dr. Zekerman at home. He wasn't listed in the phone book, so I turned to the city directory. No help there either. He must have a place out in the township someplace. I phoned Lou Gelner and he looked him up in the medical registry, complaining that he was doing all my work for me, which was true. He found that Zekerman lived out along the Eleven Mile Creek by Power Gorge. I thought that I might run out there after I went to see Martha Tracy.

The western part of the city is cut off from the rest of it by a canal to the north, dirty and full of nasty concoctions brewed in the papermills a few miles up the valley; and to the west by the river-sized stream called the Eleven Mile Creek. Except for the mansion of the chief mover and entrepreneur of the canal, built in the 1840s, this side of town has nothing to shout about. Most of the houses stand on small lots on narrow streets named after dead British colonial bigwigs. They are frame bungalows mostly with a few brick veneer specimens from time to time, and a sprinkling of pebble-dashed stucco. The coming of diesel did little to lift the grime of a century of coal-dust in the backyards along the right of way of the Hamilton-Buffalo line. Each of the houses presents either faded blinds or curtains to the outsider and all of them offer a generous veranda or porch to the inaccurate aim of the *Beacon* delivery boy.

Martha Tracy's house backed on the tracks, but put up a brave front in the form of a well-cropped privet hedge along the walk. It was stucco, with black and white pebble dash, and had a green-painted wooden porch. The second step needed fixing. My knock rattled the screen door, so I tried to get at the inside door, but it was fastened with a hook. I rattled it again. Soon I could hear footsteps approaching. The doors opened and I was looking at a woman of fifty, stocky, blonde and with a Churchillian chin.

"You Cooperman?" she said. I nodded. She unhooked the door and invited me down the dim hall, past glimpses of an unmade bed through a doorway on my right to the bright kitchen. "I've got coffee, if you don't mind instant," she said and found two mugs inverted on the drainboard.

"I want you to know that I'm not from the police."

"I've had a belly-full of them, I'll tell you," she said, raising her eyebrow significantly. "I don't know how so many people can ask the same dumb questions so many times." I hoped that my questions were better. Of course they were. I didn't get them out of a book.

"Well, I hope that these questions won't take up too much of your time."

"Time. Heck, I've got nothing but time. There's no job to do until they decide what they're going to do with me, so I'll be on sick leave for a week anyway. And it *was* a shock, you know. I'd been with him for more than five years. They always say, 'Ask Martha. She knows where all the bodies are buried.' "

"And do you?"

"Well, that's forthright! You're doing fine. Maybe, to save you time I should tell you that I was the last person to see Mr. Yates alive. I left at five to five. It had been a scorcher and everybody took off when I yelled 'Quittin' time.' I always yell that; it's an office joke. But usually it's closer to five."

"Was he alone when you left?"

"M'yeah."

"Was his bar open? Did he have a drink going?"

"You know Chester pretty well, don't you? Right, he often had a drink on the way by five, but that day, Thursday, he had been out most of the afternoon, and only got back to the office at quittin' time, so he shot himself with an unclouded brain, if that's what your little head is thinking."

"When the police got through with their investigation, did you notice anything missing from the office?"

""You should get points off for hinting to the witness. There was a bar towel gone."

"Anything else?"

"That's all. Do I get a free trip to Los Angeles if I hit the right answer? It should be easy: I outfitted that bar myself, got the set of eight glasses from Birks, kept the bar stocked . . ."

". . . and the books dusted?" She grinned at me a lopsided friendly grin that was half shrug.

"As far as you know, he hadn't planned to meet anyone after five?"

"Search me. He sometimes did, but he never told me half of what was going on."

"Speaking of knowing what was going on, did you ever hear him say anything about 'C2'?"

" 'C2'? What's that?"

"I think it was something on his mind. He doodled a 'C' with a two and I wondered whether it meant anything to you. It doesn't click?" She shook her head.

"Nope," she said.

"As you know, the police are calling Mr. Yates' death a suicide. Did you think that he was at the edge? Was he all that depressed as the papers are saying?"

"That's leading the witness again. You should learn the rules. But no. Between me and you and the gatepost, Chester wasn't depressed enough to kill himself. He had had a lot of business worries during recent weeks, but that man loved living too much to go and shoot himself. He was in a corner of some kind, but he was more the type to worm his way out of it, or change the rules, or something, than to take the way out he took. I thought I knew him pretty well, but that just shows to go you, doesn't it?"

"Ms Tracy . . ."

"Call me Miss Tracy. I'm a Miss not a Ms. I'm not one of those women's libbers."

"Miss Tracy, then, I want to thank you for being so helpful."

"You're breaking my heart. I told you I haven't anything else to do, except try to find a hat to wear to the funeral on Monday. I used to have one around here someplace. Oh, well. Now, before you get on your horse and hightail it out of here, what's all of this in aid of? Who are you working for? You beating the bushes for Bill Ward?"

"Why did you think I might be working for him?"

"William Allen Ward moves in mysterious ways his wonders to perform."

"And . . . ?"

"Well, I've never seen him ask any questions, so I always guessed that he had people collecting answers for him. He's organized that way, if you know what I mean." I had finished my coffee and had memorized the view of her long rectangle of backyard visible through the kitchen window. We both got up and she walked me to the front door. "You think that there's something that's not kosher about Chester's suicide, Mr. Cooperman, if you'll pardon the expression?"

"Miss Tracy, I don't know." I shifted my weight and held the screen door open.

"Somebody did the bugger in, eh? Well, it figures. It could make very good sense, Mr. Cooperman. Goodbye, and let me know how you make out."

"I will," I shouted over my shoulder as I went down the walk to my Olds at the curb.

I drove across the CN tracks on a rickety wooden bridge and kept on past more stucco fronts and kids playing jacks and marbles in the sunshine out Pelham Road. Beyond the rooftops, the ridge of the escarpment hogged the horizon, with the green water tower on the edge commanding the best view of the city below. The creek valley followed me out on my left. Gradually the curbing came to an end, the houses gave way to deserted farms and acre upon acre of former vineyards, all cultivating real estate signs. Occasionally, the stream below curved, and I could catch the glint of it in the sun. After a couple of miles of this, I could see the ten blue pipes running down the scarp to the creek. It was a domesticated Niagara Falls, where nearly the same amount of water fell nearly as many feet as the famous cataract, but encased in

steel, so it was a wash-out as a tourist attraction. Nobody was
interested in falling water as long as it was in pipes.

Zekerman had his name stencilled on his mailbox in such
good taste I nearly drove by his gate. It was a big, rambling
house, what they still call "ranch style" in the area even if it
rises to two floors. There were three cars in the carport, which
was an extension of the line of the green roof. I drove up his
lane and blocked at least two of the cars from getting out.
There was an Audi and two Mercedes-Benzs.

I got out of the car, stretched my back muscles and
walked up to the aluminum screen door. A red-faced woman
with tortured red hair answered the bell, and told me that the
doctor was down at the potting shed by the creek or in the
shed behind the house. I thanked her and walked around
the left side of the house, past half a dozen green garbage bags
stuffed with the outlines of cans and cartons, and a sick-look-
ing Irish wolfhound with swollen joints in his legs. He gave me
a quarter-hearted wag of his tail, then went back to his worries. By now I could hear Zekerman, or somebody, making a
racket in the aluminum-sided shed. In the gloom at the far
end, he was bashing a piece of machinery on a workbench.

"Dr. Zekerman?" I said as I came up behind him.

Zekerman filled a tall track suit with a college letter on
it without letting middle age spill through the middle. He
was balding the same as I was only I was doing it more
neatly. He had let his remaining hair grow into long ringlets
of protest against the unfairness of his genes. His foxy nose
was sweaty, as was his brow. His eyes hid behind fashion-
able lenses that he had paid a bundle for. The face, concentrated now, looked ungenerous, unyielding, as though the
cords which pulled down the corners of his mouth would
never relax, and the lines which scored his face had disappeared over the edge of stubbled chin into those of his neck
knew something far more serious than any good news you
might tell him.

"Blasted sump pump gave out. I think it's this valve,
but I'm not sure." He was looking suspiciously at the thing
which seemed to have outlets and intakes all over it. He
looked up at my face. I frowned encouragingly. "You know
anything about this make?" he asked, and I denied it in a
way that suggested even to me that I knew all other makes
on the market. "I bled it for an hour, but it didn't do any
good." I tried to deal with a picture in my mind of the

doctor treating his sump pump to a jar full of leeches. I could see I was going to be a big help. "Hold this." He thrust a flashlight at me and indicated that I was to shine it up the hole his screwdriver had disappeared down. I stood that way for three minutes or more, while he clanked about down below. "That's it," he said at last as he removed a clod of muck from under the flap of the valve, "I got it!" We exchanged grins, and I gave him back his flashlight. "Now, that we've got this fixed, maybe you can tell me who you are and what your business is."

"My name is Benny Cooperman, and I'm doing some work on the Chester Yates case." The first part of my statement didn't move him much, but the second part caught all his attention.

"What Chester Yates case? I don't know any Chester Yates."

"He was one of your patients, Doctor. You saw him last just before he died."

"Who are you?"

"I told you. My name's Cooperman." His foxy nose took on a pinched look. The mouth that in repose imitated a sneer opened slightly. His eyes began to shift about behind his glasses.

"Who the hell sent you here?"

"Nobody."

"Who are you working for?" He looked scared.

"I'm a private investigator, and . . ."

"Don't give me that garbage. Just turn around and walk away from here." He was sweating now, and it wasn't from the work on the pump valve. I'd touched a nerve. "Stop following me. Do you hear me?" He began to raise his voice. I tried to shrug and calm him down.

"Look, Doctor, don't get excited. I only want to . . ."

"Get off my land. Get away from me!" He was shouting, and the cords in his neck stood out white against his reddening face. I tried again to calm him down with a reassuring gesture.

"I only want to ask you a couple of questions. That's all. Just a couple of questions."

He backed up against the workbench and quickly shot a look to his right and left. He grabbed a blue cylindrical tank about a foot long with one hand and a thing that looked like a bent coat hanger with the other. The one struck a spark and at once the other came alive with a flame about a mile long. He lunged at me with it, singeing the arm of my coat as I lifted it to protect my eyes. "Hey, what are you trying to do?"

"Get out of here, do you hear me?"

"I'm going, I'm going." I backed to the open front of the shed, then turned and started for my car.

"Stop following me, do you hear! Do you hear? Leave me alone." I think he may have continued in that vein, but I missed it as I dashed the hundred yards or so to the Olds. My last sight of Dr. Zekerman, as I backed down his lane at fifty miles an hour, was of an irate gesticulating madman, brandishing a propane torch which nearly singed my baby-blue eyes. If that was standard practice for a shrink in these parts, I'm going to take all my future business to a chiropractor. And right then it looked like I was going to have a lot of business. I hadn't had a headache like this since I fell in the dark on top of another private dick working for the other side in the same divorce case. Dr. Zekerman from where I sat, speeding back to town, looked like he was damaged and should see somebody about it and fast.

SEVEN

Back in town I did something I seldom do: I had a couple of belts of rye and a beer chaser at the hotel. Then I went upstairs to my room and nearly brought it all up again. To hell with putting my nose where it wasn't wanted. On Monday, for sure, I was going over to see my cousin Melvyn. What I needed on a hot spring day was a cool morning searching titles at the registry office. Title searchers live a long time and hardly ever lose their sight to a propane flame. I lay back on my bed, looking up at the ceiling thinking of my resolution, when the phone rang. I grabbed it mostly to stop it making such a racket. It was Mrs. Yates.

"Mr. Cooperman? I'm sorry to bother you on a weekend, but I didn't want you to think I didn't appreciate what you have been doing. Mr. Ward was a little harsh with you on the telephone yesterday, and I'm sorry. We've all been under a great deal of pressure as you'll appreciate." Her voice sounded washed out, almost like she was reciting a chant.

"Mr. Ward's word for what I've done is 'harassment,' Mrs. Yates. I know you've been through the wringer these last three days and you're not in the clear yet. What I want to know, Mrs. Yates, is do you want me to go on harassing you? Are you satisfied to hear that your husband wasn't seeing another woman, but going to see a psychiatrist?"

"Chester is dead, Mr. Coopermen."

"Mrs. Yates, you know what you asked me to do?"

"Yes."

"Well, I did that. I was with your husband up to an hour before his death. I can tell you that his afternoon appointment was not with the Water Board as it said on his deck calendar; he went to see Dr. Andrew Zekerman. The name mean anything to you?"

"No." She said it breathlessly.

"He's a psychiatrist, across from the Hotel Dieu Hospital on Ontario Street. I've been to see the shrink, and found out that he's scared of something. He thinks he's being followed. I'd like to find out why. Believe me, it's not my imagination, Mrs. Yates. You didn't see his face when I mentioned your husband's name."

"But I still don't see . . ."

"Mrs. Yates, two hours before your husband died, he ordered a ten-speed bike for himself. You can check at MacLeish's sporting goods if you don't believe me."

"I see." She didn't sound as though she did, but I took her at her word. I waited for a minute.

"Can you tell me, Mrs. Yates, who would want to see your husband out of the way? Who would profit by his death? Did he have any enemies? Don't tell me now. I want you to think about it and let me know later on. May I suggest that we keep what I've said under your hat until I can find something that a court of law would recognize as proof? That is if you want to keep me busy, because frankly I don't think we've got enough right now to go to the police with. If you want me to drop everything right where it is, just say so. I can take a hint. But to tell you the truth, Mrs. Yates, I'll take it better from you than from that stuffed-shirt Ward."

"Bill Ward? But how . . .? Oh, on the telephone. Yes, I understand, Mr. Cooperman. Please, Mr. Cooperman, if Chester *was* killed and you can find out who killed him, I'll be eternally grateful. If it's a matter of money . . ."

"I didn't say anything about money, although I could use another two hundred. But I can wait until you get back on your feet again. Take it easy. And let me know if you think of anything that might help to shed some light around here."

"Yes, I promise. Goodbye." I heard the click, but listened to the dead line hum for a minute before I replaced the receiver. I was back in business. I might get burned to a crisp after all, but at least I wasn't going to have to be nice to that bastard cousin of mine, Melvyn.

EIGHT

I won't bore you with the rest of my weekend. One of us is enough. I could tell you about the trip to the laundromat, about how I nearly nailed the sock thief in the drier, how I pan-handled on James Street for dimes to see me through the second load after the change machine jammed. There's a lot I'm going to leave out by jumping from Saturday afternoon and landing in Victoria Lawn in time for Chester's obsequies on Monday.

Funerals make me nervous. I don't care whose they are. I watched them bury Churchill and Kennedy and Martin Luther King and the other Kennedy on television, where you could see that even when you're dead it helps to have money to bring the right tone and taste to the send-off. I skipped the church service. That's another thing that gives me the willies. Ever since I was a kid, churches and me have kept our distance from one another. I kept thinking that because of my religion they might have to have the place reconsecrated or something. I was in a religious play once. I was just a teenager, and the play was *Good Friday* by the English poet laureate, John Masefield. It was all about the trial of Jesus, and I played an old geezer who kept breaking through the crowd and pleading with Pilate to spare the life of this upright man, Jesus. And the crowd kept laughing at me and throwing me offstage and calling me a madman. That was a little of the old Masefield irony there in that part about me being mad. Anyway, while I was offstage, the director had me join in with the crowd shouting "Crucify him! Crucify!" It was a schizo situation, and I wonder how I got out of it alive and not even converted.

I walked up the gravel path toward an assembly of the city's finest, planning to watch from the background. I'd parked my car about a mile back along the twisting road behind the last in the funeral procession. I worked my way between granite headstones that caught the afternoon sun on their polished fronts and back. I could hear the Anglican priest giving Chester his last shove into the next world; he stood at the head of the grave which was surrounded by brass rails. Flowers covered the casket, and green imitation grass covered the earth on either side. Myrna looked brave, wearing a black hat and veil. She made a lovely widow, standing there, still looking less than forty. Next to her, a tall, sandy-haired man of about fifty, but admitting to forty-five, with the widow's arm on his. My guess made him William Allen Ward. Next to him stood my old pal, Vern Harrington. The other mourners included the mayor and most of the other aldermen. There were no children or even any young people. From the looks of them, I could see a lot of "ought" written on a lot of faces. Faces that "ought" to be seen to have come: colleagues, cronies, and people whose presence was expected, each wearing his face for the occasion, hats doffed, eyes fixed on the flowers on top of the coffin.

"I am the resurrection and the life . . ." The priest's white vestments were caught by a spring breeze. Squirrels went about their own affairs, and I stood at the back.

I tried to put names on the people standing there. There were few women. Most of the aldermanic wives had begged off, but there was a girl or two from his office. I noticed Martha Tracy had found a suitable hat, and stood with a clutch of office girls around her, like an iceberg with its chips.

When the deed had been done, the crowd started moving back toward the cars in twos and threes. Two cemetery workers who had come up behind me watched them recede through the tall monuments and along the gravel path. They started talking Greek to one another and set about making the final earthly arrangements for Chester's eternal rest.

I was about to turn away and follow the winding herd myself, when I felt someone sharing the view over my shoulder. It was Pete Staziak from Homicide wearing a light gabardine raincoat and carrying a green tyrolean felt hat. He put it on. It looked too small for his head.

"Hi, Benny. You sleuthing?"

"Sure, Pete. Only ... I can't sell what I have." He gave me a grin that should have been shared with a third party; it wasn't meant for me. We started back, crunching along the path. "I thought Harrow drew this case?"

"He did. And he wrote 'Closed' on the file last week. He's on something else today."

"You one of Chester's fans?" I asked, trying a line that wouldn't explode in my face in case he turned out to be his cousin. Although with a name like Staziak he had as much chance of being related to the dear departed as I did.

"Nope," he said. "But I was told that I might find you here, Benny. They had you pegged pretty good, I'd say."

"Did they send you to see if I would steal the floral tributes, Pete?"

"Sure are a lot of them. Seems a waste, doesn't it? I guess somebody makes a buck out of it."

"Pete, I never knew your philosophical side. Come on, for crying out loud, as an old friend, what's eating them downtown? What are they so worried about?"

"This isn't official."

"Naturally. You're invisible. Look I can put my hand right through you. What do you take me for, Pete? Who told you to come out here and play tip toe through the tombstones? Come on. Level with me."

We stood leaning on my car, which now looked parked foolishly far away from the grave site since the other cars had vanished.

"Benny, I could get into a lot of trouble telling you anything. But what you've been saying around town about Yates' death being murder and not suicide has got a lot of important people feeling uneasy, like you might take advantage of the funeral to make a speech or point the guilty finger or stuff like that. It don't worry me, see, because we go back a long way together, but some people worry easy." He was scratching his head under his tilted hat. I could see it wasn't easy for him to lean on me. He resented having to do it and he resented the direction from which the pressure came.

"I get you, Pete. I'll keep my bib clean. But while I'm doing it why don't you put a couple of numbers like two and two together. Why are they on my tail? Did anybody ever worry so much about Benny Cooperman before? What are they worried about over at City Hall? Doesn't their nervousness make you wonder what they're nervous about?"

"Ah, they're worried about Myrna Yates, that's all. They don't want anybody upsetting her on top of all her other troubles. You can understand that. So there, that's official."

"You mean unofficial." I grinned and he caught and returned it.

"Yeah. Okay, you understand what I'm not saying?"

"Loud and clear."

"Okay. Now. Tell me what you got, Benny. Let's have it."

"I've got a suicide who buys himself a going-away present with only two hours to go."

Pete squinted into the afternoon sun a little, like he'd seen a western sheriff do it on television. "Well now, it does sound peculiar. What else did he do before he got dead?"

"He spent an hour with his shrink."

"Christ, Benny. There goes your theory up the chimney. A shrink could have got him into a very highly excited state in an hour. He could have stirred up all that muck in his subconscious, and you know, he could have left the shrink's office in a depressed and suicidal state. Why don't you let it lie, Ben? No good'll come of your playing with it."

"Pete, look. If it didn't get so many people worked up I might let it alone, but people don't get excited without a reason. And that reason could be that there is more to this than yesterday's lunch. Why wasn't there a post mortem? Why weren't the contents of the organs sent to the Forensic Centre in Toronto? Why weren't there tissue samples taken?"

"Because there was no need. Look, we had powder burns on his head, right; we had contact marks, right; we had prints on the gun, right; and we have nitrates showing up in the paraffin test. So, where's the miscarriage of justice? Where's your case? Do you even have a client?" He leaned over me, smirklines on either side of his thin mouth.

"You'd be surprised," I said, sighing. We both looked at the other for a few seconds, not saying anything.

"Well, Benny. Take it easy."

"Sure, Pete. Sure thing." I got into the Olds and started the motor. Pete Staziak watched as I curved along the road, and I could see him in my rear-view mirror until the trees and headstones blanked him out.

Back behind my desk in my old swivel chair, things started looking the way Pete said. What did I really have? I had a wife suspicious of her beloved husband and willing to pay me good money to find out what he was up to. I had a bike-buying suicide, and a scared shrink. And the towel; I mustn't forget the towel. That was my biggest clue so far. Why I could knock down the door of the Supreme Court with a clue like that.

It was time for a very late lunch. I never eat before funerals. Around at the United I sat down at my usual place at the marble counter.

"Super Jews," the waitress said.

"What?" I said dropping my teeth.

"Soup or juice? You want to see the menu? You know it by heart."

"Bring me . . . bring me . . . bring me . . ."

"A chopped egg sandwich on white. Right?"

"Toasted," I said triumphantly, like I'd just put her king in check and discovered "gardé" on her queen. She sniffed haughtily and disappeared to the other end of the counter. In a few minutes she dropped the sandwich in front of me without a word. She ad libbed a glass of milk and I let her. There was nothing quite like lunch to make me hurry back to the office. I kept crazy hours in my business, sometimes working late into the night and once or twice a year right around the clock. Lunch at the United was what I had instead of regular office hours.

I had just dug out my shoebox full of receipts and papers from the bottom drawer of my stack of filing cases with a view to doing my income tax, when the phone rang. It was Martha Tracy.

"Cooperman? This is Martha Tracy."

"I know. I never forget a voice, Faces, maybe."

"I saw you at the funeral."

"Thought I'd see if you found that hat. The tall, sandy-haired jasper with the widow: was that Ward?"

"The one and only. The little guy on the other side was the mayor."

"Stop the press! What's on your mind?"

"They asked me to come in this morning, to clear up the junk in Mr. Yates' office. I've been knee-deep in cartons all day. Well, I ran across something peculiar. You're the expert in peculiar, I figured, so I thought I'd let you in on it. It's a list of appointments. I've never seen it before and I don't know any of the people on it. The craziest thing is that the appointments are for just about every hour of the day.

Some in the middle of the night. Are you still there, Cooperman?"

"Both ears."

"Isn't that cotton-pickin' weird? Meetings at three and four in the morning, and names like Jones and Peters and Williams." She sounded excited and was talking a little louder than absolutely necessary. "I put it in an envelope and mailed it to you. I got your address out of the Yellow Pages."

"Martha, did you tell anybody about what you've found?"

"Of course not. Think I never watch television? You should get it in the mail tomorrow."

"Depending on the mood down at the post office."

"M'yeah, you're right. Anyway . . ."

"Anyway, I want to thank you for keeping your eyes open. You're a big help. I'm getting closer to something. Or something's getting closer to me."

NINE

I'd been playing around with the receipts from my three oil company credit cards, wondering where all that oil had taken me and how much of it was for business and how much for pleasure. There was a trip to the Hamilton registry office to check the ownership in 1938 of a house on Barton Street, which in 1938 turned out to be a peach orchard. Meanwhile my client and his problem disappeared. There was the trip to Buffalo about that custom Porsche which a client's son had bought for two hundred dollars. My client, smelling dead fish, sent me to trace the ownership. In a rented room in Buffalo's tenderloin, I found the former owner. His estranged wife had done just what he'd asked—sold his car and mailed him the proceeds. I couldn't find much pleasure written on the flimsy receipts. Funny how I get paid good money to fix other people's lives, but mine always looks like a garbage bag the cats have opened up. I've got a thing about tidying things up. I should make an appointment to see myself professionally one of these days.

I was beginning to think that in another hour or so I would have broken the back of my income tax, when the telephone rang.

"Hello, Mr. Cooperman? This is Andrew Zekerman." You could have knocked me over with a burnt matchstick. His voice was a little hesitant, but he sounded as though he had something important on his mind.

"So, Doctor, you've decided I'm not trying to murder you after all?"

"I can explain about that, Mr. Cooperman, and I certainly want to apologize for my unwarranted attack on you."

"Well, the occasional attack, you know, keeps me on my

toes." I was feeling a little light-headed, and held the phone away from my ear to avoid possible singeing. "How well did you know Chester Yates?"

"He was my patient."

"For how long?"

"Since last spring. About a year. His death, Mr. Cooperman, has upset me terribly."

"Never lost a patient before, Doctor?"

"I was with him an hour before he died. That hit me very close. I was fond of Chester."

"He didn't leave your place in a suicidal depression, then?"

"Of course not."

"I didn't think so either. You think that somebody got to him, don't you?"

"Yes, I do. I know it. And you've got to get to Bill Ward and tell him."

"Right. We can't have the first families knocking one another off, can we?"

"You don't understand. Mr. Cooperman, this is too difficult to deal with over the phone, and I have a patient due. Could you come to see me here at six o'clock? I'll explain everything to you. Is that satisfactory?"

"It'll have to be. See you at six." We hung up. I looked at my watch. His four o'clock patient was just ringing the buzzer.

I was too excited by this recent turn of events to play with my income tax returns any more. I had two hours to kill and I was too het up to sit on my butt waiting for the hands to pull themselves past all those numbers on the dial. I wandered out into the sun, crossed St. Andrew and gasped at the jungle-mouth smell coming through the doorway of the Men's Beverage Room in the Russell House. It was like a taste of midsummer, and I could see the ghost of old Joe Higgins selling balloons and balsa birds on sticks as he propped himself in the lee of the stoplight on his crutches. Poor old Joe.

At the library, I went through the turnstile, and found a book on Chester's specialty, real estate. I sat down at a wide, cool table, in a quiet corner, where the fountain wouldn't make premature suggestions to my bladder. A man with a threadbare jacket was sitting opposite me reading the *Reader's Digest*. The air conditioning touched him first then moved on to me. He smelt like he'd been sleeping in old tunafish. Still, he could read upside down, which was more than I could manage.

Once I started, I soon learned how much there was to the field and how little of it I had ploughed. Mortgages to me were the things mustachioed villains brandished in front of the tear-filled eyes of the widow and her beautiful daughter. I read on, keeping half an eye on my watch.

I left myself ten minutes to walk the few blocks along Church Street to Ontario and the Physicians' and Surgeons' Building. The way was lined by leafless maples, the odd catalpa tree and next to the Presbyterian church, a ginkgo, the one with fan-shaped leaves in summer.

Inside Zekerman's lobby, I still had a minute or so in hand. I used it to study the botanic structure of the plastic yucca plant which loomed over the vinyl and chrome chairs and parquet floor. The plastic yucca comes apart in your hands if you examine it too closely. The bits that come away are harder to reassemble than you would at first think. There is always ample foliage from the larger lower branches to hide the remains of such an investigation. At six o'clock precisely, I rang the doctor's buzzer. I waited. I rang again. There was no response. I lit a cigarette, deciding that I'd caught him in the john, and gave the buzzer a good long press in another two minutes. No luck. I walked calmly to the telephone booth, dialled, let it ring and got my dime back after fifteen rings. I could feel a tenseness, born of too many movies, taking hold of the muscles in the back of my neck, as I looked for the number of the building's superintendent. It was at the bottom of all those columns of doctors. One-oh-one. I found the apartment, and as I was waiting for the door to be answered, I imagined it opening on a dark room illuminated only by the light of a television set and with a beefy man with a can of beer in his hand sitting in an overstuffed chair in front of it. Odd how reality always trips up the imagination. He was drinking his beer from a dark brown bottle. I told him what the problem was and he heaved a heavy sigh and reached for a ring of keys. He left the television running: no sense depriving the furniture of what he had to miss.

The tenth floor was cool. Ozite carpeting ran the length of the wide corridor. We tried ringing again when we got to the right door, but Zekerman wasn't answering. The super frowned for a minute at the bunch of keys, selected one and opened the door. The lights were on. But no television. It was more an apartment than an office. There was a small kitchen and a bedroom off one large room which was dominated by two large leather chairs, the sort that tilt back, slipping a footrest under your feet when you get back far enough. There was a small desk in one corner. Large french windows let what was left of the spring day into the room. Beyond was a cement balustraded balcony. I didn't get to admire the view, because of the mess the apartment was in. There were papers flung in every direction. Beside the desk the file drawers were open, and red filing folders stood half down from their moorings. In the midst of this mess, the first, not the last thing we noticed as we came into the room was Zekerman lying stretched out on one of the leather chairs. There was blood around the top part of what used to be his head. His mouth gaped open adding to the look of surprise frozen on his staring frightened eyes. On the floor, behind the chair, more blood had dripped. In the middle of it lay a heavy African sculpture, similar to several other wooden sculptures which were about the only conscious attempt to decorate the room. I stepped on something. It looked like a piece of shell-like pasta. It was a piece of shell-like shell, a cowrie shell; the murder weapon had a ring of them around its neck, and a number of them were scattered over the carpet near the body. The super stood with his mouth open in the doorway. The shock had made him automatically suck in his belly so that it no longer rested on his belt.

"Kee-rist!" he said. "Well, I'll be damned. He's dead." There was no doubt at all on that score. I tried to escape the terror in those eyes by poking my head in the bedroom. The bed was made. No sign of a search in there. When I came out, the super had still not moved. He kept repeating, "Well, I'll be damned," and shaking his head.

"Better get the police," I said. That seemed to bring him back to the world of traffic tickets and sudden death in a flash. He jumped—I almost thought to attention—and made for the telephone. "Hold it," I shouted. "Better not use that phone. There might be fingerprints. See if you can get Sergeant Staziak at Homicide. But if you can't, it doesn't matter. Just tell them the address and that it looks like there's been a murder." He left. I almost said escaped, he went so fast. As soon as I saw the elevator door close, I ran to look at the file cabinet. As close as I could make out, whole files had been removed from their places. Whoever did it

came with a box or bag to carry away with him what he
knew to be here. I probed with my trusty ball-point pen into
the files and found an interrupted alphabetical system. I
looked up Yates. Missing. I looked up Ward on a hunch.
Bad guess. I probed some of the files. Dr. Zekerman's scrawl
was impenetrable. Some of the patients were Medicare sub-
scribers. That might help, I thought, if I could get a complete list from them. At the bottom of one file drawer, a few
pages lay, spilled from their folders. I looked through the
names that came to light, trying not to touch the metal sides
of the case. Filing cabinets give the fingerprint boys a chance
to show off. A smooth metal surface is as easy as glass. Most
of the names didn't mean a thing to me, but I was suddenly
getting lucky. I recognized one of the names. It belonged to
alderman Vern Harrington. Nice, I thought, very nice.

I looked around for an appointment book. That would
tell who had been in and out of the room in the last few
hours. That was missing too. I tried to think. What else would
a good detective do while waiting for the police to arrive? I
couldn't think straight. I was concentrating on keeping my
back to Zekerman's eyes. I was putting off the job nobody
liked to do. I tried to come at him so that I wouldn't have
to look at his face. I couldn't manage it, started to retch and
just made it to the bathroom in time. By the time the dry
retching stopped, my glasses were misted up and I was out
of breath. I fetched that back and lit a shaking cigarette. I
pulled a dark blue towel from behind the bathroom door and
covered up Zekerman's head.

Now I could take him in a little better. He was wearing
soft, crepe-soled shoes with floppy wool socks; an expanse
of blue calf was visible above them. I touched his skin. Warm.
That was a bit silly, I guess, since I knew he was alive at
four o'clock. It was only just after six. A detailed medical
examination couldn't fix the time of death much more ac-
curately than that. Zekerman wore beige corduroy trousers
and an old comfortable wool sweater. He hadn't been trying
to impress today's patients with his wardrobe. His hands lay
with their backs up on his stomach. His fingernails would
have kept him from getting a job as a bus-boy in a greasy
spoon. The shirt collar made of some synthetic drip-dry material added a dash of green to the otherwise beige impression.

Then I went through his pockets with speed and efficiency. His wallet contained a thousand dollars mostly in

fifties. He had the usual credit cards and belonged to the golf club. There were a couple of restaurant receipts he was saving for his income tax. Duty entertainment. None of this looked useful, so I put it all back.

On the table beside his chair, on the right side, a pipe lay with a lot of ashes in a big brown ashtray. The ashes in the pipe were warm, but not hot. In the ashtray next to the other chair I found an assortment of butts, some with lipstick, some without, some filtered, some plain. I could see them loving that downtown.

I heard the elevator stop on this floor through the still open door, and I tried to saunter innocently to the middle of the room. The super came in still shaking his head.

"Kee-rist, how could a thing like this happen? I'll get shit for it sure as anything. They'll figure out some way I should have been able to stop it. I might as well start looking for a new job right now. Kee-bloody-rist." He seemed a bit wheezy, as though he'd run up the stairs. There was sweat under his big arms. "Anyway, I phoned, like you said. Only they're sending over some uniformed cop right away. That guy you said wasn't there. You're right about not touching anything: the cop on the phone told me that too." I handed him a lit cigarette and he took it like a junky takes a fix that's a couple of hours late. Funny how his belly stayed behind his belt like that. That took a lot of sucking. "Jesus," he said, "I haven't seen a dead man since I was in Germany in 1945. Didn't bother me then. I'd seen a few. Damn it, though, it throws you when you come on it sudden." I told him my name for something to do, but he didn't hear it, and when he took my hand neither of us put much into it.

It didn't seem more than three or four centuries until we heard the elevator door again. A couple of constables from downtown made their way shoulder to shoulder through the narrow doorway. Constables Keith and Morressey. They asked if we had touched anything, and warned us in future not to touch anything if we should be so inclined. They looked around at the mess, peeked under the blue towel and took down our names in their day books. They then asked the usual questions and they wrote down our answers. They seemed to be getting a bang out of writing up more than a description of a bruised fender or noting the failure of a brake light. I couldn't blame them; this was their glimpse of the big time.

Just when they were beginning to feel that the investiga-

tion was all theirs, someone arrived to spoil their fun. He
stood about seven feet tall in his regulation boots, which
went with a uniform although he was in plain clothes. His
freckled face frowned at the scene around him, took us in,
the body of the shrink, and the general mess. He turned to
both the super and me, introduced himself as Corporal Cahill, and warned us not to touch anything. It seemed like a
good idea.

The corporal led us both back over our stories after he
spoke with the uniformed men. He took us one at a time
into the bedroom and, sitting on the edge of Zekerman's bed,
where we weren't blurring any latent fingerprints, he nodded
his head on its thick neck as he made notes. I told him
that I'd had a call from the doctor, that he had asked me to
come at six o'clock to see him, and that when he didn't
answer his buzzer after I'd leaned on it for a few minutes,
I hunted up the superintendent, whose name was Uhernick,
by the way, and together we had discovered the corpse. He
assumed that I was trying to see the doctor on business, that
I was a patient of his, and short of foaming at the mouth I
let him believe that. After my turn, I sent Uhernick to see Cahill. Outside the big room was alive with cops in all shapes
and sizes. Flash-bulbs went off like a Hollywood opening. A
guy I took to be the coroner was holding hands with Zekerman, bending his wrist back and forth. He'd removed the
blue towel from where I'd put it and I got another look at
those staring frightened eyes. As if my day wasn't already
perfect. The fingerprint boys had dusted the telephone, door-
knobs, desk filing cabinet with talc, and were now brushing
them off again with dry camelhair brushes. The coroner
sneezed and shot a dirty look in the direction of the man
working in a crouched position near the phone. After a half
hour of this, just as Cahill had begun to think of this as his
investigation, Sergeant Harrow stood in the doorway. This
gave Mr. Uhernick and me a chance to escape the noise
again. In the bedroom, we once more got to tell our stories.
This time I didn't do so well. He remembered me for a
start. He didn't like me much. I could see that. If it wasn't for
me he would be at home carving a supermarket roast of beef.
I tried to look agreeable. It didn't help.

"What was your business with the doctor, Mr. Cooperman?"

"He called me around four o'clock this afternoon."

"Interesting. But what was your business with him?"

"He wanted to see me."

"You didn't want to see him? You're not a patient of his?"

"No. I'm not a patient, and I'm not sure about why he wanted to see me. I think he wanted to tell me something."

"About?"

"About Chester Yates' death." That got him. He didn't like that at all. He got a mean look around the jawline, but after taking a new breath, he continued the questions.

"How was Zekerman connected with Yates?"

"Chester was a patient."

"And you were bothering him about the sort of thing you told me on the phone last week?" He was losing control of his temper. He did not much want to have this neat murder slop over and muddy the waters of a tidy suicide.

"I told you. He called me." That was my best shot. "I never heard what he wanted to tell me. When we got here, he was dead."

"You're not going to leave this alone, are you, Cooperman?"

"What? Leave what alone?"

"You know what I'm talking about. You two-bit peeper. Who the hell do you think you are? I know my job, and I don't need tips from a cheapie like you. You bother me, and I don't like to be bothered by peepers. Can't keep your hands off anything."

"You find my prints and say that, Sergeant. Meanwhile ask your questions. It's past my supper time too."

"How long have you been acquainted with the deceased?" He hissed that one out from between his stained teeth. He had been smoking his butts shorter than I'd ever seen, stubbing them out with tense, nicotine-yellowed fingers.

"I've never been here before." I hoped I would get away with that, but Harrow frowned. "I saw him once before. At his house. I asked him about Chester, and he didn't want to talk about it."

"What else?"

"Nothing else. That's it, I swear. Believe me, would I try to obstruct the true course of law and order? I'm a citizen too."

He led me through the story of how we found the body again, detail by detail.

"What did you take when you sent the super out to phone?" I opened my eyes wide to show my surprise.

"Who do you take me for?" I asked.

"I won't answer that. Put your hands on your head." He then gave me a professional frisking. Now I could be glad I didn't dip into the wallet of the deceased. "Put your hands down. Now listen to me, Cooperman, and listen to me good: I don't want to see you again, and I don't want to hear from you again. Now get out of here."

When I came out of the bedroom this time, the body had been taken away and you could see the walls better without so many cops running around. The paper mess on the floor had been sorted into cardboard boxes and was disappearing out the door in the capable hands of what looked like apprentice policemen, but I doubted there was such an animal. Mr. Uhernick, who had lost his nervousness warmed to all this sudden interest in him, was telling one of the remaining constables about the D-Day landings and the carnage on the Normandy beaches that spring day in 1944. Cahill, the corporal, told me that they might need me again, so I should let him know if I was planning a sudden trip to the Fiji Islands. And that was it. My statement had been taken three times and now reposed in three notebooks. It seemed anticlimactic as I walked out Dr. Zekerman's door.

The lights of a television film crew nearly blinded me when I came out of the building. Reporters were falling over one another, while uniformed policemen tried to keep the mob of curious gray faces back. Someone with a microphone headed toward me. I thought my big moment had come, but he went by me to grab one of the fingerprint boys. The camera crew, I was happy to see, had its camera pointed at the bright receding rear end of the ambulance.

TEN

I had hoped that there would be something in the mail for me the following morning from Martha Tracy, but the postman only brought me a coupon which would give me ten per cent off on the purchase of a welding outfit. There was also a bill from one of the oil companies, which also seemed to be going in for the same kind of merchandizing on the side. Their offer was for a genuine dutch clock that would enhance the collection of a connoisseur.

I telephoned Pete Staziak to see if he could tell me anything about Zekerman's murder. He wouldn't spill anything, but I got the idea that the fingerprints hadn't proved very interesting. The only prints they had to match with belonged to the body. I guess it would have surprised even Harrow if the murder weapon bore the prints of a known wanted criminal. I told that to Pete, and he started to laugh. I asked him why, but he wouldn't say. So I had to coax him like we were in high school. Finally, he told me that the murder weapon showed a very fine copy of the prints of Dr. Andrew Zekerman. A big help. But, just to be useful, because that's the way I am, I told Pete to tell Harrow that maybe Zekerman committed suicide like Chester did. Pete liked to share a little subversive joke from time to time, but that was going too far. He deepened his voice by an octave and said he'd talk to me later. I could just see Harrow writing "CLOSED" on this file too. Harrow wouldn't see anything wrong with Zekerman clubbing himself to death with a rare African statue. Probably it was a fertility object of some sort, and the wider he spread his brains around the room, the better he'd score in the bedroom.

The bedroom bothered me, when I thought about it. I

wondered whether he was bedding many of his patients. He didn't look to me like a guy who would miss a trick like that. That fitted in with his not having a secretary or receptionist or anything. No waiting room to worry about either. The more I thought about Zekerman, the less I liked him. And now that I wasn't ever going to hear what he wanted to tell me the night he was killed, I couldn't help feeling resentful. His death was a tragedy for him, but for me it was a pain in the ass.

I put in a call to Myrna Yates. She had a woman taking calls for her. I left my number.

For a Tuesday morning, this wasn't rising to great heights. The Zekerman murder didn't rate nearly the space in the paper that Chester's death had. Zekerman got a small clutch of paragraphs on an inside page. They spelled my name right and didn't attribute anything to me that I didn't say. Harrow's statement led the reader to believe that he was on top of the case and expected to get a break at any moment. But then he spoiled the effect by asking for anyone with any information to call the Regional Police and ask for him. I felt like calling with my suicide theory, but I went out to grab a bite of lunch instead.

I'd been back in the office about ten minutes when the phone started ringing. I was trying to get a chopped egg stain out of my tie with lighter fluid, so it was a welcome change. I thought that maybe it might be my mother. Her son doesn't get his name in the paper every day. It was Myrna Yates. She asked if I could come to see her around three o'clock for tea. Jolly good, I said.

The next call was from the office of the registrar. Did I know that there had been some recent complaints against the way I was conducting my business? Was I, further, aware that the registrar takes a dim view of licencees not behaving themselves? And finally, I should be warned at once that any further complaints against my professional behaviour and I would have to face the licence renewal committee a full year before my licence was due to be renewed. I asked her to let me have that in writing, and she squealed like I'd goosed her in a crowded elevator. Harassment on the phone was one thing, but harassment on paper was something else again.

There weren't any police cruisers outside the Yates house this time. Poor Chester was old news. What was left of him was equally divided between Victoria Lawn, purgatory and probate. His wife looked as though she might be in a position to turn at least one of them to good account.

It was the sort of place that had been built for fifty thousand in the late thirties, and had changed hands enough times, been painted every five years, so now I was looking at two hundred thousand dollars worth of house. It stood solid and not altogether forbidding, rather like a cottage that kept growing, on a strip of property running from the street right down to the creek, two hundred feet away and fifty feet below. Two hundred thousand dollars worth of house, and the doorbell sounded no different than the one on my parents' condominium. And on inspection, what was masquerading as ivy on the ivy-covered walls, looked to me suspiciously like Virginia creeper.

I was braced for the stony face of a butler, but the door was answered by the widow herself.

"Mr. Cooperman. I'm so glad you could come." She was wearing a gray wool skirt and a blouse, both from Toronto or New York. The blouse was silk in a Paisley pattern, stretched tightly in all the right places. She led me, and I followed her trim ankles, into a hall where I got rid of my raincoat and hat on a chair that looked as though it had been made of thirty different kinds of wood. The floor was covered with mushroom-coloured broadloom, the kind you sink into just enough so you know it wasn't bought on special at the edge of town. She led the way through a large living room with lamps and end tables bracketing sofas and loveseats. There were a few Chinese antiques, a marble-topped table, pale jade in a display cabinet, that sort of thing. After another couple of rooms, we were out on a screened-in porch, a step below the rest of the lay-out.

"I thought we'd have tea out here," she said. "We get a nice breeze from the back." I said that I thought that that would be dandy, and that the breeze was worth the trip by itself. Something like that. She looked older than when I'd seen her first last Thursday. Her eyes were puffier, and she'd patched up the bad spots on her face with an ointment that smelled like Miriam Epstein when my mother forced me to take her to a Friday night dance at the Collegiate. On the whole, Myrna still looked better than Miriam. She had those good bones in her face which would outlast her sensitive skin. And she'd tried to cover the results with perfume.

She offered me one of a half-dozen white wicker chairs and took one opposite me. She smiled nervously and quickly took a cigarette from a silver box on the glass-topped coffee table between us. My mother has boxes like that. Only at her house she keeps stray pennies, elastics, safety pins and book matches in them.

"That was a terrible thing that happened yesterday, Mr. Cooperman. Dr. Zekerman, I mean. You were there, weren't you? Terrible. Do you think it had any connection with what happened to Chester?" She leaned over the table as she lit her cigarette with the only table lighter I ever saw that worked, then settled back sensuously in her chair as she breathed out a plume of smoke.

Just then a maid in a peach dress and starched apron swung through the narrow doorway with a tray of tea things and placed it carefully on the table. I pretended I didn't notice. The girl was Mary Slack, the kid sister of a friend who grew up to become a fireman. "Your husband had been seeing the doctor for about a year. I was talking to Dr. Zekerman just two hours before he died," I said, letting the silence that followed say what had to be said about the fragile thread of life. "He wanted to see me about something yesterday. He was excited and frightened. On Saturday, he tried to burn me to death he was so frightened. It was the name of your husband that set him off. He also connected your husband's death with your pal, Mr. Ward."

"Mr. Ward isn't my pal, Mr. Cooperman. He was my husband's best friend." I'd wanted to see if I could get a rise out of her on that point. I could. She covered her pique by pouring the tea. I generally take four lumps, but in circumstances like this I settle for two. She was able to make me feel that three lumps was social gaffe un-to-be-forgiven, and that four would necessitate my removal from the house at once.

"Tell me about that, Mrs. Yates. I'd like to know more about your husband and Mr. Ward. Can you, for instance, think of any reason why Dr. Zekerman might think that Ward might have had something to do with Chester's—I'm sorry—your husband's death?"

"That's crazy. I mean, it's absurd to suggest such a thing. Chester and Bill grew up together. They went to the same schools, they spent summers at one another's cottages. They travelled in Europe together in the summer of their senior year at university. They belonged to the same clubs, and, well, they are, or were, best friends. Everything that expression implies, including trust, confidence and respect."

"Business?"

"Yes. Up to a point. Recently Bill has been working with the city. He had had to get rid of most of his holdings. But, before that, he and Chester were as thick as ... Well, they were very close in business as well as in private."

"Tell me about William Allen Ward."

"You make him sound so very formal. I guess, from the outside, that might be how he appears. But to us, he was just Bill. He's a fine man, Mr. Cooperman, he's always had a brotherly interest in Chester, like an older brother should."

"Was he in fact older?"

"Same age, really. But you know how in any group, there's always one who takes the initiative, and one who tags along. That's the way it was with them. Chester was always a little slow off the mark. Bill was married for nearly a year before Chester asked me to marry him."

"Was Bill Ward part of that wild crowd you described to me at our first meeting, Mrs. Yates?"

"Yes, he was. But Bill was always different. He wasn't a show-off like some of them. He had a deeper side, as though he knew more about life and its seriousness than the rest of us. Not that he was a sourpuss. I don't mean that. He trained as a chemist, you know, yet he used to read novels, if you can believe it." She smiled at me over her teacup. I was enjoying my tea. It was a real treat to drink it without having to dredge up the sodden teabag first.

"Tell me, Mrs. Yates, as honestly as you can, what was your reaction when I told you that Chester hadn't been seeing another woman; that in fact he had been having therapy with Dr. Zekerman for a year."

"Mr. Cooperman, I thought I knew Chester very well. When I think back on my suspicions in your office last Thursday, I know where they began. That's clear to me. When you told me that he was seeing a psychiatrist, I knew that you must be mistaken. I'm still sure of that. I think I would know if my husband was in very delicate mental health."

"Not necessarily, Mrs. Yates," I said. This time I smiled, and she crossed her slim legs deftly with only a faint hiss of nylon rubbing on nylon.

"We went through a great tragedy near the beginning of our marriage. I told you about that. I could tell within a hair's breadth when Chester would crack. He could withstand an enormous amount of pressure, pressure that would destroy an ordinary man. He was a bear for work, and he thrived on

getting out of tough corners. I know that in recent weeks he
had been preoccupied with his business. But that was Chester.
He loved it. No, Mr. Cooperman, I'm sure that Dr. Zekerman
fits into the story somehow, but I doubt that it was because
of business worries."

"And non-business worries?"

"You mean us, our private lives?"

"Yes."

"Chester never was the sort to play around, Mr. Cooperman."

"That's not what you thought last Thursday."

"True," she said, examining the rim of her saucer
with her cup held like she was going to drop it about a foot
from her mouth. "Normally, Chester wouldn't look at another
woman. He never did. But . . ."

"This has something to do with Ward." I was guessing,
but I said it like I'd got the news by registered mail.

"Chester and Bill played follow-the leader throughout
their lives, and when Bill took a mistress, girlfriend, or whatever you call it nowadays, I, well, I feared . . .'"

"I get it. That was in the back of your mind when you
came to see me?" She nodded, and sipped the tea she'd been
holding in the air for the last two minutes. "Tell me about
this girlfriend of Ward's."

"What's that got to do with anything?" I gave her a
look, and she took a deep breath. "Her name is Elizabeth
Tilford. I've never met her, although I've seen her once or
twice. She used to work in my husband's office as a secretary.
She's a mildly good-looking redhead, tall, about thirty, with
very little sense of what to wear in an office, if you ask me. I
don't know where she is now. She went away someplace."

"Is Ward broken-hearted?"

"Bill has a way of getting over heart-break, Mr. Cooperman. You mustn't imagine that Elizabeth Tilford was the
first."

"But he still lives with his wife?"

"Naturally. Neither Bill nor Pauline want the sort of
public scandal that would result in a break between them.
They have an understanding. In some way she knows what
Bill has been doing, and in others she is able to ignore it.
She's perfectly comfortable, and has learned the value of
keeping her husband on a long leash."

"A very long leash."

"If it's long enough, you don't even know it's there."

"Yes. Well. To change the subject for a minute, did your husband ever mention C2 to you?"

"Mention what? C2? No, I don't think so. What is it? Is it important?"

"It could be. At this stage it's hard to tell what's important and what isn't." I put down my cup. "Well, I think that I've learned everything I came to find out. That's the bottom of my list of questions. I've enjoyed the tea. I want to thank you for being so frank with me." She led me back to the hall and my hat and coat. She even helped me with the sleeve I'd pulled inside out when I took it off. She was a real nice lady, and I hated asking her the question at the top of my list.

"Mrs. Yates," I asked, with my foot in the door, "would I be very wrong in guessing that you are in love with Bill Ward?"

You had to hand it to her. I thought that I'd just hit her with enough to lay her out. She stood there for a moment trying to force a smile to her lips, but her eyes told me what she thought of me.

"You really are a detective, Mr. Cooperman. Yes, I'm in love with Bill Ward. I thought I hid it better. But then I've always loved him. Good afternoon, Mr. Cooperman."

ELEVEN

I parked my car around behind my office building, which formed part of an arch of brick and stone structures put up on the high ground above the old canal at the end of the nineteenth century. The fieldstone looked green and wet on the lintel of the backdoor leading to the cellar. The unpainted wood of the door looked rotten. I walked up the lane and then climbed the twenty-eight steps to my big front door. I wasn't even breathing hard.

I put in a call to Martha Tracy at Scarp Enterprises, and in doing so, I remembered a batch of questions I'd meant to ask Myrna Yates. I was sorry that I had to take it out on her, especially since she was signing my cheques, but I needed to know more about the business end of Chester's involvements. If he was in the middle of something when he got knocked off, there must be more than several people around town sucking in air and not letting it out. Martha was out to lunch, the receptionist reported. I left my number. To kill time, I put in another call to Pete Staziak, at the Regional Police.

"What's with you, Benny?"

"What do you mean?"

"Don't answer a question with a question."

"Tell my mother. What's wrong?"

"Well, how come you're always calling me up at work lately, and for a couple of years before this week I hardly ever heard from you?"

"What are you talking? I'm always interested in how you're doing. How are you doing? There, I'm asking."

"I thought you were supposed to be a private investigator."

"What's that supposed to mean?"

"Well, Ellery Queen and Perry Mason aren't always phoning the cops to see what the latest developments have been."

"That's in books. Besides they were related to the cops or practically. Nobody tried to freeze them out. Come on, Pete, don't hold out of me. Have you got a report back from the Forensic Centre in Toronto yet?"

"Yeah."

"Well?" He took a long breath like someone who had just given in to lighting up his first cigarette in three weeks, two days, seven hours and fifty-five minutes.

"Okay. Zekerman was clubbed to death."

"Stop the presses! You didn't have to go to Toronto to find that out. I could have told you. Even that washed-up drunk Hildebrandt could have told you that."

"Leave our former shady coroner out of this. Do you want to know when he died or don't you?"

"Surprise me."

"Don't be a smart ass, Benny. He was killed just after five, as close as they can place it."

"Could it have been just before?"

"Sure. There's a margin in these things."

"So, he was knocked off by someone after getting his full hour of therapy or by someone who didn't bother to get into the nice soft leather chair."

"Looks that way. We are trying to get some help from Medicare to help us find out who his patients were yesterday, but they are reading us a lot of stuff about confidentiality and like that. They are very sensitive about that kind of thing. We got lots of his files here, but it sounds like they all could have done him in. He was seeing some weird people, Benny."

"Is that all you've got?"

"You complaining? If you weren't a private eye, you'd have to go out and get a job."

"I never thought I'd hear that from a cop."

"Hey, there is one funny thing we found about about your good dead friend the doctor: he was cooking his Medicare accounts."

"How can you tell?"

"Interesting, huh? Well, we took what was left in his office downtown and looked at it most of this afternoon. We found a few bills which didn't quite tally with the jottings about appointments. He was charging everybody we could match up with about three or four visits a month more than they actually made. No skin off the customers' noses, because in the end they collected from Medicare. Nice fellow, eh?"

"Maybe he was killed by a bunch of hit boys from the Medical Association for giving them a bad name?"

"I'll tell Harrow you suggested it."

"Don't spoil my supper. So long. I'll be talking to you."

"Don't rush. Goodbye." Pete was a good guy most of the time. But he was a sucker for a queen's side opening.

I called Martha back. I never really believe that receptionists pass out messages as liberally as they are paid to do. And with someone like Martha Tracy, I wouldn't be surprised to find people holding out on her in little ways. I was right. She was at her desk.

"Martha?"

"Who wants her?"

"Cooperman."

"Well, why didn't you say so in the first place. I just got back from drinking my lunch. Has something happened?"

"Nothing you haven't read about. But I wanted to ask you about a girl who used to work in your office: Elizabeth Tilford. Does that name ring any bells?"

"I only wish they'd stop. Sure I remember her. I put her up after she came to work for us. She stayed six months and left owing me two months' rent. I can scarcely manage the mortgage as it is, and she leaves like that without a word."

"Exactly when did she come to work at the office?" I could hear the loud sounds of finger arithmetic for a few seconds.

"I think she started around the end of July last year. She moved in with me a month after that. I had the back room empty anyway, and I thought the company might be cheerful."

"When did you see her last?"

"I told you, two months ago. End of February."

"I hear she was good-looking."

"What do you expect me to say? She had all the right equipment in just the right proportions. Red hair, long legs, smart but cold. Not what you call a good mixer. Not one to go off in a romantic fog and marry the third assistant to the boss in the mailroom. She was after big game."

"You mean Ward?"

"For a little guy, you get around, don't you? Yeah, she

picked out her man the first time she set eyes on him, and she didn't want a second or third string to fall back on. They were a hot number for a couple of months. She played him smart, like a trout fisherman. He never saw her drool once; he thought it was all his idea. That kind of smart."

"And it went on until she left?"

"M'yeah. Without a word to anybody. At first we thought she'd been fired. I remember that Mr. Yates spent part of a day talking to her in her office. That was the last day or near it. I thought she'd come out with a pink slip and a letter of recommendation. That's the way Mr. Yates did things."

"You're serious about her disappearing? I mean, she didn't just vanish, did she? Somebody must know where she went. Ward for instance."

"Ask him if you dare."

"I may have to do that. But I can't get over this business of her lamming out of there without anybody raising a fuss. She owed you money . . ."

"I'm just soft in the head, trusting people. I should be put away."

"Didn't anybody get in touch with the police about it?"

"Well, Mr. Ward wouldn't have been the one to call them in. Chester asked me if I thought that we should report her as a missing person, but, hell, she didn't seem to me to be the sort of girl that got herself raped or murdered. The other way round maybe. I thought more than likely she'd just gone off somewhere. She didn't leave much behind her. Not many clothes, no furniture, just a few books. And if you dragged me to court, I'd have to admit that even the back rent wouldn't add up to much in real money. Still, she could have said goodbye."

"What was she like?"

"When she wasn't out with Mr. Ward, she stayed home reading. She didn't have much fun, didn't like jawing like I do, or drinking, like I do, or even watching TV. She didn't even smoke. She was too serious for me. I don't know what Mr. Ward saw in her, apart from the obvious. Chester liked her too. She played up to him, and he licked it up like cream."

"Martha, you don't miss much. Be talking to you. Goodbye."

"Cooperman, come back here! What's she got to do with all this?"

"If I find out, Martha, you'll be the first to know."

TWELVE

I locked up the shop early. It was the first night in quite a few that I wouldn't be burning the midnight oil. With spring in the air, I wasn't anxious to hang around pretending I had honest work to do. Tomorrow, or one of these days, I'd have to finish my income tax. It was a month late, but as I tried to explain to the authorities in a letter, the tax must wait upon the income, not the other way around. With the longer days and warmer nights, I could see the divorce business beginning to flock in. I never liked standing under windows in the winter. People who get separated in the winter deserve to stay married. I remember once I was following this guy who took his girlfriend out for a boatride down at Port Richmond. He spent the whole day out there with her, just gliding under the low-hanging willows. They ate their lunch out of a wicker hamper. It was almost like he was treating me to a day off. Even though I didn't have a hamper, I'd been sharp enough to realize that I might need something to eat, so I was carrying a sandwich with me just in case. The lettuce and celery were wilted, but the egg was fresh. Next time, I promised myself to have travelling sandwiches toasted. They don't get as soggy.

Frank Bushmill's light was still on, but I wasn't much in the mood to talk to him. He saw me leaving though, and pulled me into his dank office for "a drap of the creature." He knew I didn't drink much, but he seemed unable to talk about anything but feet without a glass in his hand.

"How are you and the Russians getting along?"

"Too busy to do any reading, Frank."

"Too busy to live, then. Here's a book now. *The Third Policeman*, Flann O'Brien."

"I don't read mysteries," I lied.

"Read this. You won't regret it. That's an autographed copy, I want it back."

"You can have it right away. I never finish books these days. I keep dozing off." I should have seen luck when it was looking at me. Here was a chance to get away with only a book.

"Read it."

"I will. I'll start on it at once. Good night."

For Frank's sake I honestly tried, but I couldn't get the hang of it at all and I gave up about page twelve.

Wednesday dawned bright and fresh. Or I guess it did. I slept away until eight, got up, showered and shaved, and went out to get my breakfast at a restaurant near the hotel called "Bagels." They have rolls of all kinds, muffins, rye bread both light and dark, but never, *never* bagels. They just ran out, they didn't come in today, they didn't come in yet. For other people there were bagels, but not for me. I tried not to think of it as a conspiracy.

"Morning, Sid. I'll have lox and cream cheese on a bagel."

"Have to be on rye or kaiser roll. I'm out of bagels."

"Maybe you're not ordering enough." He looked at me like I said his wife was fooling around with the bus-boy.

"If I got more bagels, I would have left-over bagels. Nobody likes to eat left-over bagels. Nightmares you are trying to give me, Benny."

I opened up my office door on the sun stealing across my desk drying up the water in the plant I was trying to grow. I moved it to the shade again and pulled the blinds, which made it necessary to turn on the lights. Already I could see it was going to be one of those days. I said a silent prayer, hoping that it might help to get the season's divorces started. Once the weather brightens up and the hockey disappears from television, a lot of people take up divorce. And I had a whole filing cabinet to accommodate their business.

I jumped to a wrong conclusion. Any day that begins with mail can't be all bad. The first envelope contained a cheque for two hundred dollars signed by Myrna Yates. The second envelope contained the list of appointments that Martha had sent me from two blocks away three days ago. With a push it could have found me by itself in that time. It was a lined piece of foolscap with jottings in black Pentel. I decided to try the third envelope to see if I'd won the Provincial lottery.

The third envelope was a stiff one with Dr. Zekerman's name and office address in the upper left-hand corner. It gave me the blue devils opening up communication from the grave, or at least the morgue, so I tore it open with more than my usual number of thumbs. From inside tumbled out onto my desk a photograph, three pages of notes, nearly indecipherable, and a folded photo copy of a newspaper clipping.

The photograph was a small album-sized snapshot, a bit chewed around the corners. It showed two smiling girls looking out at me. They were dressed alike in Scottish kilts and hats, the younger one sitting and the older one standing a little behind her chair. To my inexperienced eye, they looked like sisters. The older girl looked about twelve, and her sister about ten. To me, a complete stranger, they looked like nice girls; their foreheads were large, their hair light, but not blonde, and their faces were round and open. Nothing was written on the back of the picture. Nor did the good doctor bother to scrawl a note to me. After all, he could explain everything next time I ran into him.

The photocopied clipping was from the *Beacon*, dated the twenty-eighth of February, 1964. It read:

Elizabeth Blake, 20, pretty first-year student at Albert College, Secord University, was found dead in her Pauline Johnson House room of an apparent overdose of barbiturates by fellow co-ed Susan Weiss at ten o'clock this morning.

The body of the popular student, who was enrolled in the three-year general arts program, was discovered fully clothed in her bed in the newly-opened three-storey residence. Teachers and fellow-students alike were shocked to learn of her desperate end.

Miss Blake had aroused the suspicion of Miss Weiss by not appearing at breakfast or in the Study Hall. (Classes at Secord have been cancelled because of the weather.) With the assistance of Roberta Widdicombe, a graduate student responsible for that floor of the residence, the door was opened and the body discovered.

Investigation of the tragedy has been hampered

by the violent snow storm, which has closed all
roads to the stop of the escarpment and the University. Coroner E. P. Hildebrandt, who has been
in touch with the situation by telephone, told the
Beacon today that the girl had apparently swallowed
all of the sleeping pills in a plastic phial found near
the body of the student. He will investigate the matter fully as soon as the weather permits, he averred.
Miss Blake is survived by ...

And so on. Was the dead girl one of the sisters in the photo-
graph? Or was it a picture of the fellow student, Susan
Weiss? Not likely. The Weisses aren't big on kilts. How am
I doing, Dr. Z?

Miss Blake is survived by her parents, Mr. and Mrs.
L.M. Blake of Dover Road, and her sister Hilda of
the same address.

So, we have both sisters in the picture. But which is which?
Most likely the older one went off to school first. Yeah, and
the younger was still living at home when the older girl dies.
I couldn't carry water very far in a deduction like that, so I
didn't try.

Next I looked at the three pages. My second glance
found them as hard to read as my first. They were torn from
a lined stenographer's pad, and the pencil scratchings were
all in the same difficult handwriting that had addressed the
package to me. He might as well have sent me a rag, a bone
and a hank of hair. I looked harder at the jottings. I wasn't
making it up. They were next door to hen tracks. I thought
that I might try taking them around to Lou Gelner. As a
doctor, he is something of an authority on bad handwriting.
And, to be fair, these notes looked as though they were some
kind of professional shorthand, such as the doctor might
have scribbled during a therapy session, or just afterwards.

Well, thank you, Dr. Z, you were trying hard to tell me
something. It's not your fault that I can't lip-read in the fog.
Send me another hint, please.

I turned back to Martha's find after putting the photograph and clipping in my breast pocket. It was just a list
of names, names like Jones, Peters, Evans and others each
with a time beside it.

Jones	Sàturday, 2 am
Henry	Friday, 11 pm
Bill	Friday, 1 am
Peters	Friday, 2 pm
Careless	Friday, 8 pm
Harney	Friday, 7 pm
Evans	Friday, 9 am
York	Friday, 2 pm
Henderson	Friday, 6 am
Evans	Friday, 3 pm
Peters	Friday, 6 pm
Richards	Friday, 1 am
Dodge	Friday, 8 pm
Plymouth	Friday, 8 am
Ford	Friday, 9 am
Williams	Friday, 6 pm
Roberts	Friday, 4 am

There was no continuing time sequence like a desk calendar has. Here the times were all over the place jumping from an hour in the middle of the morning to one after office hours, and then going earlier in the day again before the first appointment. Some of the appointments were made for the small hours of the morning. Chester was beginning to look like a workaholic. All work and no play, Chester, you should have known that. Yet, come to think of it, his wife hadn't complained to me of his meetings in the middle of the night. That would have put me on the payroll a lot earlier, if he had been jumping out of bed in the middle of the night "to see a man about some shares." Not bloody likely.

I looked at the names again: Jones, Henry, Bill, Peters, Careless, Harney, Evans, York, Henderson, Evans, Peters, Richards, Dodge, Plymouth, Ford, Williams and Roberts. I was beginning to think that there was less here than meets the eye. The name Bill I recognized right away: Bill Ward. But there are a lot of Bills in the world. Call out *Bill* in the Men's Beverage Room, and half the place will get up. But it was the only name on the list that was clearly a first name. That made my guess that it was Ward look a little better. There were a couple of repeating names: Peters and Evans. I couldn't make anything out of that. So I moved on. Three of the names are names of cars: Dodge, Plymouth and Ford. What could I do with a hot clue like that? So I did the logical thing, I put it down and promised that I would figure it out later on.

There had to be some way of explaining these meetings that went all around the clock.

I thought about calling my mother. I hadn't been in touch since Friday. A glance at my watch told me that it was still too early to call. I could usually count on her to be up at the crack of noon in the middle of the week, so I decided to give her another couple of hours. She had a birthday coming up next month. I made a note on my calendar. I dreaded the recurring round of trying to find out what she wanted. If I asked her directly, she would only tell me that all she wanted was to see me settled and happy. I didn't think I could deliver on that this year. Birthdays were contests that Ma and Pa waged against me with seriousness and energy. There was only one absolutely just right present in a sea of thousands of imitations, and without a hint or a clue I had to pick out the right thing. It would have been easier if she was someone who could appreciate a really good cigar.

THIRTEEN

When I got back after lunch, I could see the rest of the day stretched out before me, broken into two halves: before I called my mother, and after. They looked like long halves, and I had no desire to do my income tax in either one of them. I played with the appointment list Martha Tracy had sent me for half an hour without getting anyplace, and I phoned Lou Gelner to see whether he might be able to decipher Zekerman's handwriting. We arranged to meet for coffee at the hospital the following morning after his general rounds.

I was just thinking that it would be nice if Myrna Yates invited me over for afternoon tea, when I heard high heels on the stairs. As I said before, high heels usually means business for me rather than for Frank Bushmill.

She was a knock-out in green and rust, tall with green eyes and long brown hair that fell to her shoulders. She came through the door with the same caution that everybody else crossed my threshold, but on her it looked good. I even found myself struggling out of my chair, playing the gentleman. "Mr. Cooperman?" she asked, and I nodded. For a moment I thought it was going to be the first entry in this season's divorce business, but a quick survey of her hands, in a nervous repose in her lap after I had seated her in the customer's chair, showed no rings that told me anything. After she sat down she went through a routine of digging into her leather bag for something that had escaped her. When she dug it up, it was only a piece of paper with my name on it. I tried to offer her a calming cigarette, but she shook her head. I lit it for myself. I'll have to start stocking menthols for the women who come in here. I tried to smile, to get the conversation started. I blew out some smoke through my nose, trying to show her that I could be as nervous as she was. Only she was hiding it better. Her hands remained in her lap, and she sat up straight in her chair looking at me with her green piercing eyes. "Mr. Cooperman, I hope that you can help me. If you can't, I don't know what I'll do." Here a blush rose from her collar to her cheeks and a blue vein in her forehead began to throb becomingly. I shifted bits and pieces from the Yates case, mostly the stuff Dr. Zekerman had sent me, to one side of my desk, giving, I hoped, the impression of a man cleaning his decks for action.

"Of course I'll do my best to help you. Naturally. That's what I'm here for, isn't it?" She smiled her answer, and I thought that we were safely launched. "Let's begin at the beginning. Tell me about it first." I shuffled a yellow legal-sized block of foolscap under my nose, and removed from it the doodles I'd made while listening to Myrna Yates nearly a week ago. New customer, new paper, that's me. No expense too great, no effort too small. I began with a new series of doodles in the upper left-hand corner. "What is your name, Miss . . . ?"

"Campbell, Phoebe Campbell. I'm from Chatham originally, grew up there and I've been in Grantham for just a few months. I work for the Upper Canadian Bank. I'm just a teller. But it was there that I met someone, and that's how I got into this mess," she said breathlessly. I could see her trying not to get the story twisted. Most people let a story come out sideways, so that you can't tell the beginning from the end or one side from the other.

"I guess that you can tell that the person I met was a man." When she said that, she looked about twelve years old. Into the word *man* she put all the boogymen she'd ever heard of, and her raised eyebrow tried to tell me at the same time that she'd learned her lesson and wouldn't ever do it again, so I shouldn't judge her too harshly. That might be reading a lot into a raised eyebrow, but it was either that or watch the delicious frontier marked by the hem of her skirt and the nicest part of her knees. I try at all times to keep things on an up and up business-like basis, so I looked at her raised eyebrow.

"I met him at the bank. He came in almost every day, and always got in the line in front of my window. He got my name from the plastic sign on the counter, and started calling me by my first name. Then one day, when we closed, he was waiting for me outside. He was very nice, and asked me if I would go with him to have some coffee. I know I shouldn't have, Mr. Cooperman, but I did. I regret it now, of course, but then now I know better. You see, Mr. Cooperman, I didn't know anyone in the city, apart from the girls at the bank. Do you understand?" She looked at me imploringly with her big green eyes. I could see that in the light from the window, they had gold flecks in them, and they looked about five fathoms deep. "We've been seeing one another for about two months. First it was just coffee, lunch and that sort of thing, but later . . . I'm having difficulty telling this part, Mr. Cooperman. Need I go into details?"

"Let's say I can guess the next part. Go on to the part after that."

"Thank you. We used to go to his house here in the city. We spent many evenings there. And he gave me things: jewelry, mostly. Not really expensive jewelry, but the nicest I've ever seen. And in so short a time. I was quite bowled over. Then, last week, he told me about his wife. He'd told me about her before, but those times he talked about her as as though she were far away, part of his distant past, someone he hadn't really cared about in years. But this time, I mean last week when he spoke of her, she became real for the first time. She was a presence in his life and I could see that she was going to continue to be." She riffled her large bag for a tissue, but came up with one so crumpled and old, that I offered her one of mine. It's all part of the service.

"Did he break it off?"

"Yes."

"Have you seen him since last week?"

"No. I haven't wanted to. He's tried phoning, but I don't want to speak to him. I'm not blaming him, Mr. Cooperman, but I just want to get clear of it and start again. Do you understand?"

'Of course." I couldn't take my eyes off her smooth transparent skin. Her cheeks coloured with every difficult thing she told me. "I think we've come to the part you want me for. Am I right, Miss Campbell?"

"Yes." She dug into her bag again and extracted a package about the size of a couple of paperback books, wrapped in white paper, tied with string and patched here and there with Scotch tape, which caught the light as she passed the moderately heavy parcel to me over the desk. "These are the things he gave me. Things I don't want to see

any more. I would like you to return them for me, Mr.
Cooperman. I'll pay you, of course. Will you do this, please?"
I hefted the package in my hand, and she began laying out
twenty-dollar bills on her side of the desk like she was playing a game of solitaire. When she got to ten of them, I
called: "Whoa! That's too much. Let me try to get you
straight: all you want me to do is to return these trinkets to
your friend?" She nodded. "Look, Miss Campbell, I'd like to
help you, but to be honest, I think you can get the post
office to deliver the parcel a lot cheaper than my night rates.
Delivering parcels is right up their street. They do it all the
time." She looked at my desk-top for a few seconds.

"You don't believe me, do you?"

"Lady, your money looks real. If you believe it, that's
good enough for me."

"I'll show you what's in the box," she said, beginning to
tear off the paper.

"That's not necessary," I said. "I'll do it later myself," I
added under my breath. But the paper was already off and I
was looking into a blue box of silver bangles, a very good
dress watch with sparkling brilliants on the band, a couple of
brooches, a string of pearls and other "trinkets" like she said;
a couple of thousand dollars worth by the look of it, some of
the pieces looked like old family jewels, but of modest value.
Her boyfriend may have been getting his "trinkets" from his
wife's vanity drawer. When I looked up, I could see that she
hadn't wanted to see that stuff again, and her fingers were
already busy taping the package back together again.

"Okay, I understand why you don't want to drop this in
the mailbox. However, you could have it registered. That's
still cheaper than involving me."

"I think I can trust you," she said. Her eyes found
mine and I wanted to believe her. I'm a sucker for green
eyes. "But if there is something about the job you don't like,
I'll find another way. I'll find something." She had got to her
feet and turned away from me gathering up her bag and
parcel. I got up and came around the desk.

"I'll do it," I said. Now she wouldn't look at me, as
though she'd said too much already. "I'll do it," I repeated.
Now she turned to business.

"All you have to do is to take it tonight to the address
on this paper." She handed me an envelope. "Inside is a key
to the back door. Don't turn on the lights—I assume you have
a flashlight?"

"Naturally."

"Good. At the top of the stairs, there are two doors leading to the right of the hall. Take the second one. That was our ... a bedroom. Put the package in the top bureau drawer next to the bed. When you've finished, call me at the number in the envelope." I opened the envelope, read the address: 186 Bellevue Terrace, pocketed the key, and put the paper with the telephone number away next to it.

"Is that it?" I asked, hoping she wasn't going to add a few details like the fact that a wedding reception would be going on at the time or that the place was booby-trapped. "Whose house is this anyway?" I asked.

"The owner is Tom Twining. He works for Griffiths and Dunlop, the real estate firm. You know them?"

"I guess I've seen their ads in the paper."

"What time do you think you'll be able to phone me?"

"Oh, say around ten-thirty. I should be in and out by then. That should be late enough."

"Good. I've paid you in advance, Mr. Cooperman, so there's no need for us to meet again. Nothing personal, of course."

"That's understood." I raised my palms in mock protest. She nodded, smiled a wispy smile and turned toward the door.

"There's one thing more," I said. She turned quickly and shot me a startled look, as though I was about to ask for a couple of hundred dollars more. "You haven't given me the package." I smiled. She looked into her bag, found the parcel again, and was almost laughing as she passed it to me. In another second, she had left the room. I sat there wondering what kind of cock-and-bull story I'd fall for next, but at least this one left a pleasant fragrance behind. At least it didn't involve stealing kids from one parent for the other in a messy post-divorce case, or turning in a perfectly decent fellow just because you happened to be working for his estranged wife. At least this looked clean.

I got out of my chair, and left the office. Across the street in Woolworth's I looked for Bellevue Terrace on a tourist map of the city. It was across the valley, on the same side of the creek as Martha Tracy, but located on the ravine like Chester's place. I worked my way along the counters, past the pastel bins of lingerie, bumping into old ladies with shopping bags that should have been checked at the door and kids discovering what was new in cap guns and holsters. In passing a pay telephone, I couldn't resist taking a peek. I was right: no Tom Twining listed on Bellevue Terrace. This caper was getting to be as irresistible as Phoebe Campbell herself. I caught the eye of a salesgirl, and made the purchase of a serviceable flashlight. The batteries were extra, but what the hell.

FOURTEEN

At ten o'clock I found myself driving over the high-level bridge which connects the two halves of the city. Below me, in the dark, I knew the mingled waters of canal and creek began their joint run to the lake about two miles away. Below me too the ghosts of the old sailing fleet haunted the valley, and the echoes of a thousand hammers and adzes at the vanished drydock were enough to distract a man going about a foolish mission because of the pretty place it came from. I turned left at the first street over the bridge, and went down the bumpy, short steep hill to Bellevue Terrace. I checked the numbers. On one side ran a group of frame and stucco houses, not unlike Martha Tracy's house, all dating from the 1920s. On the other side of the street, all of the houses looked as though they'd been built within a month of one another just after the Second World War. The houses on the right and left looked at one another across a gap of at least thirty thousand dollars. The last house number I read was still too high, and by then I could see that the street continued on higher ground, the two parts joined by a hedge-bordered cinder path. To get to the upper section of the street, it was necessary to drive around the wedge-shaped beginning of a gully, which led down a dark and forested incline to the creek.

On this part of the street, at least the houses were all about the same value, with the ones backing on the ravine looking a little more desirable than the ones across the road. Still, I wouldn't say no if you offered me any of them. I picked out my house, and kept on going. The street ended in a right-angled turn to my right, with the new street slipping into working-class houses as soon as the corner had been

84

surely rounded. Squatting inside the angle itself, I could see a huge, brooding mansion of stucco and wood, with dark protruding eaves and unfriendly-looking screened-in porches. The house I was looking for stood next door to this. It was much smaller than the houses around it, without looking shabby, or suggesting that the owner sipped his tea from his saucer. It was simply dwarfed by the mansion, from which it was separated by a high privet hedge.

I parked my car around the corner in front of a brick veneer bungalow with three small square windows under the eaves. I felt my pockets; I had the flashlight and the package. I wished I had a rabbit's foot for luck.

There was no moon. It wouldn't have mattered much if there had been. There were street lights all over the place. Luckily, there were lots of shade trees and hedges. I could hear my footsteps thundering behind me; my shadow came up under me, grew, marched ahead, then faded away, as I walked along the sidewalk. The house was dark. I turned in and made my way past the attached garage, and a very noisy-looking garbage can, to the back. Here I found a screened-in porch with stacks of summer furniture lying in dusty disorder. The screen door opened easily, with a twang of its spring. There was enough light for me to find the inside door without lighting my flash. I could make out the metallic glint of the spring lock above the knob. I fished out the key, and inserted it. I was a little surprised that it turned.

I closed the door behind me, and brought out my flash. I was in a bright kitchen. The tile was real, 1930s, not plastic, and it extended down to the counter tops. The floor was terracotta. I moved forward keeping the beam of my flashlight as low as possible. I made my way through a narrow hall into the front vestibule and then easily found the stairs, which curved down at me. I went up. The walls in the hall upstairs looked mushroom colour in this light, but were probably pink. I found the second doorway to the right and went in. A large bed dominated the room. It was neat, covered with a chintz bedspread that matched the curtains. The bureau stood between the two windows. I opened the drawer. A flash of light had cut across the front of the house. I slipped the package into the drawer, which was full of rolled socks, and closed it quickly. I was half finished. The other half of the job was for myself; I was going to nose around and find out what this whole thing was all about.

My retreat took me back the way I'd come except that

when I'd reached the bottom of the stairs, I saw the light slide by the front windows again. I felt a flea crawl from my armpit down to my waist. On second thought, I'd nose around someplace else. I must have crossed to the back door in less than two seconds and without making a sound. You couldn't hear the clock as I closed the door, and in a second I had left the porch. My mind was working out where I could safely hide for a few minutes when the sun exploded in my face.

"Hey!"

"Don't move!" I didn't, although I tried to shield my face from the powerful flashlight shining in it. I tried it every way, but the light held me like the arm of an arresting officer.

"Get that light out of my eyes. I'm not going anywhere. Is this 184 Bellevue Terrace?"

"You know damn well it isn't. Stand where you are, and don't try anything."

"What should I try?" I could hear footsteps coming along the sidewalk leading from the front of the house.

"Bill?" a voice inquired.

"Yeah," said the voice behind the light. "I got him."

"Good. See if he's carrying a gun." That idea was almost too much for me.

"Look, you guys, I know what you must think this looks like, but let me tell you straight out that I can explain everything."

"I'm sure you can, sir," said the voice called Bill. A dark shape worked around the edge of the blinding light and came around behind me. I could feel my pockets being slapped, as a pair of expert hands worked me over.

"He's clean," said the voice, and the light dipped enough for me to catch sight of a dark blue police uniform standing behind it. I looked over my shoulder. The other man was a cop too. And I might have spent the evening watching television, or reading a good book, or even going to the movies.

"Turn around," said the first cop, the one called Bill. "We're going back into the house." An arm prodded my shoulder, and I followed quietly.

I opened the back door, and turned on the lights in the kitchen. To the left there was a small breakfast nook with a round table. Bill motioned me to sit down. I sat. They placed themselves at the edge of the curved red leatherette bench, blocking my escape from both directions.

"Okay," said the one that wasn't Bill, "let's hear who you are and what you think you're doing here. But remember, we've got a pretty good idea about it ourselves, so try not to waste all of our time with a lot of made-up malarkey about getting the address mixed up. Give it to us straight, and it will go better for you."

"Okay, here's the story. It's simple enough. I'm Ben Cooperman, I'm a private investigator. If you'll let me reach into my pocket, I'll show you my I.D."

"Just don't move suddenly. Take it easy." I pulled out my wallet and handed it to the one not called Bill. Bill intercepted and looked through the wallet thoroughly.

"Right, Mr. Cooperman, let's hear the whole thing from the beginning."

"Fine," I said, "fine." I took a big breath and let them know I was going to start. Bill brought his notebook into play with a lazy motion, the other fellow was more deliberate.

"Okay, you think you've caught a burglar, right? Well, how many burglars carry a key to the house they're burglaring? I know where I am and I can't remember any law against conducting private business in a private house."

"Don't get excited," said the one called Bill. "Take it easy. We haven't said anything about burglary, have we? Don't do our job for us. You were saying that you were what? Using a flashlight in order to save electricity?"

"In a private house a person can bang about in the dark if he wants to. It only becomes police business if I bother the neighbours."

"Is this your house?" said the other one.

"No, it isn't."

"Whose house, then?"

"The owner of the house is Tom Twining of Griffiths and Dunlop, the real estate company." They both wrote that down. The name tasted like artificial sweetener in my mouth. God help me.

"You were seen carrying a package into the house. Where is it now?"

"Look, I don't see where you get off asking me these questions. You saw my I.D. I'm a private investigator pursuing an investigation. How come you guys never followed me home before? Where did I get so popular all of a sudden?"

Bill looked over at the other cop, whose neck was red around his collar, and who'd missed a few spots on his chin with this morning's razor.

"Get it," he said. The one who wasn't Bill pulled his six foot length upright and disappeared. Bill looked at me, relaxing a little. He took off his cap and placed it in the middle of the table. His rusty-coloured hair was dark with sweat. My own armpits stuck to my sides. Then the other cop was back with the package. He swung his tall knees under the table and looked at me.

"Is this the package you brought into the house?"

"I didn't say I'd brought a package into the house." I felt like a politician caught telling the truth.

Bill began to tear the tape and pull off the paper. I watched in silence. At least the blue cardboard box came out without dribbling white powder on the table. From the box, Bill lifted a small, short-barrelled hand gun, about .32 caliber, with a dull blue look to it that I didn't like one bit.

FIFTEEN

It was about an hour later by my wrist watch, but in time as measured by my lifespan I had moved forward by a year at least. I felt as though I had been hauled under a bright light and slapped a few times by a crew who knew how to do it without leaving bruises where they show.

They brought me into the Regional Police office from the parking lot through a side door, the kind you open by punching in a code on the handle, and left me to cool my heels on a wooden bench for a half hour or so. It was busy with men coming and going, half of them in uniform. I found a magazine and read some movie reviews of pictures I'd already forgotten. On the wall was a bulletin board with a few "Wanted" posters on it, like in the movies. Unlike the movies, there was a handmade notice that a second-hand camper was for sale. The bottom of the notice ended in a fringe of telephone numbers. Someone brought in a cardboard box full of coffee. I was offered one at normal cost as though I wasn't about to be subjected to questioning in a Breaking and Entering matter. I thought of explaining that to the coffee man, as I fished out my quarter, but he didn't look as though he gave a damn. I sipped my coffee after levering off the plastic cap. It was bad enough to replace the traditional third degree. But just then it was warm and wet, and that's all I wanted.

When I had finished all but the last swallow, a cop in uniform came over to me and established eye contact, which I had begun to think had gone out of style since I'd been brought into the station.

"You Cooperman?" I nodded. He pointed down the corridor. "Fifth door on your right," he said. I downed the last of the bitter coffee and moved in the direction he'd suggested.

It was a very office-like office, with all of the usual furnishings, except that most of them were made of gray metal, and looked like somebody regularly went at them with a ball-peen hammer. The light came from a hanging fluorescent fixture. I took one of the gray chairs. Beige-coloured files were stuck in a metal rack and others blossomed from a file drawer. The floor was covered with rubber tile, with rust marks from where the furniture used to be, and dark smears around the cold radiator under the window. On the wall I saw some photographs in plain black frames: on the firing line with target pistols, smiles and handshakes in front of a wooden shield with a lot of silver on it, and a class picture of thirty young faces at cop college. Dusty Venetian blinds divided a view of the floodlit court house into long uninteresting strips.

When my two cops came back, they brought a bonus with them, who introduced himself as Sergeant Savas. I finally found out that the other two were Bedrosian and Kyle. Kyle was the Bill of earlier in the evening. I never did find out what Bedrosian's first name was. Savas looked like a hard man, but a busy man. At the moment he wasn't very interested in me. I was glad of that. I wouldn't ever want to be the centre of Sergeant Savas' undivided attention. He flipped through a number of reports that I'm sure had nothing to do with me and then looked up. He was almost casual.

"We checked out the telephone number you say your client gave you. Turns out to be a Chinese restaurant on Niagara Street. Pay phone. We tried it about twenty minutes ago and didn't get diddly. We checked on that name you gave us, Twining. That's another bad joke. Two Tom Twinings in town, neither the owner or tenant of that house. He's unknown at Griffiths and Dunlop. She probably found the name on a teabag. As for the gun, it's not registered. And you know as well as I do that a peeper isn't licenced to carry a piece since 1966, right? We're running some checks on it to see whether there's any priors on the weapon. Never can tell. If I were you, Mr. Cooperman, I'd reconsider telling us the name of the woman who bought your ticket to this hayride. What do you say?" I looked for a minute into his leathery face and those eyes like steel ball-bearings and tried to decide. The gun was a real surprise. She had two packages in her bag: one for show and one to go. Everything about the deal looked phoney, so probably the name she gave me was at the top of the let's-pretend list. I'd have to check that out anyway. Might as well put the cops to work for me. I'm a taxpayer, or at least I hope to become one one of these days.

"Okay," I said. "She told me her name was Phoebe Campbell. She's a tall brunette with green eyes. Good looking with a face that cries out to be believed. She works as a teller at the Upper Canadian Bank. I don't know which branch." Savas tugged on his earlobe, and motioned Bedrosian out the door to check on it. While we were waiting, Savas continued reading a report about something important. Bedrosian was back in fifteen minutes, shaking his head.

"There's no one of that name or description working at the Upper, as far as we can find out at this hour. I'll try your description around the branches tomorrow. But, Sergeant, I don't know what we'd book her on if we found her. We didn't find anything on Mr. Cooperman, and it wouldn't take much to get out from under what we're holding." Kyle looked at Savas and so did I. He was working his upper lip tightly over his teeth like he had a few strands of steak lodged between a couple of teeth.

"You know, Mr. Cooperman, in a way you're lucky your story is so crazy. We hear all kinds in a week, but you win the prize. If any of this stuff had checked out, I'd nail you to the wall with a B and E in a minute, but it stinks to high heaven, and I've been around long enough to know that all the stink doesn't come from you. Think about it. Why would anyone want to set you up like that?"

"I'm beginning to think of a few reasons. But I've got a good imagination."

"I don't want a whodunit, just facts. When you've coughed up something solid like a fact, I want to know about it. You read me?"

"Loud and clear." I wasn't going to tell him how popular I'd made myself with Harrow, or mention that I suspected a chill wind blowing my way from City Hall. If he was a good cop, and I suspected that Savas was a good cop, he'd hear about this in the morning. Savas warned me about what happens to naughty private investigators when they come up in the world and become common burglars. He told me that I'd better blow my nose somewhere else from now on, and not to leave town. And, just when I'd been prepared to curl up in the holding tank overnight, I found myself being driven back to my car by Bill Kyle, who was going off duty anyway. I couldn't imagine something like that happening in a big

city. There have to be a few advantages to living in a place
like this. It was about time I found out about one of them.

"You got a tip about me from a woman over the phone?"
I asked Kyle.

"It was a phone call. Could have been a woman; I didn't
take it. Check the dispatcher. It'll be on his sheet."

"What did you hear, then? What was I supposed to be
doing: stealing the silver, popping the safe, what?"

"The way I heard it, you were a suspicious character
about to plant something suspicious in the top bureau drawer
of the master bedroom."

"And you believed that?"

"What do you mean? I call that hitting it close."

When I finally crawled behind the wheel of the Olds, I
could feel most of me shouting, "Take me home. Enough's
enough!" and a look at my watch only confirmed that as good
advice. But something in the back of my head, which I was
seriously thinking of donating to science, told me to drive by
the office just to see that everything was in ship-shape shape.

The streets were nearly deserted, except around the Murray Hotel on St. Andrew. The stoplights always take twice
as long this side of midnight. While I was stopped at one of
them, I noticed for the first time that the pavement was wet.
It had rained while I was trading yarns with the cops. My
mother would have said, "Good, if you're a farmer." I parked
out in front of my place, and used my last strength to pull
myself up the twenty-eight steps. A three-bulb fixture hung at
the top of the stairs. Tonight it wasn't doing so well; two of
the bulbs had blown. But there was enough light for me to
see that the front door of my office stood open, and that there
was a foot sticking out of it. Again I felt that tearing at my
stomach I thought I'd left in Dr. Zekerman's office. I had to
force my feet to obey. I took out my handkerchief, and
turned on the lights. Frank Bushmill lay on his side, with one
hand thrust forward as though he had been hit by lightning
while in the act of waving goodbye. I heard my knees snap
with middle age as I knelt at his side. By now I could see that
he was breathing. For a second I felt a flash of rage run
around inside my collar. That bloody drunk had passed out
once too often. But then I saw a wine-coloured mark at the
base of his skull. He had been helped to oblivion by more
than a bottle tonight. I went across the hall and got a towel
from the bathroom and wet it. Frank looked just as out of it
when I got back. I laid the towel over his forehead and

called his name loudly. I thought I saw an eyelid flutter, but
not much. I loosened his collar, and tried biting on one of
his finger nails. He was really out. I went around behind my
desk and found the phone book and called the ambulance.

Looking down at my desk blotter, I saw for the first
time that the place had been gone over by someone who knew
what he was looking for. I knew that I'd left the three pages
of notes that Dr. Zekerman sent me sitting belly up on my
green desk blotter. I felt my breast pocket. Miraculously, the
thief had not also been there. I held at least half a head on
my shoulders. Soon I could see that Frank was making a few
low sounds, his mouth moved a little like a beached whale—
not that I've seen one—and a little more colour was beginning
to be seen in his face. I now remembered that I should have
looked at his eyes. That's the way they do it in the movies.
You can tell all sorts of things just by lifting an eyelid. By
now, however, I could hear the sound of the siren coming up
James Street. Frank would be beyond my tender loving care
in less than three minutes.

To kill the time, I dialled the Regional Police. I got a
tired desk man and asked to be put through to Sergeant
Savas.

"Yeah," Savas said, when I got him.

"It's Cooperman," I said.

"You didn't go home like a nice boy, did you?"

"No. I came back to my office. I thought you'd sleep
better if I told you what I found when I got here."

"Try me."

"Somebody's been through my place. I've been robbed.
And the guy that rents the office next to mine has a nasty
bump on his head that he still can't feel yet. The ambulance
is just parking outside. I don't think he'll be able to tell us
anything for a couple of hours. Just thought I'd let you
know."

"Kinda makes sense now, doesn't it?"

"If that's sense."

"Well, I'll come over and have a look. In the meantime..."

"I know, don't touch anything."

SIXTEEN

At three o'clock in the morning, Sergeant Savas and I started looking for coffee. St. Andrew Street was tight as a drum, and all of the usual places that either of us could think of were sensibly shut down and their operators in bed. Savas thought I was trying to be funny when I offered him a dried apricot. I always thought it would be a good idea to keep a bottle in the bottom drawer of my desk or in the filing cabinet, but with Frank Bushmill for a neighbour, and me for a tenant, it wasn't necessary.

The Sergeant had arrived a few minutes after they'd carted Frank off to the hospital. In the movies and on television, a bump on the head is a temporary inconvenience. It doesn't hold the hero up for long, and the rest of the cast bounce back just as quickly. Savas looked around my place, not taking things very seriously, since I hadn't reported the loss of the Kohinoor diamond, or the Crown Jewels. He had the edges of the puzzle that was bugging me stuck in his teeth, like bits of his dinner, and he wanted me to tell him what was going on. He didn't say that in so many words, but all those scowls couldn't have been indigestion.

"C'mon," he said, and I followed him out into a fine rain, that reflected the stoplights and street signs in a way that made me turn up my collar. The Sandman had already dumped a truckload of dirt in both my eyes, and every bone in my body cried out to be laid to rest. Instead, we got into the Sergeant's car and I could hear the hiss of the tires on the wet road. I didn't much care where he was going. I think I even closed my eyes for a minute, because when I felt the car stop, I could feel my mouth shouting for a toothbrush. It was cold and nearly dawn on a day I knew I would want to forget.

I couldn't tell where we were, but Savas seemed to know what he was doing. He knocked on a door in a one-storey frame building that came a car-length from the edge of the sidewalk. The door was opened by a short fat man with the shortest arms I'd ever seen on a grown man.

"How are you, Lije?" he said without a great deal of warmth.

"Good morning, Chris. Come on in. You're up early. I was just thinking of closing up. Nothing much doing."

"This is Lije Swift, Mr. Cooperman. Lije is short for Elijah. He's a regular prophet, aren't you, Lije. Mr. Cooperman here got himself burgled tonight while he was out burgling somebody else. You got any coffee hot?" He let us into a large dining room full of family-sized dining room tables, not the usual restaurant tables, and we both collapsed into Lije's antique press-back chairs.

"Okay, Mr. Cooperman," he said with his eyelids half closed, "what are you going to tell me about tonight? I don't want any stories, I don't want to hear any garbage, just the facts, like they say on TV. I know that I'm looking at a small part of something a lot bigger. Can you tell me anything to set my mind at rest? I want to get some sleep just as much as you do, but I know I won't sleep until I hear you say your piece." Lije brought over two large ironstone mugs of coffee. It was the best I've ever tasted. Savas knew that too. Savas was a good cop. He was a cop twenty-four hours a day and he knew about coffee.

"I can't tell you who I'm working for, and I shouldn't tell you that I've already had my ass kicked for asking too many questions and not letting the dead bury their dead. It started with Chester Yates. He shot himself. That's what it said on television and in the papers. I know, they have all the usual suicide evidence, but you know as well as I do that there are a few ways to make a murder look like suicide."

He was watching me, with the big hands wrapped around his mug and nodding in time with my disclosures. I took another sip, already beginning to feel better. "When I mentioned this to the boys in Homicide, they thought I was messing their bed. They liked it as suicide, I can't blame them. But then a couple of days later Dr. Andrew Zekerman also gets dead, this time from a bash on the head with a traditional blunt instrument. Zekerman is a shrink. Chester was one of his patients and guess whose file is missing from the doctor's office. Here's another one to try on. A girl named Elizabeth Tilford used to work in Chester's office. Two months ago she disappeared and hasn't been seen since. And behind all these deaths and disappearances is the shadow of a man who was a friend and former business partner of Chester, the boy-friend on the quiet of the girl and the last name that Zekerman told me on the phone two hours before somebody addled his brains for him permanently. There are a lot of questions I would like to get answers for, and I'm bucking a stiff wind blowing from City Hall. If I don't come up with some answers soon, I'm going to have my licence revoked in jig time."

"Tell me, Cooperman, who's the guy you think ties up all these threads?"

"I can't go public on that, Savas. I don't have a breath of proof."

"This public you can go. I'm telling you that, and I don't tell that and then make a report."

"The mayor has a special assistant named Bill Ward." Savas gave a low whistle, and bit his lower lip, which turned into a lopsided grin in about ten seconds.

"Interesting," he said, nodding, "very interesting."

"So Phoebe Campbell got me out of the way tonight so that she or a pal could go through my office. Only one thing is missing. Before he died, Zekerman mailed me these." Here I took the photograph and the clipping from my inside breast pocket. He glanced at the photograph, and scanned the clipping, then, after another look at the picture, looked up at me again. "He also sent me a few pages of jottings from his office. They looked like the sort of notes a shrink might take during a session of therapy. I was going to get a G.P. friend of mine to translate them into English for me this morning. I'll have to cancel that now. Too bad. They were important enough for somebody to go to a lot of trouble to get."

There was a slate-coloured sky looking in the front window of Lije's place. The coffee mugs were empty. I was wool-gathering. Savas had been talking and I'd missed the first part of what he was saying. I saw his mouth making the words, all right, but my own depression made reception difficult. He was talking about Lije Swift.

"He used to run a fast boat above the falls during the prohibition years in the States. The American Coast Guard used to boast that if they didn't nab him, the falls would. He ran his boat full of bootleg Canadian whiskey from below Chippewa. For a while he was a driver for a bunch of high-jackers, and drove a car right into the 1960s that had bullet holes in the back from the Provincial police." He was talking in a drone, his voice scarcely above a whisper. The story heard some other time would have been a good story. I'm not knocking Savas for trying to bring in the new day with fresh information on bootlegging operations on the border way back then. The only effect it had on me was that prohibition made some people on both sides of the border rich, and it was almost bad manners in some circles to mention that the families who made those big bucks owed so much to men like Lije Swift, who ended up running a roadhouse through the small hours of the morning.

Lije gave us both a friendly send-off. He brought over to our table a couple of eight by ten glossies of himself with his short arms around the sculptured shoulders of a late great screen sex symbol. He told us that she was a real lady, easily switching her order from roast veal to steak when the veal was overdone. A real nice lady.

Back in the car, Savas wasn't saying anything. He started the motor and a cigarette, and backed up onto the road. I watched our return to the city carefully, because I didn't have a glimmer about where we'd been. Some village on the Niagara River below the falls, with signs written in old script offering antiques for sale. There still wasn't much traffic on the road. The windshield wipers were able to make enough of the rain to keep the window clear, but it was a near thing. Out toward the industrial mile, where the grim line of black plants made a mockery of the orchards next door to them, the depression in the view would have brought tears to the eyes of Genghis Khan. I watched Savas' car straddle the railway tracks that ran along the road for a quarter of a mile. Soon he ran his car up behind my car and I got out. I was a little surprised that he got out too, and he came around on my side, so that I rolled the window down to hear what he had to say. I started up the motor, and set the wipers to work. I could see Savas' breath in the fine rain.

"Cooperman, a few hours ago I didn't see much more than a comic opera where you're concerned, but what you said about what's going on in this town made sense to me. I'd like to say I'd help you, but there isn't diddly I could do for you now except not running you in. Keep in touch.

Meanwhile I'll be reading the papers, because when this breaks I can see a lot of the houses over on Mortgage Hill starting to rattle. As long as it comes up all clean goods, I'm going to break my sides laughing. Well, goodnight. Oh, yeah, one more thing I meant to tell you about. We had to check out the ownership of that house you walked into. Don't tell anybody that it was me that told it to you, but the owner of the house at 186 Bellevue Terrace is William Allen Ward. Sleep on it."

SEVENTEEN

It was pushing noon when I rolled out of the sack. I remember hearing that phrase stuck in my head. The events of the past twenty-four hours, I'm glad to say, didn't rush back like the full tide as soon as my eyes were open. I woke into something like peace. And then my mother phoned.

"Benny, where were you yesterday? I tried to get you. I called at midnight and you still weren't home. You keeping something from me, Benny? You out with a *shiksa* when there are lots of nice Jewish girls sitting at home waiting for you to ask them out? Benny, you should think more of yourself. Have a little pride. Anyway, I thought you were going to call me yesterday. So, what happened?"

"Ma, call me back. I just got up. I've been working on a case." I upset a stack of paperbacks on a chair trying to reach out and turn around the clock.

"A case? A case of beer maybe. Look, Benny, you've got to live your own life. Your father says you haven't been to see Melvyn all week. That's your business. You got a case; I understand. It doesn't hurt to say hello to Melvyn, Benny, you hear?"

"Ma, I can't talk now, honest. I've been up all night."

"Benny, what you do with your time is your own business. I've got two glass eyes where you're concerned."

"Ma, I'm hanging up. I'm going to hang up the phone."

"A son doesn't hang up on his mother, Benny."

"I'll see you both for supper tomorrow night. Bye."

"We're having liver. I'll see how I feel. If I feel like liver, we'll have liver."

"See you tomorrow night. Give Pa my love. Goodbye."

"That's better. Goodbye." She banged down the phone

99

before I had a chance to. What the newspapers call a pre-emptive strike.

I flipped the clock back up on the blanket with a curved wrist shot that had to be seen to be believed. It was even later than I feared. My toes found my socks just out of sight under the tumbling bedclothes, and then I tried easing my legs out of the covers. I treated myself to clean underwear and went through the ball of twisted shirtsleeves and tails and pulled out a shirt that looked as though I had consigned it to the laundry on insufficient evidence. My suit smelled as though it had been simmering all night in old soup.

While I was shaving, the details of last night began to tumble into place like loose hair falling from my comb. I recalled trying to shut out the light at eight o'clock in the morning on a spring day by turning out the switch. The last thing I remembered doing was calling the hospital and finding out that Frank was out of danger: just sleeping off the effects of a bump on the head and a few earlier slugs of whiskey. I must be a decent fellow. I'll put my name up for the peeper of the year award.

I called the hospital again and asked for him without calling him "Doctor"; I don't think I could cope with any confusion this early in the day. It took a few minutes, but eventually they put me through.

"Hello, Frank?"

"Who is this?"

"It's your neighbour, Benny."

"Oh, it's you, is it. It was for the love of you that I got this wallop on the back of my head."

"What happened?"

"I was sitting in my office trying to determine whether to cut my throat or buy an expensive dinner, when I heard a noise coming from your office. I thought it was you returning, Ben, and hoped for a word or two. The door was open. I think I called out your name as I came out of my shop. The door stood wide open, but the room was empty. My last thought before the stars came out and danced a mazurka on my medulla oblongata was wondering where you'd disappeared to."

"That's all you remember?"

"Whoever it was must have been standing behind the door. I didn't see a thing. Wait a minute. I seem to remember hearing something like a whisper, a hiss a second before the whack."

"How are you feeling? How long are they going to put up with you?"

"I resent that. I think they're showing signs that I'm going to be turfed out at any moment. When the phone rang just now, the nurses flipped a coin to see whether I shouldn't be made to take it in the hall. They show no respect."

"Well, I'm glad to hear that you're feeling better. I'll drop in to see you later, if they don't proceed with the eviction. Why not pull rank on them, and demand further bedrest? Got to go. Be talking to you."

I was glad I didn't have Frank's blood on my hands, even if some got on the carpet.

I walked right by the front door of "Bagels" without looking in. Instead, I slipped into a pedestal seat at the counter in the United and caught the eye of the usual girl. She went through the routine with me. I took it toasted today, in honour of the fact that it was a full week since Myrna Yates had walked up my stairs with her suspicions. My reliable itch told me that Vern Harrington was due for a second visit. And I thought I had something this time to make him hold still.

The tulip buds in the planters by the war memorial were opening as I walked up the steps of City Hall. The girl who watches over the privacy of the alderman jumped up when she saw me coming.

"Was there something?" I asked her, as she placed her frail body between me and Harrington's door.

"Oh, no," she said. "You're not getting by me this time."

"Miss Keiller, I think you're making a mistake."

"Oh, no, I'm not. You'd better go, or I'll call a commissionaire." Her words were tough, but she was a creampuff.

"You'd better call three or four of them. And when they're here, maybe you'll all take this note in to Mr. Harrington." I gave her my friendliest grin. She moved her lower lip in confusion. She had one of those permanent waves that leaves the hair looking wringing wet. Her rouge and the rest of her make-up didn't go with the pink plastic glasses. She was like a Thunderbird with wooden wheels. She took the note from me, and held it like she thought it contained a jack-in-the-box. I tried to picture Harrington's face as he opened the envelope and read:

I think you'd better see me for ten minutes because
I might think of taking up the practice of the late

Dr. Zekerman.
Yrs,
Ben Cooperman

Something in his office fell over. It wasn't a sharp thud, but a broadloom-blunted one. Harrington was in the doorway, his face paperwhite. He was leaning on the door frame, trapping Miss Keiller inside his office. I could see her under his arm, picking up one of the slender tulip chairs.

"What do you want?" he said, underlining each word because the words didn't seem to have enough blood in them by themselves.

"Ten minutes," I said. "Just ten minutes." He huffed and puffed, and when he was finished I was facing him across his desk. Miss Keiller had cleared out.

"All right: ten minutes."

"First of all, I want you to know I'm not sore at you for making things tough for me. You slowed me down, but I'm fast and wiry. I know about you and Zekerman. And I still want to know what you know about Chester Yates' death. Just like last time."

"You carry a big stick. Ask your questions."

"You knew Chester for a long time?" He rubbed his nose on his knuckles.

"We were at school, university and for a while in business together. We played golf once a week. Our wives get along."

"Can you think of any reason why somebody might want to see him dead?"

"You mean murdered. No. Chester had no enemies. Can't name one. Not in private life or business. I know that in business it's natural to collect enemies, but not Chester. That wasn't his way. He was, well, soft, didn't like leaving blood on the floor."

"Was he depressed near the end?"

"Well, he shot himself, didn't he? That ought to prove something."

"Not in a court of law, Mr. Harrington. That's reasoning from effects to causes. Did he seem depressed to you?"

"No, not if you put it that way."

"No sign of business stress, or personal trouble?"

"Not that I saw, but he could have been . . ."

"Yes?"

"I was going to say that he could have hidden it. But that wouldn't be Chester. Chester couldn't dissemble. It was beyond him. A bad poker player was Chester."

"You knew that he was one of Zekerman's regulars too?" Harrington's eyes widened. If I'd crowned him with one of his testimonials, gilt-frame and all, his reaction would have been less telling.

"The poor bugger," he said simply.

"Zekerman bite?"

"That goddamned blackmailer could have driven him to suicide. God knows I've thought about it often enough myself." I tried not to let my delight show in my face. "Zekerman didn't have patients, he only had suckers he bled. I've been on his hook for four years. Jeeze, I didn't know Chester was on the end of his gaff too. Slimy son of a bitch."

"How do you know that he only treated suckers? What makes you so sure there were others?"

"I didn't need to read it in a book. He made me crawl to see him with my money every month. We'd go through the motions of sitting in his big leather chairs and he would ask me questions about myself, and about how I felt about paying him the money, and how that by paying I was atoning in a measure for . . . for what he knew about what I'd done. I didn't think for a minute that I was his only sucker. He had to have others, and he knew just how hard to squeeze them."

"He must have squeezed too hard a few days ago."

"Blackmail's a dirty game. If you're going into Zekerman's practice, you'll never know when you're squeezing your last sucker. It's over that fast."

"You seem to know a lot about it."

"You have no idea how glad I am that that . . . filth is dead. If I had more nerve, I'd have done it myself."

"Did Zekerman ever ask you about Chester?"

"Zekerman made me stay and talk the full fifty minutes. He asked me about city politics."

"Did he know about C2?"

"Core Two? Yes he knew about that. But I didn't tell him about it."

"Who else would know about Core Two?"

"It's a short list: me, the mayor, and, of course, Bill Ward."

"Of course." I'd had most of my ten minutes' worth, but before I left, I thought I'd better try one more shot. "Tell me a little more about Core Two." He looked a little surprised, as though I was skipping the hard questions and giving him another easy one.

"Well, it's common knowledge that we have been examining plans for a satellite business centre and city hall branch on the other side of the creek someplace. The actual location, and the details of the project are still highly confidential, for reasons that are obvious."

"Chester was in on it?"

"Certainly not. He was in a position to make a pile. It would have been most improper for him to have known anything about it."

"I see. Can you imagine how Zekerman found out?"

"Nothing that man did would surprise me. He was the incarnation of evil, that man."

"You mentioned it." Harrington was holding on hard to the edge of his desk, like he was at a political rally. I had to bring him down from the heights somehow. "Look, Mr. Harrington. I know that Zekerman had you in his vise. I think I know how tight he could turn it. But I don't care about that. I'm only concerned with finding out who killed Chester. I'm not trying to solve the problems of the world, I just want to find one murderer. That's all." That said it plain. I was still interested in what Zekerman had on him, but he didn't need to know that. And I knew that when I found it, it might only be sensational and not important. When I left Harrington standing there, it looked like he was trying to see whether he could hold his breath for a full minute. It didn't look as though he was going to make it.

As I started walking down Church Street, I saw my face reflected in a store window. There was a big grin on my kisser, and I felt as good about life as someone opening up a new bar of soap for a hot bath.

EIGHTEEN

The day was putting up an effort to help out the tourist trade, but there wasn't much heart in it, and the "Tourist Homes" along the Queenston Road would have to wait for later in the spring to make their killing. This was the time to get out into the yard and get rid of the crud that grows under the snow drifts through the winter. It was still too early for there to be much green about, except in places like City Hall where it was all laid on like *gezundheit* follows a sneeze. I went into a pay-phone booth, one of the ones with the wrap-around plastic window, and put in a call to Pete Staziak. I had to wait about three minutes until they found him.

"Yeah?"

"Pete, have they taken the phone out of your office?"

"Oh, it's you. The Cat Bandit."

"Right, and I'm going to cut you in. It's not fair that you shouldn't get your share. You do the thinking and I'll take the risks. Anything new on Zekerman?"

"I'll put you through to Harrow."

"Pete! I take it back. What do you hear? Come on, you know I don't want to go to work searching titles at my age."

"You just don't want to go to work."

"You played that card. Come on, think up a new one. You tell me something and I'll tell you something."

"Big deal. Zekerman's not mine. Why don't you sleuth a little for your old pal?"

"You can look pretty good in the Department if you know that Zekerman was blackmailing everybody and his brother. You can drop that in their laps."

"Sure, and how do I answer their first question, 'Who told me?' "

105

"Look, would I steer you wrong? You, a friend? I'd cut off my right lapel for you. Pete, believe me, I've got good goods. I had it straight from one of his so-called patients. He tells me that Zekerman was getting manna from the beaks of some of the cleanest birds in town. You brought back some of his files. Tell Harrow to start reading them in the light of a blackmail scam."

"Okay, I'll try it out on them and let you know if I come up with any crumbs to drop on your picnic. Benny, I hate to tell you, but manna just fell on the desert, it wasn't dropped by ravens. Maybe you're thinking of Elijah?"

"Since when am I a biblical scholar? And, while we're on the subject, since when are you?"

"I'll call you at your office in two hours, if I've found anything. See you in church. Bye."

I had another dime, so I thought I'd see if Martha Tracy was in her office. She was.

"M'yeah?"

"Martha?"

"Who wants her?"

"Cooperman."

"Just a shake 'til I get to another phone." I heard a click in my ear, the sound of the swallows landing on the wires outside the Caddell Building, then she was back. "M'yeah. Cooperman; how are you doing you little devil? Uncover any secret plots?"

"How's everything?"

"Well, they finally cleared out Chester's office and it's sitting there empty waiting to see which of the two people fighting over it finally inherit the space. Honestly, you'd think grown men would have better things to do than fight over where they park their desks. Would you care where they put you to do a job?"

"It's just magic, Martha. They don't make decisions unless they can wear the proper hats and wave the right wands. Who is going to be in charge, anyway?"

"Oh, that'll take years to settle. Meanwhile, there's an administrator looking after the day-to-day stuff, and a board of directors with Chester's wife on it making the policy decisions. I've still got my job, that's all I care about."

"What time will you be at home? I want to look at those things Elizabeth Tilford left behind when she disappeared."

"Elizabeth? You worried about her? She'll lay you out, Cooperman."

"Just doing my job."

"Well, I'll be home after six. Give me an hour or so to eat and you can have some coffee."

"Good. I'll see you."

I was going to phone Savas at Regional Police, but I was out of dimes. So I went into the United and asked for a coffee. The lunch rush had thinned out and it was easy to find space. Further down the counter the Mad Writer was scribbling away on his great work. My waitress looked rather too tough to wear a big blue ribbon on her rear. Some girls should have their aprons stapled on. I fished out a pack of Players and lit the last of them.

On the whole, I wasn't feeling as tough as I expected to feel. I thought that maybe, with a little luck, I'd make it an early night. Last week at this time I was tailing Chester to his last appointment with Dr. Zekerman. I wondered if Chester knew about his appointment with his murderer. It could have been accidental. Or could it? The murderer knew where he kept his target pistol. He knew that the security guard never arrived until close to six, and that the whole floor was practically soundproof from the other floors. The two of them had a drink. Martha said she'd bought a set of eight glasses; I saw only six. So maybe he left with two of those glasses wrapped in the bar-towel, probably faster than wiping off fingerprints. But why take both? Why not leave one of them on Chester's desk, as a jolt of Dutch courage to stiffen him for the fatal act? No, he had to take both glasses because he had handled both. He poured the drinks and brought them to the desk. It would be easy to use the bar-towel while pouring the drinks, with his back to Chester, but it would look too foolish to carry both drinks with it.

I started thinking about the clipping that I was still carrying in my inside breast pocket about the suicide of Elizabeth Blake. I thought it wouldn't hurt to take a quick run out to Secord University. The library was crowded with students, and as far as I could see there was no running water to distract the avid reader. I filled in a pink form and ordered the 1964 volume of the Secord *Standard*, the school paper, and found a place near a window to plough through it.

I found an account of Elizabeth Blake's death that added nothing to what I already knew. There were pictures of an ice fort built during an unexpected school break, when the campus was closed down for a week by a record snowfall. I flipped through the rest of the fat, black-bound volume to kill ten minutes. I felt guilty returning the book in less time than it took to find it in the stacks and sign it out to me. I read a few smart-ass movie reviews that didn't find much to like in anything. The football games sounded like the ones today. The name of a kid who went on to write comic pieces in one of the Toronto papers was prominent in nearly every issue. Then I hit it. A twenty-four-year-old honours chemistry student named Joe Corso took a drop of six storeys from the balcony outside one of the chemistry labs. 1964 was certainly the year for it. A couple of his pals said that he had been broken-hearted since he'd been turned down by the scholarship committee at M.I.T. That sounded fair enough. I nearly cut my throat when I flunked grade two. The cute bit of information came in the last paragraph which named Corso's two pals: Chester Yates and William Allen Ward. As chummy a pair of chief mourners as you could wish for.

I made a couple of calls from the library phone. The first got me the Alumni Association, which got me the representative of the 1964 graduating year. Within ten minutes and four dimes later I had a link which joined the dead girl and the dead chemistry student. Yes, they had dated and yes it had been serious.

At the Diana Sweets I ordered a vanilla marshmallow sundae and a vanilla milkshake. With that on my stomach, I thought I'd call Savas. It took about six rings before he answered.

"Savas," he croaked.

"You sound like you've been up all night."

"I'm up all night every night, shamus."

"Don't try to make me feel guilty for your sins. I've got enough of my own. What happening?"

"Cooperman, we checked out your Phoebe Campbell. She's made of smoke. We covered the waterfront on this. Not only isn't she anywhere now, she never was anywhere. Not under that name and not with that description. Sure you're not seeing things?"

"I've got two hundred dollars in my wallet that she gave me for last night's B and E. Is that evidence?"

"Two hundred dollars' worth. Doesn't buy much."

"Savas, you ever hear of Joe Corso?"

"Sounds like a football player. Who does he play for, the Cleveland Browns?"

"I know that you guys are tripping over all the suicides that have been happening, but I've got another for you. I was up at Secord University this morning looking into Elizabeth Blake's death in the school paper. Nothing new there. But a couple of weeks later a chemistry whiz named Corso took a long walk on a short balcony of the Chemistry Building and didn't live to graduate head of his class. There are a couple of things about this that might interest you: the pals that told everybody that he was feeling blue because he missed a big scholarship were Yates and Ward. The topper is that his girl-friend was Elizabeth Blake."

"So he killed himself out of sympathy? So what?"

"Come on. Nobody's that sympathetic."

"Look, Cooperman, all this stuff isn't worth peanut shells without a story to tie it all together. I bet you can find that Dr. Zekerman was the head of the Chemistry Department under an assumed name or something. Do you get me? I can't touch this stuff without a trunk full of old-fashioned evidence. You can't get anywhere on a murder charge with a bunch of affidavits. Hang in there. You're a good peeper, Cooperman, but you'd make a lousy cop. I'll be talking to you. Goodbye."

I'd killed about as much time on the phone as I could profitably do, so I cut across the street and took a run at the twenty-eight steps leading to my door. I had a little over an hour before Pete's call was due, so I drew up a list and started drawing arrows from one name to another. Before I messed it up with doodles, it looked like this:

Elizabeth Blake .... 1964 (suicide)
Joe Corso ....1964 (suicide)
Chester Yates .... present (suicide)
Andrew Zekerman ....present (murder)

To this list I added:

William Allen Ward
Elizabeth Tilford ....present (disappeared)
Phoebe Campbell ....present (disappeared)
Vernon Harrington
Myrna Yates

I guess just about any of them might have had a motive, even Myrna. As the widow with a lot to gain, she could throw the law off by pointing to me as the sleuth she'd hired to look into her husband's untimely end. Phoebe Campbell fitted into this crazy web in some way. The story she told me about Twining could fit Ward just as well. He was a well-known sniffer of girls' bicycle seats. But I couldn't see why she'd want to beat that African carving to splinters with Zekerman's head. And why kill Chester? If she was disappointed in love, why not go after Ward? Same with the Tilford woman. She was pushed out of bed by Phoebe, or so it looks. Tilford knew Chester, knew the office lay-out, but, according to Martha, she got on with him fine. Besides, she looked less like a doer than a done to at the moment.

It was at Ward's name that I looked longest. He had a dirty finger in the eye of everyone on the list. He was at the University at the same time both Elizabeth Blake and Joe Corso were killed. He knew Chester since they were both in Pampers. He was in on the bottom floor of the Core Two development. Myrna Yates has been in love with him since the year one, and he had had affairs with both of the missing women. Ward could have been one of Zekerman's suckers. Zekerman sounds as though he was pumping Harrington for information that would give him leverage on Ward or on Chester. Funny, how I keep calling Yates "Chester." I never met him, but he seems an altogether more likeable bum than Ward. Nobody's obliged to speak well of the living.

NINETEEN

The light comes into the office on a slant through the dusty windows. Somehow it bugged me, and I didn't like being bugged by things I couldn't do anything about. The window cleaners came twice a year; for the other three hundred and sixty-three days of the year, the windows were filthy. I couldn't keep my bottom on the chair; I couldn't concentrate. I went out, thinking vaguely of getting a cup of coffee or a pack of cigarettes, when I got an idea. In another three minutes, I was in the Olds and driving along the Power Gorge Road. Traffic was light, and the sun licked at the curves of the creek on my left all the way. I passed Zekerman's mailbox and took the next turn to the left, which took me down into the creek valley. I crossed the creek and turned the car around in the next driveway.

I stopped the car on the Red Bridge across the Eleven Mile Creek. It wasn't red any longer, but it had been when I was a kid and used to watch the fast gray water moving under its timbers. From where I stood with the motor idling evenly, I could see up to Pelham Road, where at one end Myrna Yates' father used to run a car wrecker's, and at the other I could make out the elaborate ranch-style shape of Dr. Zekerman's place. I could see the aluminum shed where we had met so explosively and down by the water was a smaller wooden shed—the potting shed. I'd been thinking a lot about that potting shed since my last conversation with Harrington. If I was going to try my hand at extortion or blackmail, I think I'd like a nice quiet potting shed to keep my dirt in.

As I got nearer I could see the shed more clearly. It was made of plywood, with a small gable roof. A bunch of red letters screamed at me "Beware of the Dog." I'd seen the tired old Irish wolf-hound last weekend, and wasn't impressed. The door faced away from the creek. It was a Yale lock, which gave fairly easily after nicking the corner off a credit card. Inside, I was looking at the creek through an iron mesh safety shutter and the kind of glass that imprisons chicken wire. It was a potting shed, all right. The place was liberally supplied with clay flower pots of all sizes and shapes. It smelled of dead leaves. A pair of gardening gloves caught the light on a counter that stood waist high against one wall. On it lay all of the implements you would expect to find, but which I wasn't looking for. The drawers under the counter showed more of what I wasn't looking for. The walls showed no cupboards, the floor no trapdoors.

It was small, so I didn't have to do much searching when I'd lifted up the last of the pressed paper starter boxes. Under the window, a bunch of geraniums were languishing, like the ones back at my office. Mine were in a bad way because they badly needed to be replanted, but these stood in a large square bin of moist potting soil. I tested the bottom with a green bamboo tomato stake. The bottom was less than three inches from the surface. It began to look more interesting. I examined the edges of the bin and found small holes on the insides near the corners. I looked around me for something to go into the holes, and at the same time began to get the feeling that I might not be left undisturbed for very much longer. In one corner I found a set of wires ending in hooks, attached at the other end to a nylon rope. I flipped the yellow strand over a two-by-four above the bin, set the hooks in place, and pulled on the slack end of rope. The bin lifted clean out of its setting, and when I got it up a few feet I tied off the rope and took a look. What I saw was a rather rusty well-type filing cabinet. It just fit the hiding place, with enough room for the lid to clear when I opened it up.

With all the care Zekerman had taken in preparing this surprise for me, he might have hidden a fortune in gold, or the missing Russian Crown Jewels or something. What I knew I could expect were the sordid secrets from the lives that Zekerman leeched from. I riffled through the red files. There was one marked Vernon Harrington. What had he done? Nothing more than a hushed-up hit-and-run charge. A black eye for a politician and for the cop who put the lid on it. The next file told the story of a drunk-driving charge that had been kept quiet so that another leading citizen could go on with important civic work. I wondered whether they were all sleeping better since the good doctor had permanently ceased practising. In the file marked Chester Yates, I found the original of the Xeroxed clipping sent through the mail. Then I hit pay-dirt: a file marked *William Allen Ward*. A great big birthday present. But right away somebody spilled chocolate milk all over the tablecloth. I heard a car stop on the near side of the bridge. I grabbed something from the file. My feet were already moving me to the door.

Once outside, I beat a retreat to the bushes along the creek. A muskrat frowned at me from the waterline, but didn't advertise my presence. The bushes smelled of decaying leaves and the water of garbage. The clay of the bank was rubbed smooth by the bellies of the animals going in and out of the water. I could hear voices, but the shed itself masked my view of the path. The voices reached the shed and stopped. After a few hour-like minutes on damp knees with the sound of the creek almost as loud as the thumping inside my jacket, I heard the voices again, retreating. At the same time, I could make out smoke curling around one wall. I heard a sudden popping noise, and flames could be seen on both sides of the shed. I was far enough away so that I knew I was safe from the fire, but it had come so unexpectedly, I felt like I was still inside. It burned quickly, like a burning school-house firework. When I heard the other car start and drive off, I began moving along the creek towards the bridge where I'd left mine.

It felt good to hear the motor catch. Through the rear-view mirror, I saw that the flames had found every draughty cranny of the shed and forced their destructive way through. There was nothing to do but press my foot firmly on the gas.

When I pulled into a gas station not far from my office, I took my eye off the spinning meter long enough to examine the handful of paper I'd saved from the fire. At first glance it looked like any old piece of newspaper, only it was in German. The name at the top read "Zuricher Zeitung." The date was 26 January 1976. At the bottom of one of the pages, two nearly identical cartoons appeared. My German was good enough to guess that you were supposed to discover the minute differences between them. I was nearly tempted to return this fascinating document to the shed on the creek, when I saw the picture. A group of men and women dressed in the very best skiing togs was standing chatting near a chair-lift.

The caption identified the group. One of the couples named was *Herr William Allen Ward unt frau von Kanada*. I looked up at the picture again. *Und frau* was Myrna Yates.

As I opened the door of my office the phone rang. It was Pete. I asked him to tell me the latest news.

"Harrow told me that they have Ward's name in Zekerman's handwriting a couple of times. They also have about six or seven dozen other names, so they aren't going to pick up Ward right away, if it's all right with you. They also have a full list of patients treated by Zekerman during the last five years. Ward is there too along with Yates and a hundred other names, including some of our first citizens."

"Could I see the list?"

"I'll drop an illegal Xerox off to you. Hell, no! I can't do that. Benny, I keep forgetting you aren't with the firm. Join the cop shop and see the world." I could picture him, shutting his eyes while he thought. "Can you come by my office right away? I think I can arrange for it to be sitting some place conspicuous when you come in. I may not be there. They've detailed me to look into that quarry skeleton some kids dug up out by the escarpment. I can see that this case is going to be a feather in the coroner's hat. Most of the work will be done out of town at the Forensic Centre. If I see you, I'll say hello."

"Not if I see you first. Be talking to you."

I got my car out and drove as directly as the one way street pattern would let me to the parking lot behind the Regional Police Building. I was stopped by the door with push-buttons on it, but not for long. I went in as a constable came out. He even held the door open for me. I walked right by the desk as though I knew my way around and had urgent business, but was hauled back before I'd gone many yards down the corridor. When I said that Staziak had asked me to wait for him in his office, the sergeant looked at me, trying to see if he recognized either my front or side view, and finally showed me where Pete's door stood open. I sat in the chair at Pete's metal desk and looked down at an open file. The open page was a print-out from a computer, containing about a hundred names and Medicare numbers. Most of the names I didn't know. A few of them I'd seen in the paper. Harrington was there, so were Yates and Ward. I didn't have time to write them down. Nor was I a whiz at the memory game.

I dropped my eyes from name to name, trying to imagine the hold Zekerman held over each of them. And each one, a possible murderer. When I'd scanned all the way to the bottom I was none the wiser. I now had double confirmation that Ward was a patient and I knew that he had been the subject of oblique questions aimed at Vern Harrington. I was happy with that. But I knew that a law court wouldn't find one name any more attractive than the last. So, I was going to have to find out a little more about William Allen Ward. I think I already knew enough about him to make it a very interesting conversation.

That should have been a very satisfying thought. But my mind was somehow distracted from it. There was something in the list that had failed to register on my first look at it. I looked down the row on row of names once more. Then, about a third of the way down, hidden, innocent-looking, there it was:

Hilda Blake

the sister of the girl who'd been killed by the overdose of drugs back in 1964. The other girl in that photograph, maybe. Probably. So she was getting squeezed by Dr. Zekerman too. He had his needle into everybody. Bad enough losing a sister to a suicidal overdose, but now having to dish out hard-earned money to the greedy doctor. It didn't seem fair. I hadn't thought of her as being still in the area. I'd try to look her up as soon as I had both hands untied.

I turned out the desk lamp on Pete's desk and let myself out. There was no switch to turn out the overhead fluorescent fixture. Probably needed an Act of Parliament.

TWENTY

Martha hadn't got around to fixing the broken second step leading to her chipped green porch. I noticed this with the satisfaction of a non-property owner. Maybe, when all of this was over, I thought, I'll fix it for her. I wasn't really a handyman, but I had generous impulses. She opened the screen door wearing a chenille housecoat and holding a glass of beer in her red hand. I went in, the screen door slapped back into place, and I followed Martha into her kitchen at the back of the house.

"Sit down, Cooperman. Take a load off your feet. Do you want the coffee I promised or would you prefer a cold beer?" I smiled.

"I get gas from beer. Thanks just the same." I was brought up to believe that beer was the people's drink and that I was a cut above the people. A few years ago I went home for Friday night dinner at my parents after a few drafts in the Harding House with Ned Evans—Ned was trying to get me involved in a production of *A Midsummer Night's Dream* to be staged under the stars in Montecello Park. To hear my mother talk, you would have thought a brewery had come through the door. "A drunk and his family are soon parted," my mother observed, while my father shook his head from side to side. To him, to them both, my taking a drink was only a final confirmation of the fears they had when they found me eating bacon with the O'Reillys when I was four.

"I'll have coffee, Martha."

"It's instant," she challenged.

"There's another kind?" I guess she saw me looking at

her as she crossed to the counter, piled high with dirty dishes, to plug in the chromium kettle. She looked at me, then at her housecoat.

"Don't get any ideas; I've got trousers on underneath. Say, while the kettle's boiling, I'll show you Liz Tilford's room. I never cleaned it out when she left. Thought I might get my rent if I left things as they were. But I don't think she'll show her dimples around here again. She's moved on to bigger game, if you ask me." She led me to a small, bright room at the back of the house. Through the window came a clear view of a water-soaked lawn struggling to become green again. It had reached the dirty straw stage. There was a black maple silhouetted against the sky, with the cut of the railway line on the other side of a ragged wire fence.

In the room stood a bed—neat and businesslike—and a small table and chair. What pictures there were looked like they came out of a Sunday Supplement. The place had a barracks-like feel. On the bedside end of the table, held together by wooden bookends, stood half a dozen books in paper bindings. She'd been dipping into Plutarch's *Lives,* the plays of Corneille, speeches of Cicero, a biography of Charlotte Corday, and Rousseau's *Social Contract,* in English translation I was relieved to discover. What would a fellow like Bill Ward have seen in a serious girl like this? I couldn't imagine Liz Tilford knocking back one-liners in front of the TV on hockey night.

Martha was standing behind me with a cup outstretched. I took it and shook my head at the books.

"Funny, eh?" she asked. "And she didn't read magazines or the papers either. Don't blame her there, really. There's nothing in them these days. I told you she didn't go out unless it was with Ward. And he didn't call more than a couple of times a week. As far as I know, Liz didn't write to anyone, or call anyone. She didn't hear from anybody either. As a room-mate for me, she was next door to living alone. I always suspected that when Bill Ward took her out to eat in a restaurant, if he didn't pay attention, he'd order for one."

"But, Martha, you said she was a knock-out: long legs, red hair, a good body. She didn't have to tell jokes or make with the clever chatter, all she had to do was be there."

"Yeah. Some people have it rough," she said with a sigh mixed with a mock come-hither look then disappeared back towards the kitchen. I glanced again at the books. None of them was old. They all looked as though they'd been picked up on the same expedition. She hadn't written anything in any of them. When I gave one a hefty shake, a sales slip tumbled out. It told me that she had bought five of the books for sixteen dollars and fifty cents on March third of last year, at the Basic Bookstore, 986 Queen Street West in Toronto. I pocketed the slip and shook the other books too. Nothing. I went to the closet. Not very much here: a well-worn raincoat—time she bought a new one. A couple of pairs of summer shoes lay strewn about the floor of the closet like dead puppies, and a wool skirt hung from a hook on the back of the door. The pockets of both skirt and coat yielded nothing. I looked at the labels. Nothing distinctive, except a Toronto name on the skirt.

I was just turning away, disgusted with myself for not being able to pull Nero Wolfe out of one pocket and Philip Marlowe out of the other, when my beady eye spied something in a dusty corner, half-hidden by a shoe. It was a laundry ticket with a South End address on it. Now I didn't feel so empty-handed. I had two clues. With any luck, they might lead me into interesting dead ends.

I sipped at my neglected coffee and returned to Martha in the kitchen.

"Find anything useful?"

"Could be. Won't know until later. I wonder if you'd mind my helping myself to these books for a few days? They might help me to get to know her better."

"Help yourself. No skin off my shin if you don't give them back."

"I won't forget to return them. Remember, you may never get that back rent. Tell me, Martha, is there anything else about her you haven't already told me."

"She was the last person to talk about herself. I think I got the idea she went to university. But it wasn't from anything she said, it was just the crests on the book ends she has in there. She wasn't a Niagara of information. More coffee?"

"Nope. Gotta run." Martha walked me to the door, tried to keep a yellow cat out with her leg as she opened the screen door for me. I angled out, leaving the cat pouting on the porch.

"So long, Cooperman. If you find that tramp, tell her to remember her friend and to hell with the back rent." That came through the screen at me as I reached the car door.

From a pay-phone in a candy store the size of a three-hole outhouse, I phoned the hospital. Frank Bushmill had been discharged. Then instead of driving back to my office by way of the high-level bridge, I went down the hill to the canal. To my right, as I approached the bridge, somewhere up in the gloom, stood the mansion erected by the canal's builder. I guess he could stand outside on his widow's walk at the top of the Victorian turret above the main entrance and count the profits lock in and out of the system, a bit like my father sitting behind the cash register watching the customers pull out the suits and dresses from the racks.

On the other side of the road, and on a street parallel to it, I could make out several good frame houses dating from the last century. They'd been built for the nobs of yesteryear who wanted to watch their goods move up and down the canal. Now they were full of three and four families each. They were the sort of houses you pay admission to get into at one of those pioneer villages in the States. Someday they'd be flushed out and made comfortable for the nobs again. The car went clunk, clunk, clunk over the bridge; the black water ran dark and close underneath, sliding away toward the lake. It was dark now and the night air was heavy with sulphur; white froth from the papermills glowed on the surface of the water tempting the authorities to lay a legal action against the polluters. The road began to climb now, under the dark girders of the high-level bridge, circling around at the top and joining St. Andrew Street where Ontario Street made a large well-posted intersection.

At the United, the counter was clear. One of the girls was perched on a stool, her knees bracing a folded newspaper. She frowned at a crossword puzzle.

"What's a six-letter word for Spanish wine?" she asked.

"Port," I suggested.

"Can't count. You going to have your usual?" I bought a paper, flipped through it, but found nothing new on any of the far-flung fronts I was trying to cover all at once. I turned to the back of the paper and began scanning the want ads. Under "Positions wanted" I had begun to notice that the *Beacon* had started letting in the sort of ad that it would have discouraged a few years ago. I wondered whether the decent family papers were starting to get corrupted by the intellectual papers with the wild ads I'd heard about. One ad read:

WASP seeks opportunity part-time in public rela-
tions, experienced in French and Greek.

It sounded lewd to me. Maybe it's my dirty mind.

That reminded me of Dr. Andrew Zekerman and his
money-making schemes. What did he hold over Chester and
Ward? What did he have on Hilda Blake? Was it connected
with the death of her sister and the chemistry hot shot, Corso?
I patted my pocket with the laundry ticket in it. It was the
master key that was going to unlock all the hidden doors.

I paid my check and got into the car. It was early
enough so the parking on the street was limited. I turned
off into the lane which separated my building from the
former home of a dead bank. It has been a long time since
a bank went under, or belly up, as they now describe it, but
the shock of seeing huge square stone letters spell out the
name of a bank that can't measure its assets in paper clips
makes a fellow think. My headlights picked out other letters
on the fieldstone front of the factory: "Rutledge Textiles."
The letters were large, old-fashioned and wooden, gilded
and unilluminated except by the lights of my car. Above the
door a plaque had been fixed into the stonework reading
"Established 1868." A dark, fortress-like place, it had been
built so far from the street in order to take advantage of
the hydraulic power which first ran the machines inside.
Yellow light seeped from the heavily-grilled windows. I
turned off the lights, got out and locked the door. The
papermills were heavy on the night air even here, about
twenty feet above the canal. I could hear the low rumble of
whatever was going on inside the factory, as I turned and
started to walk up to street level.

I'd taken only a half dozen steps from my car, when I
saw two heavy figures walking toward me. I knew they were
big because with each step they took, they blocked out more
of the streetlight coming from behind them. As they got
closer it was becoming a very dark alley. I didn't like the
way they were closing on me; black unfriendly silhouettes.
I turned back, thinking to make for the wooden stairs that
led down to the front entrance of Rutledge's. The steps were
better lit than the alley, I thought I might do better in the
light. Coming up the wooden steps at about the same speed
as the two palookas were walking towards me, but with a
big unfriendly grin on his kisser, was another out of the
same package. He was wearing a light ski-jacket and his

muscles made the cloth stretch tight in far too many places. He was looking right at me, coming up steadily. I thought of getting back into my car. Even if I couldn't get it backed up and out of there, I could at least lock the windows and doors. Not a very good idea. Not only were these three not very respectful of private property, from the looks of them, but I could see on the ground a dozen or so ways to break a car window open. Besides, I knew I wouldn't even have time to get my keys out before they had me. My only chance of escaping them seemed to be the well-lit front door of Rutledge's. Once inside, I thought, I would be safe. But I couldn't head there directly. The guy on the steps would be waiting for me having caught his breath from running down only a dozen steps. No, I had to allow him to get to the top before I made my move.

I walked past my car, slowly, as though I hadn't anything better to do than to examine the back of my office building. I looked over my shoulder, casually, I hoped. The two from the alley had turned after me. The one in the ski-jacket was about three steps from the top of the stairs.

To my right, the bank sloped away down the factory and the canal. To my left, stood the haggle-toothed backs of the stores of St. Andrew Street, some longer than others, some with their back ends supported by steel girders. Everywhere I looked I saw the black metal of fire escapes hanging just out of reach. Ahead of me the path narrowed. I had about a hundred yards to go before my way was finally blocked by two large bulk loaders. I saw what I would have to do. I would continue to walk slowly until I got to the loaders, then cut down the bank where I would try to lose myself in the bushes and stunted trees. When my way was clear, I'd head towards the front door of the factory. Not a great plan, but my own. Once behind the door of the factory, I would be safe enough. There would be people, a telephone, maybe even a few security men.

I had already begun to think I was sitting pretty, when I was sapped by the sudden thought that the front door might not be open at this hour. I could hear the low murmur of the machines. There had to be a good chance that the door would not be locked. I tried praying, like the time I tried to rescue my Saturday allowance, which had fallen through a grating, with a wad of gum on the end of a piece of string. On that occasion, now that I thought of it, a passing stranger asked what the trouble was and when I told him, gave me the money from his wallet. I didn't see him standing near the door of Rutledge Textiles.

I made my move suddenly. I leapt from the packed earth of the path over the edge of the embankment and soon I was rolling among the empty wine bottles, broken glass, damp cardboard and other garbage of the slope. I came to rest against a tree trunk, and nearly lost an eye trying to climb through the thicket of fresh shoots that grew out of a nearby stump. The ground was all give, with no sure bottom to it. Sticks, stones and mulching leaves were hard going. There was nothing sure to get my feet on. Every step was its own hard-luck story of scraped ankles, twisted knees, ripped trousers and gouged eyes.

Behind me I could hear them shouting to one another, and smashing through the scrub. I heard curses, and I hoped they'd fallen into a tiger trap I'd overlooked. One of them let out a yell, and I could tell he had found a new home for some discarded broken glass. I heard my name called, but I was moving more surely now. My eyes were getting used to the hazards, my feet expected very little. I didn't look back.

They were about half way down the hill above me. They'd crashed into the bush as soon as they saw that I had. That slowed them up. They weren't very bright. Now I stood on the edge of a grass margin with nothing between me and the door but a flat straightaway with a cement sidewalk inviting me the last fifty yards. If my three friends came straight down, I would be well ahead of them by the time they were in the clear. If they tried to come down on a slant in the direction I was running, I'd be home and dry by the time they reached the door.

I took a deep breath and made a dash for it. I could feel a pulse in my ear clipping me faster than I was running. Voices above me, and the sound of gorillas breaking through the undergrowth, dogged my steps. Over my shoulder I saw one of them break clear and pound after me. His face was twisted by the distorting overhead light at the beginning of the sidewalk. But I made it to the door. Further back, the two others had came out into the open, and were barrelling this way. I tried the door. The handle turned and the door gave inward. In a moment it was closed behind me, and, for the moment at least, I was safe.

TWENTY-ONE

I wished that there had been a big, old-fashioned bolt for me to slap home behind me, but there wasn't. I dusted myself off quickly in a vestibule of dark stained wood, with a display cabinet showing the new miracle fabrics that Rutledge is making part of our everyday lives; on the opposite wall hung an oil painting of the factory from the front, showing the immaculate slanted approach to the front door in the early 1900s. Through a frosted-glass double door I found myself in a hall leading, over a part-metal part-hardwood floor, towards a silver-painted heavy fire-door to both left and right. But in front of me lay an office with a geezer looking through the plate glass window at me. I smiled and sauntered into the industrial green charm of this refuge.

" 'ello, wad can I do for you?"

"Oh, I was just passing," I said, rationing my breath and trying to look calm and businesslike. "Rutledge around?"

"You gotta be kidding. Dere ain't been no Rutledge 'ere for fifteen years. We keep the name, dat's all."

"You from Montreal? How'd you like Ontario?"

"Look, I was born in Ontario, spent all my life in Ontario, and dose bastards in Quebec can murder demselves in dere beds for all I care, and dat's fur sure. Now, what do you want 'ere dis time of night?" I felt the door behind me open.

"I'm working on a project for school, and I wonder if I could bring my class through to see the machines?"

"Sure ting. Dey do dat all de time. I'll show you around. Make you a hexpert." I saw him looking over my shoulder at the newcomers. "We're sure getting busy and dat's for sure. You looking for somebody?"

123

I turned and saw the trio for the first time close up. I recognized the hefty one with the blue ski-jacket. There was blood on his shoe. The other two I'd only seen in silhouette against the light at the top of the alley. One was dark, the other darker. Both were wearing the sort of jackets hunters wear over plaid shirts, with twill trousers. The darker one displayed a large moustache over a blue chin and a black leather cap. The other was bareheaded with heavy acne scars. The chase through the bush had been kinder to me than to these guys. There were burrs on their trousers, scratches on their hands and faces. They were controlling their breathing well. The heavy with the black cap answered the foreman.

"We're with him," he said smiling at both of us.

"You sure look like you came down 'ere the 'ard way. Okay," he said throwing down the clipboard he'd been holding since I walked in on him. "I'll show you de working looms on dis floor. Upstairs it's de same ting all hover again. Dat way," he nodded toward my right, "is all finished now. Just storage, no machines. Dis way we 'ave hold machines, and den in de next room de new machines from St. Louis. Best in the world." He led his docile group to the fire-door and hefted it with his shoulder; it rode uphill on tracks, so that it rolled down into place when we walked through it. What we walked into was a blast of noise from about fifty looms, in five rows.

It was like the screech of a high-powered engine as the engineer hears it. It looked like a scene out of a movie I went to once about the workhouse in Merrie England. The looms just had to be manned by orphans. Each machine set bobbins of yarn dancing overhead as an automatic shuttle ran back and forth. Every once in a while a take-up reel weighing a ton lurched a notch or two to keep the tension right. Above us, waterpipes ran over each aisle, sending out a fine spray into the already noise-clogged air. I saw a few women walking around, but they didn't look like my idea of weavers. Nobody tried to talk in that din.

Directly across from the door we came in by was a new steel shutter door set into the old wall. The foreman pulled a chain that dangled to one side. He started a motor and the door began to lift slowly. Here was another room full of machines. As we passed into this room, an addition to the original factory, I saw that the chain for closing the door was on my side. The foreman had swaggered quickly to the middle of the room, I hung back. Then I made my second wild dash of the evening. I sprinted to the door, pulled the chain, tossed it over a high bracket on the wall, and ducked under the closing shutter. I hoped that it would take a minute for them to figure out how to open it. I could hear them shouting behind me, the foreman, for some reason, more plaintive than the rest. I was pushing open the silver-coloured fire-door when the other shutter stopped in the closed position. A moment later I was out the other doors and running ahead of my wind up the wooden steps. I was shooting up the lane when I heard the factory door slam closed behind me. My heart might burst from the effort of that uphill scramble, but I was miles ahead of them as I came up St. Andrew Street. I never loved this messy, gaudy, nearly superseded stretch of pavement so much in my life before. I headed across the street into the jungle-mouthed atmosphere at the Men's Beverage Room of the Russell House. I walked through the smoke, enjoying the comparative quiet of the blue hazy room, past figures hunched over amber drafts on black-topped tables, until I found the bathroom. I passed a terrified face in the mirror as I went by. I felt better after splashing water on my face. The roller towel wasn't much help; it offered a choice of filthy and filthier.

As I turned, thinking of phoning somebody, anybody, I became aware that the doorway was filled by something that wasn't a door. It was one of my fleet-footed friends from down below.

"I've got a friend wants to talk to you. Nobody's going to get hurt, just come peaceful."

"Bill Ward?" I asked, not believing what I was hearing.

"Smart guy, eh? Got all the answers. Well, maybe you got a couple answers for him. Let's go."

"Bloody hell! Why didn't you say that Bill Ward wanted to see me. I've been meaning to see him for a week!"

TWENTY-TWO

A few mintes later I'd been stuffed into the back seat of a green four-door sedan between the heavy with the ski-jacket and the one with the black cap. The driver was the acne-scarred figure who had followed me to the hotel. There was no room in the back seat to manoeuvre. I thought that if I had to send my regrets to Bill Ward, the fastest way to leave the scene would be past the gorilla in the ski-jacket. I thought I might clear a path by stepping heavily on his recently cut foot.

Nobody spoke. The driver headed south, towards the green eye of the water tower, through the best of Mortgage Hill, along the country road that climbed the escarpment, skirted the university and continued to Malham. Black cap produced a small, dark flask. He removed the top and took a long drink. The sign that followed told me it tickled all the way down. He wiped the rim of the flask and passed it to me. I shook my head, and got a jab in the ribs for my can-dour. I took a gulp. Rye whiskey. Straight. I wiped the rim and passed it along to the mug in the ski-jacket. He drank carelessly, letting some of the booze trickle down his chin. He too wiped the rim and passed it back to me. I tried to hand it back to the owner, but he nodded to me in a manner that strongly suggested that I'd better have another swig. I did so. Only then could I pass along the flask. Black cap had another, then it was my turn again. It didn't seem to be in the cards that I should get to exchange seats with one of them. By the time I'd had five turns at the flask, black cap had had three and the ski-jacket only two. For an alcoholic I was in a wonderful spot. Unfortunately I'm not.

By the time the flask was empty (I'd had seven to four

and three respectively) I was ready to start singing "There's a Long, Long Trail A-winding," but my comparatively sober mentors simply exchanged a glance and I shut up. It was perfectly timed. The driver pulled off the main road into a long lane. I recognized the pillars on either side of the entrance. Funny. I hadn't seen those pillars since they pulled down my old art teacher's house to make way for the Physicians' and Surgeons' Building. I'd heard that they'd been taken out here, to mark the lane to the Otterpool Golf Club, because Sam Zimmerman, the junk dealer, had tried to get them to mark the entrance to his junk yard. In the 1940s it was junk. Somewhere in the 1950s it became steel. And the golf course was still a golf course.

There were a few lights on in the front of the club house, but I was taken in the back. The sulphur in the air was purer up here, and off in the distance I could hear the pounding of a drop-forge. I was half carried, half shoved, into a deserted snack-bar with a white linoleum floor. I took some courage from familiar things on the tables: ketchup bottles, salt and pepper shakers, napkin holders. I couldn't come to a bad end among such ordinary surroundings. I was pushed into a red-bottomed chair with metal legs beside a dark window. I think I may have closed my eyes. I remember feeling wonderfully refreshed when I let my cheek lean against the cool window-glass. After a few years sitting like this, I became aware that there was someone standing in my light. It was Bill Ward. I think I said, "Hi," and went back to my serious work which was trying to catch the little motes that kept swimming up inside my eyelids. There were red ones and purple ones. Mostly they were magenta.

"Cooperman, you're in a lot of trouble." He sounded like a television quizmaster telling a guest he had only ten thousand points and was about to be taken out of the final round.

"I'll shape up, you'll see."

"You've got to lay off, Cooperman. I told you once, and I'm telling you again. That's more than fair."

"No coaching from the studio audience. Do you know why Chester was killed?"

"Don't start that again. Chester killed himself. He wanted to get clear of his worries, his depression. Look, I've told the police to go easy on you. Sergeant Harrow is all for demanding your licence after the funny games you've been playing. I tried to calm him down."

"Okay, okay. But give me a minute on Chester. If he was going to kill himself, would he have bought himself a ten-speed bike a couple of hours before shooting himself? You were his pal, you answer me. Is it likely?"

"That's unsubstantiated idiocy. There are a dozen explations, and each of them makes more sense than what you are saying."

"Everybody says he was depressed. What was he depressed about?"

"Business pressure. He'd been expanding too quickly. Growth wasn't keeping up. Money was getting scarce. He was two years ahead of the game, and he didn't have the capital to wait two years." It sounded fine, but I didn't believe a word of it.

"Is this the first tight corner he's been in?"

"Of course not. But this was different."

"Tell me. Tell me when the game gets so tough that you put your brains on the rug."

"It's no use talking to you. I'll speak to Harrow."

"You do that. But since it's settled, how about answering some of my questions?"

"I'm a reasonable man, Cooperman. I've never met anyone so persistent. What do you want to know? These groundless assertions of yours are a waste of valuable time."

"I suppose you've never heard of Phoebe Campbell?"

"That's right."

"Would you be surprised to learn that she paid me two hundred dollars to plant a gun in your house on Bellevue Terrace?"

"Be serious, Cooperman."

"I'm telling you. Phoebe Campbell paid me to enter your house on Bellevue Terrace. She gave me a package to leave in a dresser drawer. The package contained a .32 calibre hand gun. The police have it now. Maybe Sergeant Harrow forgot to mention that. Why would someone want to plant a gun at your house? Somebody doesn't like you, Mr. Ward."

"Let me get this straight. You actually went into that house? How did you know it was mine?"

"The police told me."

"What do they know of this?"

"Only that there was an attempted break-in. Your office probably has a report about it."

"What did she look like, this Phoebe Campbell?"

"Tall, good-looking, brunette, long legs, clear skin, well-spoken."

"This is insane. I never met this woman. It's a mistake."

"If you didn't tell Phoebe Campbell about this hide-away of yours, whom did you tell?"

"Nobody knew about that place. I picked it up when a business associate went under. It was business. I accepted the house and let certain charges and debts ride. I hardly ever went there. I meant to dispose of it before long."

"Did Pauline know about it?"

"I don't want to hear my wife's name in your mouth, do I make myself clear? Of course, she knew nothing of it. She knows nothing of my business affairs."

"What about your affair affairs?"

"What exactly is that supposed to mean?"

"You're too modest, Mr. Ward. It is well known that you break a lot of hearts in a year."

"Stand up! Stand up and repeat that!" He looked like he was going to pop his cork. I didn't think these fellows socked people who weren't wearing the old school tie, so I got up, and he glared at me. I hoped he wouldn't hit me; I was still dizzy from the car ride. I remembered seeing a fight at a party over a girl: two men in their thirties exchanged glancing blows and then both got down on their hands and knees looking for dislodged partial dentures, glasses and a contact lens. Ward still looked angry when I got him into focus, but he didn't look like he was going to knock me down any more.

"Mr. Ward, could I have a glass of ginger ale. I don't feel so good."

"What . . . ?"

"I need something to clear my head. I don't want to get sick." He dropped his fighting stance, threw me a contemptuous look with nothing personal in it, and went to the bar. I drifted off, after finding my chair again, to where people drift off to. In far too short a time, I saw that the bubbles tickling my nose came from a tall glass under it. Ward sat down across the table from me.

"So you think someone killed Chester and you think I had something to do with it."

"Could be. You were as thick as thieves as far back as you can go. In a business way you've been in bed together before this. I think Chester was holding your end while you were playing around at City Hall. I think you might make a handy sum on this Core Two project, under the table, of course, and in a way that will look kosher on paper after the fact. I think you would steal pencils from a crippled beggar if you saw some advantage in it. But I don't give a damn about your character, Mr. Ward. I only want to find out who bumped off your pal. You'd think that as his friend you'd want to give me a hand. Instead you call Harrow. Don't get me wrong. I don't mind. I'm used to being leaned on from one direction or another. Funny thing is that he's your pal, not mine." I took another sip of the ginger ale.

"Look, it's ludicrous that anyone would kill Chester. But supposing he was murdered, I still can't think of any motive."

"You had a lot to gain. He was in your pocket. Wouldn't you gain the upper hand in what you were planning to split on Core Two?"

"That's the second time you mentioned Core Two. I don't know where you heard about it, but you've been misinformed. I work for the city. I'm not a cheap speculator."

"Who said you were cheap? There's big money riding on Core Two. And the way you're playing it, it isn't speculating."

"You're drunk, disgusting, and way beyond your depth. Core Two is a city matter. I'm just an advisor to the mayor and the council. I get paid a fixed salary."

"Yeah, about as much as a postman, I've heard, with perks, of course, with perks. But something like Core Two doesn't come along every day. And there you are with Chester ready and waiting to help you again, just like in the old days. There'd be money in it for him too, naturally."

"This is just talk; you can't substantiate any of this."

"I can prove that Chester knew about Core Two. So, at the very least, you're the best guess as to who told him about it. That's a breach of trust, before we get to any money. I've got that much in Chester's handwriting. I've got more. I know you were being squeezed by Zekerman. He was also interested in Core Two. Zekerman was a greedy man, Mr. Ward. He found out about it from Chester. Chester wasn't hard the way you are. Chester could be gotten around."

"Shut up. You don't know anything. It's all bluff."

"Well, if it is, why don't you throw me out instead of

taking it out on that ball-point pen." Ward looked down at his hands. Two halves of the pen he was holding would never fit together again. Blue ink stained the heel of his right hand. He looked at his hand like it belonged to somebody else. In a moment, he shot a look at me. He had recovered and was going to counterattack.

"You don't really know very much, do you? Not when it comes to courts of law and proof. You don't have anything with much weight."

"Two men are dead, that should raise some eyebrows."

"Chester killed himself. No eyebrows are being raised on that one."

"That leaves Zekerman. He didn't club himself to death. The most likely murderer would come from among his patients. You were one of his patients. Did you kill him?" He shook his head, not disguising his affection for me very skilfully.

"No, I didn't kill him. He was a greedy man, but a small one. It was easy to pay his greed out of petty cash. Why should I have dirtied my hands with Zekerman's blood?" He gave a snort that was supposed to show contempt for my accusation and me all at once. I thought it was time to shift ground.

"Let's change the subject. Tell me about Liz Tilford." He blinked like I'd asked him if he'd seen any good movies lately.

"There's nothing to tell. It was a private matter. She is an attractive, intelligent young woman. I hoped to be of help to her, getting her launched, getting her established." He looked out of focus to me as I looked across the table at him, fuzzy at the edges, but I could see that he was directing all his attention at me. I was in focus. "What has Miss Tilford got to do with this anyway?"

"She's disappeared, that's all."

"That's a little dramatic. She left town, that's not against the law. She's in Toronto; I think she went to Toronto."

"Did you have a fight?"

"You insist on implying that our relationship was of a personal nature. A man like you can't understand ..."

"Ward, it's late, and I'm not that shockable. You've been seen together. It's on the record, so include me out of your play-acting. Why did she leave town? What happened?"

"Nothing happened. She just went away."

"You're sure she isn't buried out there in the sand-trap of the sixth hole, or wearing a cement overcoat at the bottom of the lake?"

"Liz? You've got to be joking. Why would anyone want to kill her? She didn't know anything."

"Interesting way to put it. Unlike the dear dead doctor. He made a business of knowing. In fact he didn't know when to quit."

"You're kidding yourself if you think you can drag Zekerman into this. It won't wash."

"He didn't think Chester was depressed. He was his shrink. If he was lying to me, what was his game?"

"So far you're the one with the answers."

"You said that you could pay off Zekerman out of petty cash. My guess is that that's a lot of petty cash. He knew about Core Two. That's just the start. He also knew about you and Myrna Yates."

"You bastard!"

"Let me finish. I got to the potting shed ahead of your boys. I know about Switzerland. So don't get your indignation in an uproar. That's two things he knew, but there was a third. He knew about what happened at Secord University during your last year. He knew about Elizabeth Blake."

Ward looked sunk. His mouth fell open. He didn't shout at me, he didn't even look angry. I could see him better now. The effects of the flask were wearing off. The fuzzy edge had been sanded away leaving an outline that was sharp enough for a portrait painter. I remembered the sandy hair from the funeral. It was the sort that turns gray without anyone noticing. His face looked boyish from a distance, but now, up close, I could see that these broad youthful lines were criss-crossed with thousands of small wrinkles. His blue eyes looked out from under heavy brows, and there were signs around the chin that collapse of the firm jawline was only a matter of hours away. A minute slipped off the table. The ginger ale stopped bubbling.

"You know all about that?" he said finally.

"It's all there if you know where the pieces are. I've been up to Secord. I've nosed around. I know about Elizabeth Blake, and I know Corso was in on it." Ward nodded, like he was weighing an offer to purchase City Hall. Finally, he said:

"Corso made the stuff, you know. Chester and I stayed clear of that."

"But there was more than just making."

"He was a good chemist. But it was all Chester and I could do to handle him."

"Where did the Blake girl fit in?"

"She bought some of the stuff we were distributing on the campus. She got into us early. She wasn't an addict, just interested in the experience-bending aspects of L.S.D. She wasn't a thrill-seeker, like some of them. She found out that Corso was making it in one of the labs. At first we thought that she wanted to shut us down. But no, she wanted to find more ways to change perceptions. I called her the Mad Redhead. She had a strange intensity. She and Corso were working on variations, and she was his eager guinea-pig. One night, something went wrong. Joe called us. It was a terrible night. A blizzard was going on outside. She didn't come down. She raved for hours and then collapsed. At first we thought that she would come out of it. But there was something funny about her breathing. Her eyes were open. We were scared. Corso went to pieces, so Chester and I carried her back to her room through the snow. It was well past one o'clock.

"There was no one around in that weather, but if anyone saw us, it must have looked like we were helping a drunk. We tucked her into bed, and as an afterthought, I emptied a phial of sleeping pills I found on her table into my pocket and left it empty by her bed. Then we got away as quickly as we could. I figured that if she woke up, the empty pill-container wouldn't mean anything; if she didn't wake up, we needed a smokescreen. Nothing like this had ever happened to us before. We both came from good families. Our parents were a respected part of the community."

"Good for you. Decent chap. Tell me, did Elizabeth Blake ever talk about her sister?"

"Seems to me she mentioned she had one. I don't know. Yes, there was a sister who was always imitating her, couldn't grow up fast enough. She was supposed to look a lot like Elizabeth, but I never met her."

"That sister, Hilda Blake, is still alive. I've seen her name. She was one of Zekerman's patients. I can't guess what the good doctor was holding over her head. Can you?"

"Of course not."

"Could it be about Corso?"

"She couldn't know anything about that. Her sister was dead. She didn't know us."

"What might she have known?"

"I told you: nothing. Corso got frightened. It was too much for him. Then he missed getting a scholarship."

"How very convenient."

"Cooperman, I hope you're not suggesting that I . . ."

"I'll say it plainer. I'm telling you. Chester and you arranged for his taking that fall. You were both in on it. Only you as usual led the way. You went up to the lab where he was working. You got him to come out on the balcony to see something. It was then easy for you both to grab his legs and push him over the rail. I'll bet you were back in the elevator before he hit the ground. But I don't mean to suggest anything."

"You can't prove that. You haven't a shred of evidence."

"Right now I'm not interested in evidence. I'm just trying to focus on this. Now tell me, how did you keep Chester quiet after that? Was he trouble?"

"Chester always believed what I said and did what I told him. He was always like that, from riding school on. I was always looking out for him, one way and another. After Corso's death, things quietened down. We took our degrees, started in business. Chester went into his father's factory. I did some business courses in the States. We both got married. It was years ago."

"And you all lived happily ever after until Dr. Zekerman began to show an interest."

"I could handle him."

"Somebody certainly has handled him."

"Well, guess again, if you think that was me."

"Zekerman didn't think Chester was depressed. How did you know that Chester was on his list too?" Ward blinked his electric blue eyes.

"Andrew told me," he said. The air was slowly leaking out of him like he was a forgotten beach ball.

"He was on the take from Harrington too. I caught up on a lot of reading at the potting shed down by the creek just before arson struck."

"At least all that filth is gone." He was staring at the blond fuzz on the back of his right hand.

"I suspect that I'm not the first with the news."

"So, what? I don't think you are going to turn me in for that."

"Not even for trying to scare Zekerman before I ran into him the first time. Your boys did a first-rate job of frightening him, but he was so scared he decided to trust a cheap peeper like me. He needed an ally, and he couldn't be choosy."

"You won't get far in his shoes, Cooperman. Not without Andrew's files."

"Is that what you think I'm doing? Look, my name's Cooperman, not Zekerman. Maybe from your side of the table there's not much difference in the sound. If you think all cats are alike in the dark, you're crazy. To me, Mr. Ward, you are not the centre of the universe. I used to be able to live for hours on end without hearing your name. I liked it that way. I look forward to going back to that."

A couple of minutes passed. Ward had got up and was facing the black window, running his fingers through his pallid hair. He went to the sort of barber who gave an English cut: no sign of clippers on the side. At length he turned to me. "Some people might not like your mixing in, Cooperman, however pure you claim your motives are. Some people might try to protect their legitimate interests. People have accidents all the time."

"I thought you might get around to that." I tried to muster an agreeable expression.

"Nobody knows you're here."

"You don't have to convince me. But accidents can be insured. I'm a great believer in life insurance."

"You didn't arrange this meeting, I did."

"Are you a card-playing man, Mr. Ward? If you are, you know that there are times when you have to put your money where your mouth is. You're right; I didn't expect this meeting tonight. But I expected it. When you expect something in my business, you take out insurance."

"What kind of insurance?"

"A letter to be opened in case of my sudden death or disappearance, placed in hands that will not ignore it."

"I say you're bluffing."

"Good. It takes more opinions than one to make a poker game."

"Supposing you walk out of here?"

"You know I'm working for Myrna Yates. If you killed Chester, watch out. I'm after you." Ward looked like he was weighing the proposition. Far off a phone was ringing. I could hear the deep voice of one of the boys taking the call. Ward looked in the direction of the closed door. One of the other torpedoes had taken over the call. I couldn't make out any words. There was silence for a moment, then a soft rap at the door. Ward opened it, pinning me to my chair with a look first. Whispering at the door, then Ward's voice on the phone, affable, reasonable, a friend to all. Further whispers at the door. The eyes of his two hoods on me.

"That was a lucky call for you, Mr. Cooperman. I'm going to have to break off this discussion. I've got business to attend to in town." I nodded. It seemed reasonable enough: he was going to give me a stay of execution because he had other fish to fry. But I think he'd bought my insurance story. "I'll have one of the boys drop you at your office." He was climbing into a Burberry raincoat while he was talking. One of the boys, the one with the acne scars, moved in my direction.

"You're all heart, Mr. Ward," I said. "You know what I mean? By the way, since we're both laying our cards on the table, I have a message that Chester was writing just before he was killed. The message is in code."

"Unless it has my name on it," Ward said, smiling, calmly adjusting the belt of the trenchcoat, "I'm not interested. Besides, Chester and I have been exchanging ciphers since we were kids. You detectives always trip over the ordinary looking for the unusual."

I got up and walked past Ward toward the door I'd come in. By this time the letter I called my insurance was looking pretty real, even to me.

TWENTY-THREE

I woke up and it was Friday. The first thought that came to me was Friday night dinner with my mother and father. Then, when my eyes were well and truly open, I remembered how close they'd come to being closed permanently. Ward wasn't the fellow to change his game plan because of a little guy like me.

There were a few things I wanted to clean up before the weekend settled in on me, so I kept after myself until I was washed, shaved, breakfasted—a bran muffin at Bagles—and on the road to Toronto. It was an hour and a half drive at the best of times, and I didn't want to get stuck in weekend traffic. It was going to be a warm couple of days, I only wished that I could afford to take a few off.

The highway was busy but not in a snarl. I headed arrow-like towards the head of the lake, through orchards and vine-yards with the escarpment following my every move through my left window. Up and over a windy bridge, that managed to rise at least a mile and a half higher than anything that might conceivably run under it and I was on the second half of the journey, this time through mile after mile of one-storey factories and assembly plants. The highway added a couple of lanes as we approached the blue silhouette of the Toronto skyline, and, when traffic slowed to the thickness of warmed-over stew, I began to get my old hay-seed feelings about the big city. I never arrived in Toronto without feeling like I was some rube off the farm come to sell my goats at the market. I let the phallic CN Tower lead me into town, wondering as I drove up Spadina Avenue, how it was that most cities are female except Toronto. Chicago, New York, Paris are the experienced old whores who know all about breaking in a new stud. Toronto somehow missed that cue, and doesn't know where to get a sex change at this late date.

Spadina Avenue looked the same as when my father first brought me here as a kid. Every other Wednesday he used to buy stock for his store in the wholesale outlets south of Dundas. He'd do a little buying, a little gin rummy, have a corned beef sandwich and gossip with his crowd. He'd catch up on the news: who was in Florida, who dropped dead, who was going out of business. He would save up the best bits to take home to my mother.

"Sophie, did I get a shock today on Spadina Avenue."

"Manny, I don't want to hear about it."

"And him just back from Miami."

"Manny, I don't want to hear."

"I just saw him two weeks ago, healthy, in his prime."

"I don't want to hear."

The Basic Bookstore at 986 Queen Street West was wedged between a cleaner's and an optician's. As locations go, it didn't look very promising, unless you were looking for a tax loss. The guy behind the counter wore his hair long and blond. There was a suggestion of a moustache, which looked like a young lawn with signs saying "please" on it. He was in faded blue jeans. Maybe there are no other kinds today. Deep in the fiction department, I saw a guy in a whole suit of blue denim, a three-piece suit at that. His solid leather hat added a gauche touch. I started out lamely.

"I'm looking for a girl." I immediately wanted to start over. I put the sales slip down on the cash counter. "The girl I'm looking for bought half a dozen books, real classics, here a year ago last March. A good-looking girl with red hair. Is there the remotest possibility that you might remember something about her. She bought some Rousseau, Plutarch, Corneille and Cicero, all in paperbacks. She might have bought a biography of Charlotte Corday, you know, from the French Revolution, here too. Any chance you might remember her?"

"If she was all that good-looking, I'd remember her. Some days, man, the only thing that happens all day is that a good-looking chick walks through that door. But, like, I've only been here a year. So she was before my time. Was she an out-patient?"

"A what?"

"Out-patient. Like, you know, that's the Queen Street Mental Health Centre across the street. They're the only people buy English books in this neighbourhood. If she bought books here, it was because she was a patient with street privileges, or she was a visitor. And if she ended up with the books, like, the chances are she was one of the shut-ins out for a walk."

"You ever work for Pinkerton's?" I asked. I was always careful to watch the competition.

From this side of the street, the Queen Street Mental Health Centre looked like the sort of building that was designed by the same committee that designed the camel. It consisted of a series of wings shorn from the bird. Later, somebody told me that the old asylum on the same lot had been one of the marvels of early Toronto, and like the rest of those marvels was pulled down. Some of the wings had been built before the old structure was destroyed, and now they leaned away from the space it had occupied as though it was a way of avoiding contamination. There were a few visitors—maybe they were patients; who knows?—walking in and out of the place. I bellied up to the Information desk. Behind it, a black woman with a pencil through her hair was cleaning her glasses on a piece of tissue.

"How do I go about finding a patient?"

"When did he come in?"

"I'm not sure. It's a she."

"Same difference. What's the name?"

"Elizabeth Tilford." She ran a long finger down three plastic-shielded pages of names.

"Uh, uh," she said. "She's not in here. You sure she here?" I nodded, and she shook her head. It wasn't a contest I could win. So I asked her to direct me to the medical records department where I very quickly learned that I couldn't expect to see any of the files without spending eight years in medical school first. Somehow, I doubted whether Myrna Yates would see me through more than pre-meds. I was on the point of leaving when the clerk who had been so forthright in reading me the rules asked what it was I was trying to find. I could see that he had now taken off his cold efficient clerk hat and was sporting one marked "concerned human being." I told him that I had reason to believe that a woman who might be needed as a material witness in a murder investigation may have been a patient in that institution. He made sympathetic noises, joining me in railing against hidebound rulebooks and the inflexibility of small functionaries. He told me that I'd have to get a doctor to do my research for me, and that even he would have to have a good reason.

"Have you any idea how long this woman was supposed to be here?" he asked.

"I don't even know when she left. She was in Grantham by August of last year, and that's all I know about the movements of Elizabeth Tilford."

"Well, you get a doctor to drop over, because we keep complete files on everybody, mental history, charts, treatments, everything. Did you say Elizabeth Tilford?"

"I did. Why?" He was biting on his nail as though the answer came from there.

"It's just that name. Elizabeth Tilford. It strikes a chord. I know I've seen the name, or heard it. Just a minute." He lifted a conspiratorial finger in the air and disappeared. After about two minutes, timed by my pulse, which I could feel beating without placing hand over heart, he came back with a grin that threatened to cut his head in two unequal pieces. "I knew I'd heard the name before, and now I've checked. Liz Tilford wasn't a patient here, she was a nurse. They'll tell you all about her in personnel. You don't have to be a doctor to find out about staff." He thought it was a big joke, and I left him there to enjoy it.

Personnel was a big woman with a plastic tag on her white coat that said "Ferrante." I told her who I was looking for and she looked encouraging. From a file drawer her expert fingers drew a card to which other cards were attached with paperclips.

"Elizabeth Tilford. Yes, she was a nurse here for many years, worked in just about every department, it looks like, except the kitchen. She took courses on vacations. Looks like she was an all-round good nurse. What were you looking for specifically?"

"When did she leave Queen Street?"

"She took her superannuation in February last year."

"She took her what?"

"Superannuation. Retirement. She left because she'd reached the mandatory retirement age."

"How old's that?"

"Sixty-five. Some take it earlier. Depends how long they've been here. We have a formula based on the number of years worked and your age. If they add up to eighty-five, you can retire with full pension. Does that help?"

"I'm afraid it confuses me. I've been looking for a young woman."

"Why don't you talk with Mabel Kline, she's senior nurse. She might be able to tell you about Miss Tilford."

"Where can I find her?" She consulted her watch, and then dialled an inside number with four digits. There was a pause. The upshot of the conversation was that for ten minutes I found myself walking down corridors looking for a certain room number. At every junction, there were arrows with numbers pointing in all the possible directions. I simply had to follow the arrow with the number group that included mine. Easier said than done. I was beginning to believe that my grasp on the fundamentals of arithmetic was slipping, when I blundered into the right wing. I asked directions from a gray-haired man in a wine-coloured bathrobe, and soon found myself knocking on a door with Mabel Kline's name on it.

The door was opened by a man of about forty. He was wearing a sweatshirt over a soft shirt, and looked like he'd just come from a gym.

"Is Miss Kline around?" I asked.

"She'll be right back. Have a seat." I made myself comfortable in one of the straight-backed chairs on the visitor's side of the desk, and offered a cigarette to the man.

"No thanks," he said. "I've given them up completely now. I've seen the recent tests on tars, and I'm convinced that there is no way to eliminate all the noxious carcinogenic matter. Did you know that in one unfiltered cigarette, like the one you are now lighting, there is enough tar to destroy about fifty cells in your lungs."

"Is that a fact."

"After smoking a package of unfiltered cigarettes, just like the one in your hand, there have been tests to show that pre-cancerous anomalies can appear. They showed experimentally, not clinically of course, that once pre-cancerous conditions exist, that in roughly half the cases the cells finally produce malignancies." I butted my cigarette in the ashtray provided, and was beginning to feel certain pre-cancerous anomalies forming under my ribs, when a tall gray-haired black woman came in briskly in a starched white uniform. She smiled at me, and gave a dirty look at the health fiend next to me.

"Richard, what on earth are you doing here? I told you

I would look in on you after rounds this evening. Now, run along and behave yourself." Richard got up, nodded at me and left. "Richard is one of my star patients."

"Patient?" My chest immediately responded to treatment. The furry feeling under my tie cleared up, and I offered Miss Kline a cigarette.

"No thanks. I've just put one out. I'm trying to stop. Not doing very well. Clara Ferrante said on the phone that you were looking for Liz Tilford. May I know why?" She blinked her bright eyes and smiled. Her high cheekbones were becoming. She sat very straight in her chair, giving me her complete attention. I could feel her efficiency in the way her hair was drawn back from her forehead by a no-nonsense band of tortoise-shell. I liked her. I explained that the Elizabeth Tilford I was looking for was a good-looking red-head in her twenties, not a registered nurse in her mid-sixties.

"So you see, I'm probably here under false colours."

"Sounds highly unlikely to me as well," she said helpfully. "Still it obviously is a different woman. No question about that?"

"None. No. It's just a dead end in my investigation. I want to thank you for your help."

"Don't get up yet, Mr. Cooperman." (I'd given her one of my cards.) "I've just had the strangest notion. Liz Tilford was one of the best nurses I've ever worked with. She knew her job, but that was only part of it. You know, this place can get you down after a few years, especially when we were still in the old building. But like very few other nurses, Liz Tilford really cared about her patients. Most of us feel that when you've rubbed one back, you've rubbed them all, that patients, especially here, are somehow inhuman unconnected bothers. To Liz Tilford, every patient was an individual. She didn't just remember a few things about her patients and so josh them along and set up a friendly bantering relationship. She really got to know most of the people who were under her care for any length of time. It was a gift. She was missed when she left, I can tell you."

"What happened to her?"

"For a while she lived here in Toronto, in a small apartment not far from the hospital. Then, I heard she went to live with a married sister in Sault Ste. Marie. I don't know the name. But, you didn't let me finish. What I was going to tell you was that during her last few years here, she became very fond of a patient who answers the description you gave of the woman you are looking for. Liz was good to everyone, but there was a special bond between Liz and this young patient. Do you think that might be helpful?"

"It very well might. How can I tell, Miss Kline? I feel like putting my name down to be committed. What happened to this young woman? The patient you mentioned?"

"It seems to me that she left us over a year ago. Yes, now that I think about it, it was just after Liz retired. The last few times I saw Liz was as a visitor to see some of her special patients. Yes, and here's the link I was going to mention, when the girl left us she went from here to live with Liz Tilford. I think I remember hearing that Liz had helped a few of the former inmates find their footing in the outside world again. You see, she was an extraordinary person."

"Yes, I can see that. Thank you for all your help, Miss Kline."

"Mrs.," she said, with a turn of her head and a smile. "What will you do now, Mr. Cooperman?"

"I'm not sure. I might go over to that apartment building and talk with the super. I'd like to find out the name of the girl Liz Tilford was living with."

"Oh, you needn't go to all that trouble to find that out, I think I can save you steps there. I remember the girl's name very clearly, because it's the same last name as my favourite English poet. Her name is Hilda Blake."

TWENTY-FOUR

I headed directly from the highway to my parents' condominium. It was pushing seven when I walked into the tangerine grotto that was the family living-room. There was no sign of anyone on this floor. In the kitchen, the light was burning, but I couldn't see any sign of activity in the oven. It was Friday night, but I didn't recognize any of the signs. I followed the noise of the television down into the family room.

"Oh, you did come?" asked my mother.

"Did I say I wasn't coming?" I looked at my father for judgment, but he was too clever to get involved. He kept watching the last dregs of local news.

"Well, in that case," said my mother, as though my arrival had made alternate plans necessary, "I'd better put some meat in the oven and peel some potatoes. I haven't even lit the candles yet. Benny, you didn't even phone."

I rolled my eyes heavenward in my usual helpless way, and followed Ma upstairs. She preceded me into the kitchen. By the time I arrived on the scene she was pulling out slabs of paper-wrapped frozen meat and dropping them on the floor like bricks. It was like a bowling alley, the racket. She found the brick she wanted and flung it un-wrapped into a pot with a resounding clang, added a can of tomato juice, paprika, an onion, and put the lid on. "There," she said as she slammed the oven door, "that will be done in two hours. I'll put the potatoes around it in an hour."

She'd placed two brass candlesticks in the middle of the tablecloth in the dining room, inserting stubby white candles and lit them with her lighter. Then she covered her face with her hands and mumbled some words under her breath.

144

"Ma," I asked, "what is it you say?"

"You've been asking me that question since you could talk. How many times do I have to answer you?"

"Tell me again."

"It's a blessing." She was back in the kitchen, collecting knives and forks and spoons from the dishwasher.

"I know it's a blessing. Tell me the words."

"Why do you want to know? You want the job?"

"I'm just asking." I took the plates she handed me and walked around the table putting one at each place. I got out some glasses.

"Not those," Ma said. "Use the ones from the china cabinet. I thought we'd have some wine."

"Don't change the subject. What are the words you say with your eyes covered?"

"I say, Benny, what my mother taught me to say before you were born. That's what I say."

"And the words she taught you were? Tell me."

"Why do you want to know? You got a customer for the information? Benny, stop nagging me. Here, put the salt and pepper on the table. And when you've done that, open this jar of pickles. Put it under the hot water if you have to."

I gave up. Before I could retreat, she thrust a bottle of wine and corkscrew into my hands.

"Before you go, open this. Your father will kill me if it hasn't breathed."

I went downstairs to see my father again. I leaned over and kissed the top of his head. He'd been in the sauna. I don't know what it is about a sauna. I sometimes think it's a redwood time machine. You enter at two in the afternoon, you leave half an hour later and it's five-thirty. I don't blame Pa for spending his time there. It keeps him away from the card table. He looked up at me, put his head to one side and said, "So, you went to see Melvyn, like you promised?" He'd seen Melvyn who'd told him that I had not been in to see him about getting work searching titles. This was Pa's way of saying "So, you didn't go to see Melvyn." He had a way of saying everything so that it didn't matter whether the sentence was positive or negative, it still meant the same thing.

"No, Pa, I've been busy. You don't believe me, but I've been having a very good week. Here." I took an aluminum cylinder from my pocket. "Here's a cigar I bought for you in Toronto."

"What were you doing in Toronto?" He was actually looking at me. The TV was blaring away unnoticed for a second.

"Just business. But I thought you might like the cigar."

"If I'd known you were going, I would have had you pick up a box of them for me. I've got an account at Shopsy's."

Then there was dinner. It was always like seeing a scene from an old favourite movie. Conversation drifted back to Melvyn, reports about the Bar Mitzvah the week before, and certain hints were dropped to let me be reminded that they were known as the Coopermans whose son lived in a hotel, while other Coopermans that they might name had just sold their two-hundred-thousand-dollar house in order to buy one worth four hundred thousand.

My last sight of my mother on this occasion was a glimpse of her through the kitchen window placing ice cubes on her potted plants. I'd questioned her about this practice before, but, as with most questions I asked her, received no satisfactory answer.

After running the gauntlet of the fast-food chains on Ontario Street, I decided to drop by my office for a half-hour. I climbed the stairs remembering how Frank had looked lying in the doorway last Wednesday night. It was ten years ago.

Frank was sitting in his own waiting room, with a half-finished bottle of rye on the magazine table in front of him.

"How are you, scout?" he asked, brighter than I'd seen him on these occasions. "Pull up a seat and have a jar with me." I sat down, but placed my hand over the glass he held out.

"How's the head?"

"Oh, the head's fine. They put me back together with vinegar and brown paper. I've been on the look-out for you all day. Where the deuce have you been? I've heard the hard flat feet of the constabulary on the stairs and other heavy treads. You've missed a record day."

"I drove to Toronto this morning, and spent most of my time at the Queen Street Mental Health Centre."

"Don't they dress it up nowadays? Have they struck the word asylum from the dictionary?"

"Do you remember anything more about who zapped you the other night?"

"No. I remember not seeing or speaking any evil, but I may have for a moment heard some. Like a whisper. I told you. What brings you back at this hour, man, you should have been tucked in long ago?"

"Just wanted to check the mail, the answering service, that sort of thing. Sooner I get at it," I said struggling to my feet and making noises of departure, "the sooner I'll get home. Take care, Frank. Good night."

"Good night and God bless, old son."

The mail was disappointing. I'd expected to have to ask Frank to help me push the door open against the pressure of a huge stack, but I was wrong. A circular about a downtown business association, trying to get the few businessmen left in the area to stamp out the dry rot along St. Andrew Street. There were the expected bills from the oil companies, the telephone company, and one I wasn't expecting—insurance. After Thursday night, I didn't think anyone would take my money for insurance.

The telephone answering service was more interesting. There was a call from Myrna Yates; one from Bill Ward; and one from Savas. I decided to try them in reverse order, so that could pass on any new tidbits to Myrna.

It took about three minutes for Savas to grab his phone, and I was just thinking of calling it all off, but there he was with that voice that spoke of too much coffee and too many cigarettes.

"Savas."

"Cooperman. You phoned?"

"Yeah. What kinda office hours you keep? Why didn't you tell me you were independently wealthy and could close up shop whenever you felt like it?"

"Sorry. I was in Toronto on business. What have you got?"

"We checked on that piece you tried to deliver to Ward's place Wednesday night. For the size of it, it has a rare history. The Forensic Centre tells me that it was used in a shooting at the university back in early 1964. Guard got hit in the hip when he interrupted a couple of thieves in a drug warehouse in the basement of the chemistry building. They shot him and then zapped him to keep him quiet." Then I got a lecture on how lucky we were to get anything on the gun, because usually they only save slugs when there's been a fatality. A ballistics hotshot narrowed the field down to happenings in and around Grantham. "They were wearing stockings over their faces, and they got clean away."

"That was in the days when stockings came one at a time. Nowadays, burglars have to work in twos."

"You should know, Cooperman. How come you haven't been picked up in the last thirty-six hours? You getting cagey?"

"Nope, I've seen the light, Savas. I turned over a new leaf."

"Any leaf you turn over wouldn't be worth diddly. Keep honest."

It was easier getting to Ward. My name suddenly cut through two voices like unsweetened chocolate and there he was. Again I had to explain that I was out of town all day.

"I've had a call, Mr. Cooperman, from Miss Tilford. I've arranged to meet her tomorrow night."

"Don't be crazy, Ward. That's walking into a trap."

"I can handle her."

"Listen to me when I'm talking. You can't meet her. I spent the day in Toronto, and after a lot of sleuthing, I know who she really is. She's poison to you, Ward, I'm telling you."

"Yes, but you see, I now know who she is too. And I'm ready for her. My boys won't let anything happen to me."

"I'll never talk to you again. She's out for your blood. Even Zekerman was trying to warn you about that."

"Yes, that's ironic, when you think about it, isn't it. Goodbye, Cooperman."

Myrna Yates answered the phone herself. She wanted to see me. She sounded irritated, so I promised to drive right over. I'd been hoping for an early night, my eyes were tired from the long drive and my stomach was already beginning to protest again the assault of my mother's dinner. I took a couple of stomach tablets. I parked the car on the street outside the house. Funny, the smell of the papermills up in Papertown was just as strong here on Mortgage Hill. My steps echoed against the house as I came up the walk.

She answered the door herself. The butler was always out in that place, or maybe it just looked like they should have a butler to look after things. She took my coat and led me into the living room. She was wearing a navy blue linen skirt with a green shirt. Her sandals had raised heels and left a track in the broadloom as I followed her. We sat in a corner of the big room, with a table at knee-level between us. I searched her face for some answer to the irritation in her voice, but couldn't find any.

"May I get you something to drink, Mr. Cooperman?"

She was up again and on her way to a honey-coloured pine
cabinet which hid every kind of drink in the catalogue.

"A gin and tonic, light on the gin, please. In fact, you can
leave it out. I'm having stomach problems."

"You probably could use a home-cooked meal."

"Thanks," I said. She handed me a tall glass and carried
another back to her seat on the edge of a chintz-covered sofa.

"Mr. Cooperman, have you been to see Bill Ward?" She
looked at me over her drink, but she wasn't playing games.

"I saw him last night at his golf club. Why?"

"I got the strangest call from him an hour ago. He was
asking me whether I'd ever heard of that Dr. Zekerman who
was killed. He wondered whether he'd tried to get in touch
with me. Of course I told him that I'd only just learned that
Chester had been seeing him. He was, what do you say, pumping me for information. I didn't like it. May I ask you what
happened last night?"

"As long as you're paying my bills." I told her about
Ward's subtle way of arranging the meeting. "Zekerman was
blackmailing Ward and your husband about some events that
reached back to their university days. Zekerman was a nasty
piece of work, Mrs. Yates. He also knew about you and Mr.
Ward. He had a picture in a Swiss newspaper. I've got it
now."

"I see." She could have looked startled, she could have
said thanks, but she didn't. "Do you know why he is acting
this way? It isn't like him."

"I wonder if he isn't getting desperate. Would you say
that he's been acting strangely, before today? Has he been
more attentive, perhaps more ardent?"

"We're very close, as you know. And since the funeral,
I . . . Well, I don't know what I would have done without him.
He handled everything."

"Yes, I remember. He said I was harassing you."

"Yes, well . . ."

"Speaking of harassment: tell me about why Liz Tilford
left your husband's office. You had something to do with that,
didn't you?"

"I don't know what you mean. What has that to do with
anything?"

"Did you ask Chester, I mean your husband, to get rid of
her?"

"Mr. Cooperman, if you mean to . . ."

"Please, Mrs. Yates, this is more important than you

know. I suspect that you didn't enjoy seeing your successor every time you visited the office. I'd probably have done the same thing."

"Well, as a matter of fact, I did speak to Chester about her."

"And?"

"And Chester said he'd speak to her. He told me that they'd had a good talk and that he'd made her understand he wanted her to start looking for a new job. He said that she took it very well, and said she would begin hunting. But she didn't come back after that day. She didn't show her face in the office again ever."

"Did Chester, I'm sorry, did Mr. Yates guess why you were concerned?"

"No. I just told him that I didn't think she dressed suitably and that she seemed to waste a good deal of time on three-hour lunches."

"Did you often take such a personal interest?" She shook her head, as she tamped down a cigarette on the lid of the silver cigarette box on the table. It was a nice gesture, very feminine and irritable at the same time. "Then Chester knew you didn't approve of Ward parading his after-hours business under your nose." I lit the cigarette and she looked at me closely through the smoke as she answered.

"Chester knew that I disliked Bill's behaviour with women. He lacked discretion."

"But he was discreet about you; no one knew about the Bellevue Terrace place."

"He had his moments, Mr. Cooperman." She wasn't surprised that I knew about Bellevue Terrace. After Switzerland, their affair had continued here in Grantham. He probably ended it when the good doctor began to show an interest.

I heard a muffled slam coming from the front of the house. It was followed by footsteps on the carpet, very quiet footsteps. When I looked up at the double doorway leading into the front room, I saw Bill Ward standing there removing his trenchcoat.

"Hello, Myrna. Good evening, Mr. Cooperman. I didn't expect to find you here. I wondered whose car that was." He went directly to the pine cabinet where he poured himself a double scotch with Perrier. Then he collected Myrna's glass and refilled it expertly. "Is that gin you're drinking, Mr. Cooperman?"

"I'm just fine, thanks," I said. "As a matter of fact, I was just leaving." Mrs. Yates frowned to show that she was sorry to see me go so quickly, careful not to show any surprise at Bill Ward's sudden appearance. I turned and said goodnight to Myrna, and then said to Ward, "I still feel very strongly that you shouldn't keep that business appointment you mentioned." Ward shrugged and smiled. I wouldn't say he looked likeable just then, but it was his least hateful pose to date. Myrna came with me to the door.

"I know what you think," she said.

"I know you know," I said, grinned and said goodnight. I dragged myself back to the hotel and to bed. I'd forgotten to ask Myrna for another cheque, but I thought that she'd be good for it. It was hard getting her voice and eyes out of my head as I tossed and turned under the covers with the neon winking at me through the half-drawn drapes. The cars outside drew crazy shadows across my walls. I was glad when sweet oblivion finally grabbed me and dragged me off.

TWENTY-FIVE

Once again, I won't bore you with the details of my weekend. The secrets of the laundromat will die with me, as will those of the car wash and an attempt at stapling the hanging hem of my trouser cuff.

The Saturday paper was full of Core Two. Even the Toronto papers devoted generous space to this multi-million-dollar civic development. Stories told how parcels of land had been carefully assembled over the past year, forty-two separate pieces. Ward was quoted briefly and Mayor Rampham at length. Both were pictured wearing smiles and hard hats. Another blow for progress.

On the business page, I head about the details of the financing. Elsewhere, a couple of developers who had been quietly bypassed were calling for an inquiry, and yelling "fraud." But an Ontario cabinet minister was quoted saying that Grantham was showing the way ahead to the rest of the province. It was a big day for Grantham. It was a big day for Bill Ward. He had made the killing he'd dreamed of. He was no longer just a wealthy man as we understood wealth in this Niagara backwater. I took my hat off to him, the bastard. He'd brought it off in spite of Chester's death, Zekerman's interference and my snooping. I took my hat off to him.

I managed to kill a few hours on Saturday evening reading through Liz Tilford's library. It was quite a collection for a serious-minded girl with nothing better to do on Saturday nights. Then I dug out the page of appointments that Martha had mailed me. After an hour or two, it began to get interesting.

Monday morning found me still in bed when the phone

started ringing. Since few people had this number, I was confused to hear it jangling away on top of my copy of *Improving Your Chess*. I stretched out an arm from the bed and the noise stopped.

"Hello?" I could hear the pajamas in my voice.

"Cooperman?" It was Pete Staziak.

"What do you want, Pete?"

"Get your ass down here right away." He wasn't fooling around. He sounded like he'd been up all night, so I suppressed an instinct to tease him. At the best of times, Pete had a sense of humour like I'll bet Harrow's mother insists Harrow has, but there are some days when it's best to let it lie undetected.

"What's happened?"

"The short answer is that Bill Ward's dead. Looks like a couple of his bimbos knocked him off. We've got them here telling stories that should win prizes at a national fiction award. I'd appreciate it if you'd drop in. Okay?"

"I'll be right over."

It took no time at all to get myself organized. My breath tasted like I'd been baby-sitting somebody else's false teeth, and when I sneezed my sinuses smelt of mildew. I grabbed a raincoat and pulled it on as I ran down the stairs. When I got outside, I could see that I wouldn't be needing it. It was going to be another beautiful day. The sun was already glinting on the tops of cars parked in the market square. The Regional Police office is just a block and a half from the hotel. I was standing in front of the push-button door in less than ten minutes. Well, fifteen.

I asked for Sergeant Staziak, and the man at the desk pointed the way, not that I didn't know where it was, but the last time I'd set about finding Pete myself, I'd felt the full weight of the law descend on my shoulder. When I walked into that small metallic alcove, he was sitting there with a cigarette dangling from his thin lips. A reddish stubble on his chin caught the light coming in off the parking lot.

"Thanks, Ben. I appreciate this. Here's what we've got." He picked up a report from the blotter in front of him and began ad libbing from it. "Sunday morning, around noon, a farmer and his wife from out in the township thought they saw something suspicious on their drive home from church. Up on the escarpment, the Old Stone Road takes a sharp left in front of an abandoned quarry. They saw that the fence had been shattered, and when they stopped to investigate, they saw a car thirty feet below lying on its back. They phoned the police at, at, at," he sifted through the report, "twelve thirty-two, and the initial report from the two investigating officers said that the body of a man was found wedged behind the wheel. So, we were called in. To make a long story short, Ward didn't die in the crash. The coroner is certain that he was dead when the car took the fall. In fact, Ward died of carbon monoxide poisoning. We went out to the golf course and asked a few questions. Eventually, we brought in two of Ward's bodyguards. These bodyguards, to wit Bruno Marchetti and Thomas Pacifico, have been grilling most of the night, and their stories are now so far apart that we don't know which one to book. Ward was carrying a bundle of bucks with him, so we don't suspect any of the usual scam. Likewise the effects of carbon monoxide poisoning are easy enough to recognize. Whoever pushed Ward over was either not on the bright side, or didn't care much about being found out. How'm I doing?"

"Just fine. I still can't see why you got me up, though." Pete looked at me for a moment, and then lifted his report again. He had long ago stopped taking his cigarette out of his mouth to flick the ashes off. Even at school, I had admired the way he could blow the ash off the end without bothering to use his fingers.

"One of these bimbos says he heard you and Ward having a violent argument late last week out at his golf club. He's trying to get us to lock you up for popping Ward, so that he and his pal can get back to weeding the fairway. Now I don't put too much stock in what Bruno Marchetti has in his deposition, but I don't think he made up the part about you seeing Ward like that. I'm not likely to read into his statement what he wants me to read, but I'd like to hear from you how much of this is up and up. Did you see Ward late last week?"

"I saw him Thursday night for over an hour around ten o'clock. He sent three of his boys to grab me, and they caught up to me after I'd done my best to give them the slip. If I'd known it was Ward who wanted to see me, I could have saved a lot of running."

"You were talking generalities? The fluctuation of the dollar, the position of the French franc compared with the Deutschmark. Come on, Benny, don't ration it."

"We discussed the deaths of Chester Yates and Andrew Zekerman, both of whom he knew. I asked him some questions about Core Two, and about the disappearance of a girl he used to know. When we finished talking, one of his boys drove me back to my car. It was around midnight, as close as I can remember."

"Okay. You saw him Thursday night, and maybe these are two of the three that set fire to you. You didn't want Ward dead, neither did they. Ben, I can't figure it."

"How are they taking all your questions?"

"Nervous as a child bride. Only Marchetti has mentioned you."

"Do you know when he died?"

"Yeah, as close as the Doc can put it, around twelve-thirty Sunday morning, about twelve hours before he was found. Figure that one out."

"What are you talking about? What's to figure? You don't think these galoots killed Ward? Okay. Then somebody else did, unless he did it himself. He didn't have any more reason to kill himself than you do. Overlooking the fact that he had to face waking up in the morning as William Allen Ward. Now why would these two tough guys want to pop Ward? He was their boss, and I guess he looked after them. Is it likely they got a notion to freelance? The only muscle they have listed down at the labour exchange is the kind they've been avoiding all their lives. The way I see it . . ."

I was just about to wax poetic on my private views concerning this unfortunate state of affairs when Harrow thrust his big face in the doorway.

"Well, we finally got something on you, did we, cheapie? Good for us. I just had my day made for me." He was grinning with his stained teeth. I don't know where you can get teeth like that.

"You not working tonight, Joe?" Pete Staziak asked. His way of saying "push off" to a fellow officer. But Harrow kept his face in the doorway until he'd smoked his current butt down to his cuticle.

"It's not work when we get a chance to see justice done around here. Couldn't leave it alone, could you, peeper? You knew better than the whole department. Had a little fight with Ward, and decided to even the score. So you set up this amateur-hour accident and expect us to buy it. It stinks, Cooperman, and so do you." He left his butt, such as it was, in a Styrofoam cup, and walked away only moments before Pete slammed the door in his face.

"I'm going to slam my door on his fingers, next chance

I get. I'd love to throw him an electric toaster when he's in the shower."

"Take it easy, Pete. I don't chip easy."

"To hell with you. Where does he get the idea he can stick his snout into my investigation?"

"Has he found out who killed Zekerman yet?"

"Stop it, Benny. I don't want to feel sorry for the no-good crud."

"Right, where were we? Yeah. I was about to tell you that I think I have this thing figured out. I *think* I have, but you're going to have to get the story out of them, because I can't prove a word of what I'm going to say."

"You think you know what happened, Ben? That's great. Let's have it, and if it doesn't leak all over us, we'll have the horse collar on Harrow for sure. You want coffee?" He ducked out into the hall for a minute, and put the arm on a constable who didn't walk with sufficient concentration to avoid Pete's instructions. When he got back, I pulled out a fresh package of smokes and stripped it of the wrapper.

"Friday night," I began, "I got a call late at night, ten-thirty, eleven o'clock from Ward. Wait a minute. I'm trying to keep it simple, so right away I'm telling lies. At the time I said I came back to my office, I phoned my answering service. There was a message to call Ward. Before I got to him, I had to go through two deep male voices. Ward wanted me to know that he had had a call from a woman he used to see. She disappeared from the scene a couple of months ago. Really disappeared, although nothing was reported. Ward knew that I'd been looking for her. I thought that Ward would have known more than he did about where she'd gone. Anyway, on Friday night, out of the blue, he got this call from her asking him to meet her. I warned him that such a meeting might be dangerous, but he just laughed off the suggestion. I think he met the girl and by half-past twelve Saturday night, Sunday morning he was dead, with his boys sitting on their hands parked outside not knowing a thing about it. They see nothing suspicious, and do nothing until early next morning, when they come across the body, an apparent suicide."

"Another apparent suicide. We're collecting a matched set." Pete intercepted the fresh-faced constable with the coffee, and handed me a warm Styrofoam cup. "I used to try to drink tea out of these things, but the lemon melts the plastic and wets my trousers. Cheers." I pried the cap off my cup and looked for a place to drop it. I followed Pete's lead, and left it on his desk where they became emergency ash-trays.

"Picture the boys sitting it out. Their boss has told them to expect him by a certain time. That time has passed, and when they start looking, they find trouble. Trouble in that their boss was dead, trouble that he'd killed himself, and trouble about where he'd done the job. So the boys, as a parting ges-ture, decide that they can improve on things. One of them drives Ward's car, and the other follows. They both know the lay of the land up on the escarpment like their tongues know the sockets where their molars used to be. With any luck, they hope that the car will catch fire. So then they go back to the golf club and that's where you picked them up. The question now is where did Ward take the girl and where did she go. I suspect it was the Bellevue Terrace house, where I was picked up last week. Savas knows all about that. It has an attached garage with a connecting door to the kitchen. Let's say she tells Ward something that hits him so hard, he wants to end it all. She leaves and he does himself in in the garage. Neat? Or try this on. She gives Ward a needle of some kind, some-thing to knock him out, and leaves him in the car with the motor running. She goes out the back way, leaving the body-guards watching an empty house and putting in time while their boss is sucking in the fumes. Either way, the boys think they're improving things by sending the car into the quarry. Why don't you try that on your two friends?"

"They're hard nuts to crack."

"They may feel differently about it if they think that it's a murder they're implicated in and not just a suicide. Trying to make the boss's suicide look like an accident's one thing, dressing up a murder is serious business with very nasty long numbers on conviction."

TWENTY-SIX

The sun was unusually brilliant; the spring, which had arrived such a few short days ago, had settled in and made itself at home. The few trees downtown were fattening at the ends of their twigs. Soon there would be buds and leaves. The tulips I'd noticed in front of City Hall had blossomed into red and yellow blooms. They'd had help, but there were a few other green stems by the court house, weeds to be sure, but I'm generous by nature. Green is green until August in my book. Then it's every man for himself.

I went around to the United to pick up some lunch. For once, I picked up the menu and read through the businessman's lunch. A couple of things looked tempting, but the waitress got to me half a minute too soon and I funked, ordering a chopped egg sandwich on white toast. Today I took an order of coleslaw on the side, and felt immediately better for ordering it. Breaking fresh paths is a heady experience.

I climbed the stairs to my office. I must be getting old; the experience of getting to the top and seeing my name on the glass doesn't hold for me what it once held. There's been a fading away of the lustre, just as the gold-leaf lettering was beginning to flake.

Once inside my door, I did something I'd intended to do a few days ago. I'd been thinking about what Mrs. Kline, the head nurse, had told me. I reached for the telephone book, and looked up Mrs. L. M. Blake on Dover Road. The odd piece I'd been holding now slipped into place. The laundry ticket I'd picked up in Liz Tilford's room at Martha Tracy's house, bore an address on Dover Road. So, that was it. Elizabeth Tilford, also known as Hilda Blake, had disappeared where a hot-shot detective would never have thought of look-

158

ing for her. She'd gone home. The listing was under her mother's name, so her father had died and she hadn't remarried.

I drove out Queenston Road, a curving extension of St. Andrew Street. It held the bank above the old canal for about a mile, then cut out toward Niagara, as soon as the canal took a bend to the south. Wherever a street joined Queenston Road, in this early section, I could glimpse a vista of grim broken promises. The canal had held out party favours and presents to the men who sunk their capital in setting up mills along the hydraulic races, fast running channels of water which would drive millstones, operate saws, churn butter, or power fifty looms whenever the water dropped to the level of the next canal lock in the series. But now the party was over. Most of the buildings stood derelict—some looked stunned— with broken panes of glass in the rotting window-frames, boarded-up doors, buildings that had once dominated the horizon with towers and the hum of industry.

The road curved along the edge of the old canal now, climbing with it the gentlest face the escarpment presents on the Niagara Peninsula. At the top of the hill Papertown sends out a few streets of welcome. One of them, curving along the top of the escarpment, is the Dover Road. From the backyards along its length, you can see north to the lake, and I guess on a clear day, you can see the purple office towers of Toronto and the CN Tower in front of them. But the Dover Road is also the location of the huge green water tower, itself the focus of attention from down on the lake-shore plain.

I checked the number. The house I was looking for was constructed of modest gray brick with a roof with a gentle slope to it. There were curtains in the front windows, and in the back, a low shed. The green tower stood a lot or two away, with the gigantic structure blocking out only the least pleasing view to the lake. It was a small property, in need of some repair to the shutters and the cracked cement of the front walk, but I could think of worse places to spend my declining years.

I knocked on the front door. I could hear an immediate response from inside, probably from the front room, but the door wasn't answered for nearly a minute. When the door opened, and then only seven or eight inches, the woman with frightened green eyes asked me to name my business.

"Mrs. Blake," I was guessing, "I'd like to speak to Hilda,

if I may. Is she here?" I gave her the best of the Cooperman smile, and let the sunlight catch all my dimples.

"What made you think you'd find her here?" She wasn't openly unhelpful. She was being unhelpful in a helpful-seeming way. I smiled again.

"I think you'll find that she's expecting me. The name is Cooperman. Ben Cooperman."

"Why don't you leave the girl alone?" the old woman asked. She was solid and short, with gray hair going a little yellow in its tight curls. She wore an apron over a flowered dress. A brooch, in the shape of a thistle, sparkled on the neat lapel of her collar. "Haven't we suffered enough?"

"I wish I could answer that, Mrs. Blake. I don't know all the answers. I hope that Hilda might help me to find some. I need her help, Mrs. Blake." She looked at me, made what appeared to be half a pout, and then stood back from the door allowing me to pass her stout figure.

The room was full of caged birds of all colours. I counted at least twenty cages, some suspended from ornamental stands, and others set on tables and suspended from wires. The birds were the usual birds, with the usual bright colours that caged birds run to. There were blues and greens and yellows, an occasional glimpse of red, black, pink and even white. There wasn't a song bird in the lot. Not a cheerful note in over fifty little feathered breasts. The space in the room not devoted to livestock was taken by a couple of comfortable chairs and an over-stuffed sofa with a picture above if of cheerful song birds. On the mantelpiece of an imitation fireplace stood two Dresden birds in china, on each side of a group of stuffed cardinals in a bell jar. It was the sort of living-room that had probably never seen a barrel of Kentucky-fried chicken.

"You're admiring my birds," she said. It wasn't a question. I nodded a lie. "I have more than fifteen different varieties, not all here in the living room, of course. That black one with the short bright beak is a minah bird, of the eastern passerine type. Some of them can be made to talk, but I don't hold with teaching animals to do tricks. Some people see no harm in it, but I find it disgusting and degrading. It degrades both the animal and the teacher, if you want my opinion." I stopped trying to feign interest in her exotic birds, hoping that she might come down and perch somewhere close to my reason for being here. She stopped leading me from cage to cage and said, "You really have to see her, Mr....? I'm sorry, I've forgotten your name."

"Cooperman. Ben Cooperman. If you could tell her I'm here. I think you'll find that in a way she has been expecting me."

"Well, if you say that she knows you're coming, I guess that will be all right. I hate to see her upset. She's been so brave since she came back home."

"Brave? In what way?" I guess I turned on her a little more directly than I'd intended. She blinked her eyes a couple of times before trying to answer.

"We've had a lot of grief in this family off and on, Mr. Cooperman, and Hilda has kept her little head held high right through the worst of it. At times things looked black for the whole family, but Hilda kept us going, like a little jenny wren fighting off a bluejay. Who would have thought that the cost would be so high? And how I missed her when they'd all gone. First Elizabeth, then Morris, that was my husband— the shock of Elizabeth's death killed the lamb in less than a year. Then Hilda became sick, but how she fought back. I was very nearly distracted myself, I'm telling you. If it wasn't for my little friends here, I should have miscarried in my head, I'm sure." She paused, and looked over my shoulder, as though she could see through the wall at my back. "She's out in the garden, Mr.... There! I've forgotten it again. I'm getting on in years, and my memory isn't what it was. I used to be able to remember all of 'The Wreck of the Hesperus' by Mr. Longfellow, the poet. Nowadays I can't remember my own name, so please don't take offence." She led me through the house, our way lined by more bird cages, to the kitchen. Through a window I could see her, seated in a lawn chair, looking out over the view from the heights.

TWENTY-SEVEN

She was wearing a soft blue cotton dress with buttons and a collar. The brilliant sunlight caught it, and her long red hair, hanging loose; she seemed to glow as she leaned back in the old-fashioned canvas lawn chair. Beside her on a white wicker table was a full crystal pitcher of lemonade, with the condensation forming droplets which ran down the sides. Around her, the garden was blooming with the enthusiasm of early spring. I don't know the names of the flowers; irises, maybe, and crocuses. They were all there, in spite of the marauding shadow of the water tower which once a day must brood over these flowerbeds. At this hour, the great green shadow was elsewhere, and the picture in front of me could not have been more idyllic if it was in some English garden in a painting. Except for the far end of the yard. There, the escarpment dropped away suddenly. At my eye level, I could see a hawk turning, a hundred feet above the rooftops of the city below.

I walked around and stood in her light. She lifted her hand to her face. "You're blocking the sun, Mr. Cooperman. Come over here and sit beside me so that we can both enjoy it." I settled into another lawn chair, and brought it closer to Hilda Blake. "I've been expecting you," she said. "I thought that you'd come this morning." I grinned, helplessly. "You met my mother?"

"Yes, I just saw her."

"She's been very good to me."

"Does she know, then?"

"Oh, of course not. Her support was of a general kind. I'm surprised if you thought, even for a moment, that I could have shared my task with anyone, even Mother. She's

really a very strong person, though, complex and special like
the rest of the family. Can you imagine anyone named Blake
keeping birds in cages?" I tried to match the smile she tossed
me. "He said 'Everything that lives is holy.' Do you believe
that, Mr. Cooperman?"

"I guess I do, in a way," I said, a little out of my depth.

"I used to believe it with all my heart." She looked at
me with her green eyes very round. The sun had illuminated
the golden flecks in them and the blue vein in her forehead
was throbbing. "Yes," she said, looking out away from me.
"I used to believe that and a hundred other beautiful things
that I have had to put behind me. I'm cut off from fine sen-
timents now, but I feel the wound."

"Why don't you tell me about it?"

"Oh yes, I will. And you are going to tell me things as
well. But first, may I pour you something cool?"

"Thank you very much." She filled two of the tall glasses
on the tray from the pitcher, the ice cubes protesting like
distant chimes, and handed one of the glasses to me. I let her
sip her drink before I began to drink mine, a delay that she
noticed and smiled at.

"Please give me a little credit, Mr. Cooperman. I'm not
that sort of person. Do you really think I intend to poison
you?" I felt like a schoolboy caught cheating in an exam.

"Well, you must admit that I might have reason to be
cautious."

"I wouldn't do anything now that would spoil what I've
done. You are not part of my mission, Mr. Cooperman." She
looked at me like she was explaining why she'd failed to
castle early in a simple king's pawn game. Her mission. I had
to concentrate on the men she'd put in the cemetery.

"Tell me," I said. "Tell me about before you had a mission." She looked over the edge of the escarpment; for a
moment I thought she hadn't heard me. There were two
hawks wheeling now, slowly in great circles.

"It began such a long time ago. Try to imagine it, sitting
here in this garden where we spent so much of our time. My
grandfather built the brick shed over there. He used to raise
mink. The old house on the property belonged to his father's
farm. It was one hundred and fifty years old, but it had to be
destroyed when the land was subdivided. My sister told me
stories of the old house, how she'd played in the rafters under
the roof, or crept from one bedroom to another through two
closets that joined. Granddad worked, when he was younger,

for the canal company as a lock-keeper. He filled Elizabeth with canal lore, and she passed it on to me. One time he showed her where an abandoned railway tunnel, nearly a quarter of a mile long, ran under a basin between two locks on the old canal. This morning I caught myself thinking that now I'll be free to look for that place. It's fascinated me since I first heard of it as a child. I was forgetting your visit, Mr. Cooperman." The smile that nearly didn't make it at all faded quickly from her eyes. She went on with the story.

"The city made Father sell off the mink Granddad left. They tried to force him to take down the shed, but he convinced them that it had historical interest."

"Your sister was special, wasn't she?"

"Oh, yes. But that doesn't really tell half of it. We were close, of course. Even though I was younger, I tried to keep up with her. Elizabeth was a first-class student all her life. I think she was a genius. She was always right up there with the top three. And then, suddenly, without any warning, she wasn't there any more. She was only twenty, Mr. Cooperman. She had so much to give to life, and they spoiled it. They murdered her." Her face had coloured during the last part of this. She paused thoughtfully, forgetting that she had company, and sipped from her glass.

"You knew that she was taking drugs, didn't you?" I asked, trying to bring the real Elizabeth Blake back again.

"Yes, but she was never an addict. Youthful experiment, maybe. Everybody was doing it then. It seemed natural, a part of growing up. Don't you see?"

"Oh, I see all right. But I also see that she was more than an innocent victim of the pushers. She was one of the pushers herself."

"Elizabeth was good, and honest, not a bit like what you are thinking. If you'd known her . . ."

"Hilda, you knew she was involved in that drug ring. She knew who was making the drugs; she helped distribute them. She was there when the security guard was wounded. With the gun you gave me."

"I remember that night." She was leaning forward with her hands on her cheeks. "I was doing homework in my dressing-gown with the roses. She came into my room; I could see from her face that something was terribly wrong. She rushed over and held me for a long time." Hilda stopped speaking like she'd suddenly caught a high note in her ear and she couldn't go on until the vibration ended.

"Hilda? Tell me about the gun."

"The gun?"

"The one Elizabeth brought home. The one you got me to take to Ward's house." She was frowning at me slightly, as though she'd just suddenly noticed that I was selling magazine subscriptions. When I asked a question, I got a vague response. We danced around that way for a while, and then the note, or vibration, or whatever it was, must have gone away. She picked up the story again with a half apologetic smile.

"She cried and cried in my arms. We'd never been so close. She'd never needed me before. For a while it was as if she was me and I was her. All the while, she was babbling. Most of it I didn't catch. But I recognized names: Joe, Bill and Chester. I heard about a gun that went off, that someone was hurt. Elizabeth went back for the gun. Bill Ward had dropped it. She was bone-white with fright. I held her close until morning." Hilda looked little and crushed in her chair.

"But, Hilda, the gun?"

"The gun?" She looked away from my face. "Oh, I just kept it."

"Was Elizabeth in love with Joe Corso?"

"Joe was the only one who did anything. The rest was sordid business. Joe had discovered how to make things in the lab. He could do anything. He was brilliant."

"And Elizabeth worked with him?"

"Yes. That was why she stayed in residence that term. She wanted to be near Joe. She told me how they were often up all night waiting for the results of a group of tests. You don't believe me, do you? You're like all the others."

"Hilda, I have difficulty accepting the hero status you're trying to give both of them. They were in it either for the kicks or the money. Can't you see it for what it was, a dirty piece of business at best? If they'd been caught, there would have been jail terms for both of them."

"You don't understand how what happened next wiped all of that away."

"The security guard was shot a few months before your sister died. They came within an ace of killing that man, but they kept on making and pushing the stuff."

"Haven't you ever seen pictures on television or in the papers showing the wives of accused men walking to or from the courtroom? Have you studied the faces of those women as I have? They shout hatred at the cameras with their eyes, and defiance to the world. Questions of right and wrong are for courts and strangers. They have no place under the roof of the accused."

"When did you see your sister last?" The question sounded like a parody of something just out of my reach. Hilda Blake smiled at me. It was a smile that could almost make me forget why I was there.

"She was busy with her final exams, so she hadn't been home for more than a week. Of course, she telephoned nearly every day. She was full of talk about the papers she was working on, and Joe, and her plans for the summer. She was full of life, and brimming over with enthusiasm. Two days later she was dead. The inquest was a farce. They say the coroner was drunk. He called it suicide, but I knew they were all lying. I tried to say so, but the doctor gave me something to make me go to sleep.

"Mother wasn't well enough to go to the funeral. I went. I tried to tell the people what happened, but I was taken away. I can't remember by whom. Isn't that odd? I just remember a strong hand on my arm. But I remember vowing over her coffin that I wouldn't let Chester Yates and Bill Ward get away with what they had done. I knew that I would live long enough to send both of them to hell."

"And you would do it the way they did: make their deaths look like suicide."

"They murdered my sister, Mr. Cooperman. I saw them escape any shadow of blame. I knew that they wouldn't escape me." We sat quietly for a minute. I thought of lighting a cigarette, but there was something about this garden and this afternoon that frowned on such an idea. I took another sip of lemonade.

The sun had moved a little since we began talking. I was aware of shadows in the garden, but the warm spring afternoon continued. In her sun-drenched dress Hilda talked as simply as though we'd been discussing the plot of a novel, or the exploits of somebody who'd lived three centuries ago. I had to keep reminding myself that until recently we executed murderers like Hilda Blake.

"After Elizabeth died, Joe tried to get in touch with me. We talked on the telephone once."

"Did he tell you what had happened?"

"He didn't have to. He sounded frightened, and it could only be Ward and Yates that he was afraid of. They killed him too. I should have guessed that they would try to kill Joe. Then, a month later, Father had a stroke. He didn't die right away, but he couldn't speak any more. From his hospital bed, he looked at me the way he used to look at Elizabeth, and he told me things that he'd never been able to say before. I can't describe those wordless conversations. There was an ecstasy about his eyes. I felt for the first time worthy. And I could take responsibility for what I knew he was telling me to do.

"The time after that is confusing. I'm not sure what happened next. I remember dropping out of school. I remember another funeral. I remember doctors and nurses and drugs. In the calm times I can remember hearing voices. Nothing to do with me, just people talking about their cats and dogs and family. I remember hearing two doctors talk about a nurse as though I wasn't in the room. They were saying terrible, private things, as though I wasn't able to hear. Then I can remember long corridors, and sunlight on balconies. I remember sitting in a garden watching the flowers. I think I could actually see them growing. The buds were slowly unfolding as I watched them."

"Was it then that you met Liz Tilford?"

"Oh, I forgot. Yes, of course, you'd know about her, wouldn't you?"

"I've had to keep my eyes open."

"I'm glad it was you, Mr. Cooperman. What's your Christian name?"

"My first name is Ben. But I'm Jewish."

"Ben. I like that name. Ben. It suits you. You are a Ben. Liz Tilford would have liked you. She was my friend. I was closer to her than to anyone after Elizabeth, my sister. Funny, their both having the same first name. It was a good omen."

"She found you in the hospital on Queen Street, while she was still on staff, am I right? She took an interest in you, didn't talk to people as though you weren't in the room. She remembered things you told her, and later, when you began to get better, she brought you things."

"Yes, we spent long afternoons taking society apart and putting it together again. I didn't realize to what a degree I was occupying her time until later. She seemed to know that I was special right from the beginning. It was as though we'd known one another all our lives. It was like having an older sister again.

"I forced myself to stop walking around in a daze. I stopped worrying about things I could never quite fit together, things glimpsed at the corner of my eye, that always disap-

peared when I turned my head. I paid attention more. Tried
not to think of Elizabeth or about Bill Ward and Chester
Yates. I think they reduced the number of drugs they were
giving me to keep me going. I started liking some of the doctors. We even had our own jokes. My bad dreams began to
go, I was getting well, and I liked the idea of being well
again."

"At the beginning of last year, did Liz tell you that
she would be leaving the hospital?"

"Yes. For a while I could see that something was bothering her; she could never hide anything from me. She had
one of those faces that can never keep a secret. I asked her
what it was, and she told me, making a long sad story of it.
But I knew that we needn't be separated for long. I was getting well, and with time off for good behaviour, I might look
forward to leaving within a few months. I could feel the bur-
den of strength in the relationship passing to me that morning. Do you know what I mean? I had changed what she had
seen as a parting into promise and hope. I became the older
sister, in a way. We began to make plans about what we
would do when I was well.

"When she retired, she came to see me every day. The
other nurses joked that the only way to get Liz really to retire would be to give me my walking papers. And that's what
they did eventually. They declared me as sound as a steel
hull, and toasted my launching with champagne in the nurses'
lounge. Against the rules, of course, but as Liz would have
said, very gratifying."

"You shared an apartment for several weeks only."

"Yes."

"Do you want to tell me about that?"

"You're just like some of my doctors, Ben." She looked
at me, smiling in a rather sleepy way, then took a deep
breath for courage and continued. "Liz and I planned to go
on a camping trip as soon as I got out of the hospital. It was
a thing I'd never done. She came from Sault Ste. Marie, and
it was second nature to her. I didn't think for a minute that
the route she'd picked—a trail up the Montreal River, a
hundred miles north of the Sault—would be too much for
her. Despite her age, she was tireless. I don't know anything
about her previous medical history, Ben, but she didn't wake
up the second night out. I'd never seen a dead person before.
I was frightened. I took her purse with her driver's licence
and papers to show to the authorities, and left Liz in the tent,

zipped up inside her sleeping bag. We were about a mile from a very faint path, but before I left, I tried to memorize exactly where the tent was, so that I could lead back a rescue party.

"I must have walked for two days without sleeping. I won't bother trying to describe what it was like. If I hadn't gone through the experience of being crazy, I would have nothing to compare it with. Eventually, I stumbled on to the highway about a mile above where we'd left the car. As I climbed into the driver's seat, I locked the door behind me and fell into a deep sleep. When I woke, it was dark, but the moon was full. I remember seeing Liz's bag lying in the moonlight on the passenger's seat. I think that that was when I realized that I wasn't going to report Liz's death. I knew that it was a gift of fate or something. It was Liz's gift to me. She'd been dearer to me than anyone I'd known after my sister. To her, I'd been the family she'd never known. And now she was giving me the tools I needed to complete my mission.

"From that day, I became Liz Tilford. I cancelled the apartment, mentioned vaguely in a couple of places that she'd gone to live in the Sault with a married sister, and moved first back here to my mother's house in order to make my plans. I knew that my time was limited. Someone would find the tent in the woods. Someone would suspect something from the uncashed pension cheques. I knew that I had to act quickly, and I did."

TWENTY-EIGHT

Hilda Blake paused in her story, giving me a smile that mingled both pride and sweetness. It was with difficulty that I kept myself from identifying with her. I found I was silently cheering when circumstances made her task easier and damning the obstacles to her revenge. She had made herself totally the weapon of her hate, and yet she remained somehow uncorrupted by it. Her account was precise and unaffected. She was incredibly calm.

The afternoon shadows were lengthening. I was beginning to be glad I had my jacket. Hilda held her elbows with the opposite hands. She sighed a little. "Ben, I've been talking far too long. It's your turn. Tell me how I did it."

I hadn't expected to be challenged so directly, as if this was some television play or a party game. But these last few days had been full of surprises. Did I honestly expect Hilda Blake to behave like anybody else? I kept telling myself that she was as crazy as a tailor with two customers and one pair of pants. If I wasn't careful, I thought, I could fall into her vision and get lost.

"You came back to Grantham a year ago, the end of March, beginning of April. For some reason, maybe it was habit, maybe something they'd said to you in the hospital, you decided to see a therapist. You were certain, and sure of your mission, or destiny, but you wanted to be sure that you would remain well enough to execute your design. I don't know how you happened to pick Dr. Andrew Zekerman."

"I tried three others and couldn't get an appointment. Then I tried him." From the way she said "him," I could tell that she didn't like this part of the story.

"Zekerman found you a fascinating patient, but not for

the reasons you might guess. He discovered in the story you told him about your past certain unprofessional interests of his own. He began to take you over and over the same ground. He wanted to know all about what happened at Secord University."

"He told me that it was to make me accept what had happened." There was a tremor in her voice for the first time. She was agitated by Zekerman's presence in the story.

"Dr. Zekerman was a blackmailer. You were a source that gave him information about two people who were rich enough to make him find the practice of psychiatry dull and unrewarding. He used what you told him, and what his own research turned up, to squeeze a lot of money from both Yates and Ward. And he was about to try for higher stakes." Hilda's hand had gone involuntarily to her throat. The clear skin of her cheeks and neck coloured. At first I thought that since Zekerman's schemes had nothing to do with hers, she could feel normal outrage for the victims. But the look on her face was closer to anger or anxiety.

"He nearly spoiled everything. I didn't know why he pushed himself in uninvited. It still bothers me to think about the way he tried to confuse and change what I had to do. He was just greedy, as you say, he had no special purpose as I had."

"As Elizabeth Tilford you applied for a job in Chester Yates' office. He took you on. That put you close to Chester so that you could watch his every move. You discovered that he kept a loaded target pistol in his cupboard, and that he enjoyed a drink at the end of the day from his hidden bar."

"He boasted about being an expert shot," she said. "Anything Bill couldn't do, Chester gloried in."

"The job put you in the right place to be noticed by Bill Ward, who could never resist a pretty face. He invited you out. You played up to him, flattered his vanity, laughed at his jokes."

"Do you despise me for that?" She was sitting straight in her chair now, challenging, her red hair quite dark in the failing light.

"I don't come into this at all. I'm just an investigator. I'm no judge or jury."

"You think it was a low trick to take advantage of them that way. I can tell. But I sacrificed myself as well as them. You must see that?"

"All I can see is that you let Ward make love to you on

and off for two months in his little place on Bellevue Terrace, while you studied the way the locks worked and discovered the best way to cut through the hedges and back lanes, all for future reference.

"In order to be free to move as you chose, you thought it best to disappear from the office. You left just after Chester warned you that he would have to let you go. You'd nearly finished with the Liz Tilford identity anyway. But people like Martha Tracy remembered you. Martha tried to be your friend. But you didn't have time for that. You were getting ready for your job by reading about how Brutus killed Caesar for the good of Rome, how Medea sacrificed her children for the good of her self-respect, and how Charlotte Corday assassinated Marat for the good of France. You saw yourself in a noble tradition, not just a murderer, but a dedicated avenger. Your own sacrifice was part of the mission from the beginning.

"You picked Chester first. You went to the building a little after five that Thursday afternoon. You hoped to find him there having a drink at the end of the business day. You knew that your sudden reappearance would spark his interest enough for him to drop whatever business lay on the desk in front of him."

"He was surprised to see me. He got up and invited me in, quizzed me about where I'd been hiding. He offered me a drink, but I said I'd get one for both of us. Chester liked to be well looked after."

"You used the bar towel so you only touched the glasses. You put something into Chester's drink that you'd brought with you. Chloral hydrate is the usual stuff in detective stories, but you'd been talking to Liz Tilford. Maybe she told you that knock-out drops aren't all they're cracked up to be. Maybe she told you about the new short-acting barbiturates. Something like secobarb would be just the thing. You'd be taking a chance that someone might order a full-scale post mortem. The drug would turn up fast enough in a toxicology examination, or if samples of the tissues were sent to the Forensic Centre. But by now you were taking a lot of chances.

"You brought him his drink, and watched the drug take hold. As soon as he passed out, you went to the cupboard, picked up the gun with the towel, and pressed it into Chester's right hand. You placed his finger in the trigger guard, lifted the gun to his head and applied a little pressure to his finger. It was easy. Now all you had to do was put the towel-wrapped glasses in your bag. You took the stairs to get out, I think, and you'd been clear of the building for half an hour when the security man came into Chester's office looking for a free drink." I didn't know how I was managing to tell Hilda all this without taking a smoke. I guess that looking at her taking all this from me was intoxication enough.

"I think that it was on the day of Chester's funeral, you kept a regular appointment with Dr. Zekerman. Zekerman knew nothing about Liz Tilford or her disappearance. Hilda Blake had never disappeared. You saw that he was frightened. Chester's death upset him so much that he was even afraid of you. He told you about sending a few choice items out of your past to a private investigator who had bothered him on the weekend. There are even fewer private investigators in Grantham than there are shrinks. Maybe he boasted my name."

"He did. He ranted about how he'd insured his life. He didn't accuse me, he just talked." She was rubbing her wrists automatically. Zekerman had a way of doing it to her.

"You couldn't be sure what it was he sent me, but you knew that you had to try to get it back before you turned your full attention to Ward. I don't know where you got the name Phoebe Campbell. I suspect it goes back to the hospital."

"She was a patient; she still is, she still is."

"The details about the job at the bank were very convincing, as was the brunette wig. It took me a long time to see that your green and rust outfit had been chosen to go with red hair, not brown."

The light had started to fade from the sky, and the city below the escarpment was debating with itself whether it was dark enough to turn on the streetlights. When I was a boy, I used to try to have my eyes glued to the lights on our street so that I could see them go on all at once. I remembered that and the fact that I was never looking at the right moment.

"You came to my office with a ruse to get me out of the way so that you would have time to look for whatever Zekerman had sent me. As you discovered, he hadn't sent me much, a few indecipherable pages of routine notes. But I'm glad you didn't get this," I said, reaching into my breast pocket and showing her the picture of the two little girls in their kilts. She took the picture from me and looked at it for a long time.

"May I have it now?" she asked, trying to disguise the urgency of the request. I nodded. I wouldn't need it any more. And I didn't think that at this point Hilda Blake would begin destroying evidence. She propped the picture against the side of the pitcher, which was now only a third full. By now it had grown too cool for cool drinks.

"By giving me the gun that had been used to wound the security guard, you were putting something incriminating into Ward's house. I was stupid not to see that you'd switched parcels. You knew that I wouldn't take a package with unknown contents around the block without looking first. You wanted me to be detained at the house while you went through my office. You had to do it that way because there's no telling when I'm likely to show up: three in the morning or three in the afternoon, they're all the same to me when I'm working on something. At the same time, you wanted the cops to get the gun. I don't know for sure what you hoped to accomplish. But I guess the gun meant something to you: the interrupted robbery, your sister's death, and most of all, Yates and Ward. You hoped that the police would be able to read the gun like a book, get them to start asking questions about those good old Golden Rule days at Secord. You couldn't know that it was only by an extraordinary piece of luck the gun was linked to that robbery. But the trail ended there. The registration of the gun led nowhere. It didn't lead to Ward. Bad luck.

"More bad luck when you ran into my boozy neighbour, Frank Bushmill. He heard you ferreting around in my office. You heard him call out in time to hide behind the door. When he came in, you hit him. Very professionally. What did you use?"

"I had some shot inside two pairs of woollen socks. I hope I didn't hurt him too badly?"

"I'm not sure I know what you think is badly enough." Hilda looked confused by the word games. It had been a cheap shot, and I was sorry. "Anyway, he's fine now, completely restored to his dipsomania."

"It's dark. The lights are coming on down below."

"Yes, so they are. I missed seeing it. I'm nearly finished."

"In a strange way, Mr. Cooperman—Ben—I'm enjoying this. It's one thing to be found out when you intended to get away with something. But since I never meant to fool anyone for long, I at least have the satisfaction of knowing that I will not be misunderstood. You can be my witness."

"Now we come to Bill Ward. He told me that you'd telephoned him. I warned him to be careful of you, but he wouldn't listen. By then, he knew who you were, and may have believed that you were involved in Chester's death. He thought that his bodyguards would give him ample protection."

"We went for a drink, first," Hilda said. She wasn't looking at me, but staring out over the edge of the escarpment where the hawks had been flying in the afternoon. She was curled sideways in her chair for warmth, hugging herself with her arms.

"Will you take my jacket?"

"No, let's finish. He was pretending that he didn't connect me with the past, but he'd been drinking; he got careless. It was nearly midnight when he drove back to Bellevue Terrace."

"Just as he'd driven you there so many times before. He drove into the garage and closed the door. Somehow you got him to get back into the front seat of the car. Then you distracted him and while he was in that condition, you jabbed him with a needle, another memento of your friendship with Liz Tilford. He may not have felt a thing."

"He did, actually. I told him it was a pin in my dress. He made a joke, I forget what, and then he began to get groggy."

"After he passed out, you found his keys, let yourself into the house and returned them to him. The last act was to turn on the car's ignition. You let yourself out the back door of the house, cut through the hedge to the lane and eventually made your way back here. You couldn't know that in the morning his bodyguards would attempt to save Ward's good name by driving him away from what might be seen by the authorities as a love nest, and sending him into the quarry. That spoiled the fine finish you'd planned, but at least it wasn't your fault. And once the police began stripping away the sham of a not very convincing accident, they had what looked to them like another suicide." I paused and took a minute to catch my breath. Hilda's penetrating eyes were fixed on me. I'd finished, but she was waiting for more. For what? A verdict? A sentence?

"You've done what you swore to do, and you did it selflessly and with dispatch. Your sister's death, Hilda, is thoroughly revenged."

"I didn't expect anyone to have understood so well. I never feared being caught, I expected that, but I was afraid of the story getting twisted, afraid they'd dismiss me as a lunatic."

I didn't see her get up, but when I brought my eyes back

from the place where the garden dropped away, I saw that her chair was empty. I rose involuntarily. She was standing in front of me in the gloom. "I'm glad it was you, Ben. And I want to give you something." From her collar she unfastened a small brooch, which she pressed into my hand. I could feel the hair on my arms prickling. She put her hands lightly on my chest and kissed me. In a moment, she was back in her chair as though nothing had happened. "I'm quite calm now," she said. I looked out at the dark shapes above the glow of the city. Minutes went by, falling over the edge.

"What are you going to do, Ben?" The voice was tranquil.

"You know very well."

"Yes," she said with a sigh, "and I know what I must do." She sounded content and peaceful. There wasn't a thing I could say. She smiled at me there in the dark, and I looked at her for a long time without moving. Neither of us said anything more. Below us, the lights of traffic were snaking between the straight lines of streetlights. There were thousands of lights down below, but somehow they didn't cut through the darkness.

TWENTY-NINE

It was the night of the day after. We were sitting at one of Lije Swift's tables on the road to Niagara. It was well after midnight and I'd been drinking. Pete Staziak and Chris Savas had taken me under their wings. I'd been roped into coming out to Lije's for a real feed, Pete called it, and it had been. Cheese stuffed into the hollow of celery sticks, then there was duck from some lake in Quebec, covered with orange slices, a mixture of supper and breakfast.

The French wine helped. It helped a lot. I could hear Pete and Chris talking over me while I concentrated on getting the last of the crisp skin off the final piece of breast. I didn't try to pull any of the sound close, I let it sail past. I'd become sick of the sound of my own voice lately, always telling about suicides that weren't suicides, and all those women who were really the same woman.

Lije appeared at the table holding a bottle in his chubby hands. They hung on the shortest of arms. I tried to imagine him at the wheel of a speedboat somewhere in the upper Niagara, between the coast guard and the falls, with a boat full of bonded Canadian booze. He was inviting us to have some cognac. I said sure. Why not? Last night I'd felt pretty gloomy, but now I was enjoying the food, the drink and the company. I took a sip of the cognac, and it bit my lip. I took a bigger sip, to bite it back, and it snapped at my gullet all the way down.

Peter was leaning forward on his arms which had pushed away his dinner plate. "How you feeling, pardner?" he said to me.

"Doing fine, sheriff. What time's the hanging?"

"No neck-tie party today, pardner. We're plumb out of

177

suspects. The only thing we got is Harrow's goat, and I think we'll roast that nice and slow. He didn't much appreciate the help you gave him on this case, did he?"

"You noticed that?" Savas chimed in, worrying his teeth with his tongue.

"The surprise is that the bugger didn't create a royal rumpus when we dumped it all on the table." I grinned at the love birds on the willow pattern. "The thing I still can't get straight," Pete said, dredging up the last of the cognac in his glass, "is Zekerman's death. Benny, run that one by me again." I groaned, and pretended to collapse, but both Pete and Chris protested. I had to reach for the rusty gearshift and try to engage my wits with my mouth still loping along in neutral.

"All right, you guys, but this is the last time."

"Right."

"Okay. Zekerman's death didn't have anything to do with Hilda's holy plot to punish the other two. You understand that she couldn't accept the truth about her sister. She couldn't even see that her death was accidental. Elizabeth took too much, or from a bad batch. She was still alive when Ward and Yates took her back to the residence, but only barely. Ward set the stage for the *suicide*. But Corso, who'd been closest to Elizabeth, started to crack. Ward and Yates must have found out that he was in contact with Hilda. They knew that the secret had to be contained. So they popped Corso.

"And nothing happened for a whole bunch of years. Corso and Elizabeth were dead. Hilda was in a mental hospital, and Ward and Yates went about making lots of money and joining expensive clubs. They got married, they became as respectable as their parents had been. Chester was always turning a sod or talking to the Canadian Club; Ward was always cutting ribbons or whispering sound advice into the shell-like ear of His Worship the Mayor. Then this neat little world of theirs was threatened by the past. Zekerman had found out about extracurricular activities back at Secord University. Hilda Blake, fresh out of Queen Street, spilled all the sordid details to her shrink. He heard about the illegal drugs, the interrupted burglary that ended with the guard getting hurt, the deaths of Elizabeth and then Corso. I'll bet he couldn't believe his luck. He already ran a profitable business. There are plenty of people in this town who are glad Zekerman is out of the way. So, for a long time, Zekerman milked Ward and Yates like an ant milks an aphid; he was reasonable, not pressing them too much on any one occasion because he knew that there was going to be a next and a next.

"Then he heard about Core Two from Chester. Zekerman was a greedy bastard from the day he slipped off the delivery table trying to steal the forceps. He wasn't satisfied with a monthly hand-out any more. He wanted a share of the profits."

I reached into my pocket and brought out an envelope. In it I'd placed the page of appointments Martha had sent me and a piece of paper I'd been scribbling on. I passed the original sheet to Pete.

Jones	Saturday, 2 am
Henry	Friday, 11 pm
Bill	Friday, 1 am
Peters	Friday, 2 pm
Careless	Friday, 8 pm
Harney	Friday, 7 pm
Evans	Friday, 9 am
York	Friday, 2 pm
Henderson	Friday, 6 am
Evans	Friday, 3 pm
Peters	Friday, 6 pm
Richards	Friday, 1 am
Dodge	Friday, 8 pm
Plymouth	Friday, 8 am
Ford	Friday, 9 am
Williams	Friday, 6 pm
Roberts	Friday, 4 am

He looked at it for a while and then passed it without comment to Chris Savas. Savas examined it, smiled and returned it to me.

"When I first saw it," I continued, "I couldn't make heads or tails of it: all of those ordinary names, the car names, names that meant nothing, or very little, to Martha Tracy, Chester's secretary. Then one night I decided to forget about the names. They might be there only to confuse things. So what's left: a bunch of appointments for a Friday and Saturday running right around the clock with no time off for things like sleeping or eating. The meetings are all helter-skelter so it's hard to see who's coming next. But then I got the idea that the order was the key. That phrase I just used

'around the clock' hit me again. I drew a circle and represented on it the numbers on the face of a clock. Now, if each
hour represented a letter, then you'd have to go around
twice to include all but the last two letters in the English
alphabet. The last two letters would take us into Saturday.
Friday 1 am equals A; Friday 2 am equals B; and so on
down to Saturday 2 am equals Z. Well, I tried it out." Here
I passed around the table the second piece of paper:

Z WANTS IN FOR A THIRD

I heard Pete's low whistle as he passed the sheet to Chris.

"My guess is that this is a rough copy of the message
Chester sent to Ward, a message which tipped Ward off to the
stakes the greedy shrink was playing for. Ward was a practical
man, he knew that he would have to do something about
Zekerman."

"But didn't the picture change when Yates caught it?"
Pete asked.

"How could it? Chester's share would be paid into the
company. Ward's interests were legally guaranteed no matter who headed up Chester's company. But Chester's death
decided Ward to act as quickly as he could to eliminate this
bloodsucker. He knew that Zekerman kept no secretary or
receptionist; he knew that he wouldn't run into any other
patients. He just kept his regular appointment, and when he
found a moment, he clobbered Zekerman with his own
African statue. When he'd made sure that he was dead, he
went over the office carefully, taking the appointment book,
a group of files including his own and Chester's, and anything
else with his name on it. In another two minutes, he was walking back to his office.

"Funny thing about that: as soon as he examined the
files, he knew Zekerman hid his dirty secrets elsewhere. Ward
and I both started wondering where that might be just about
the same time. I got to the blackmail files only minutes ahead
of his boys."

"So Hilda Blake had unwittingly tipped Zekerman to
the prospects of blackmailing the same two she'd sworn to
kill."

"Yes, but Zekerman was pretty sure that it was Hilda who
killed Chester. That's another ironic thing about this case.
Zekerman was so greedy to get his third of the profits from
Core Two that he wanted to warn Ward about Hilda. He

told me on the phone to watch out for Ward. He didn't mean that I should be careful of him, but that Ward should be on the look-out himself."

"Tell me, Ben," Savas said, leaning across the table, "when did you get all those women straightened out?" I thought about that one for a moment, enjoying the cognac and the concentration in the four eyes opposite.

"Well, Phoebe Campbell worried me right from the start, but I felt I had to run with that in order to find out what was going on," I lied. "I didn't start putting all those faces together until I got an itch at the back of my knees when I saw the Secord University crest on the bookends in Elizabeth Tilford's room. I had Hilda Blake in the back of my head from then on."

"Did you ever find out what that whispering was that your neighbour, the chiropodist, heard just before she hit him?"

"Easy. He heard the rustle of her skirts, and was just about to turn, when she connected."

"Here's to the rustle of skirts!"

"Long may they rustle!" We drank to that and didn't talk for a few minutes, each of us attuned to the sound of a different rustle. Pete broke the silence.

"It's a good thing there won't be a trial," he said. "They would have locked her away this time for the rest of her life."

"Yeah," I agreed. "The funny thing is, that after she'd successfully assassinated those two, she was as sane as I am, which isn't saying much, I admit. But she had planned all the chapters—even the last. I saw the phial of pills in her hand when I said good night. I knew that I'd never see her again. And she saw that I knew. One of those circles of knowing."

"She was dead when we got there. How come it took you until midnight to remember our phone number?" I shrugged, and examined the bottom of my empty glass. I didn't like the idea of Hilda being dead. I could still picture her sitting in the garden, watching the cares drop away from her as she made her confession.

"Where's Lije with that cognac?" Savas asked.

"So, that's it?" Pete cocked his head in my direction. "Now it's all up to the lawyers. It could go on for years."

"Especially now that the cat's out of the bag about the scam Ward was practising on an unsuspecting city council."

"In the end, Myrna Yates is going to become a very rich widow. With her looks, she won't be a widow for long."

"Harrington's resigned. The mayor has been running scared, won't talk to reporters, won't make a statement. There were questions asked in the Legislature. There'll be a cabinet shuffle at the very least. There's been talk of a Royal Commission to investigate."

The cognac must have been getting to me. Pete and Chris kept on talking, but I was taking in only every other word. Hilda had dreamed for years of killing off Yates and Ward. Now she'd done it. And her revenge was still working away like a mother of vinegar. Both men had been totally discredited. Their reputations had been through the shredder. Their clubs not only removed their names from membership, but fixed it so that they'd never been members. One large firm, with nothing to do with this story, quietly dropped the name Ward from the hyphenated name. The old family crests had fallen off the wall. At a boy's private school the plaque which displayed the names of the winning school "eight" for 1960, was mutilated so that now there were only six. The thing that Ward feared most, the motive that had carried him from one coverup to the next, family disgrace, was still at work. Hilda's revenge was a continuing process, not something over and done with. I don't think Hilda had counted on that.

Savas was talking: "A lot of people were involved all right, but since Ward's dead, he'll get most of the blame."

"Myrna deserved better than Chester from the start. Better than Ward too for that matter."

"Funny the way Harrow took it all so calmly at the end. I thought he'd have our guts for garters," Pete said. I shrugged. I hadn't mentioned to Pete or Chris that I'd had a word with Sergeant Harrow. I wasn't going to run afoul of him any more. He'd been the policeman who'd helped Harrington cover up that hit-and-run job. Harrow knew I wasn't launching into the extortion business, but he knew when to bet and when to fold, so when I told him that I was on to him, he smiled a yellow smile and threw his cards in the middle of the table.

"Hey, Benny! Come back to the conversation." Both of them were looking at me.

"Sorry. You were saying that Myrna Yates is going to be a rich widow. I didn't miss a word. As a matter of fact, she's already playing Lady Bountiful."

"What do you mean?" asked Pete, wiping his chin on a crumpled napkin.

"Well, I got a message through Martha Tracy asking

me if I would accept, in addition to a fair settlement of my outstanding account for services rendered, the gift of a brand new ten-speed bicycle."

The boys grinned and Lije came round with the cognac again. I liked the idea of the bicycle. It was what I needed to change my luck. There was a whole cast of characters I wanted to forget and couldn't, pictures I saw at night that I couldn't turn to the wall. Maybe the bike would get me out into the country more. I could use the exercise. I had a whole summer of warm weather to look forward to, and with it I was hoping that a fresh ripple of divorce business might find its way up my twenty-eight steps. The summer should be good for that.

ABOUT THE AUTHOR

Born in Toronto, but raised in St. Catharines, Ontario, HOWARD ENGEL was for many years a freelance broadcaster for the CBC in Canada and in Europe. In 1967 he joined the CBC permanently and until recently was editor of the literary flagship *Anthology*. He lives in downtown Toronto and is now working on a second Benny Cooperman novel.

ODD'S END

by
Tim Wynne-Jones

Winner of the $50,000 1980 Seal Book Award

A superbly written psychological thriller in which an insidious net of terror winds about the victims, with tension building to a harrowing climax.

The idyllic life of a young couple, living in an isolated house by the sea in Nova Scotia, is shattered by the poison of suspicion and the fierce power of evil, as they are forced to skirt the thin line between sanity and madness.

"Tim Wynne-Jones' novel is easily the best...ideal...it combines mass market appeal with literary merit..."
Toronto Star

The Mark of Canadian Bestsellers

OETWJ

SEAL BOOKS

Offers you a list of outstanding fiction, non-fiction and classics of Canadian literature in paperback by Canadian authors, available at all good bookstores throughout Canada.

The Mark of Canadian Bestsellers

SB-5